PARTINGS

LEONID BORODIN, who born in 1939 in Irkutsk, was released in 1987 after serving four years of a fifteen-year sentence imposed by a Moscow court for "anti-Soviet agitation and propaganda". The sentence was something of an unintended tribute to the force and quality of Borodin's writing, and it was the second time that he had found himself in prison for his political views and his writing. From 1967 to 1973 he served in "strict regime" camps for his part in the illegal "Social-Christian Alliance". Between sentences he wrote three books, all banned in the Soviet Union but published in Russian in the West. In 1983 he was awarded the French PEN Club's Freedom Prize for an earlier novel, *The Story of a Strange Time*. After his release in 1987 Leonid Borodin rejoined his wife and daughter in Moscow.

Leonid Borodin

PARTINGS

Translated from the Russian by
David Floyd

COLLINS HARVILL
8 Grafton Street, London W1
1988

Collins Harvill
William Collins Sons and Co Ltd
London · Glasgow · Sydney · Auckland
Toronto · Johannesburg

BRITISH LIBRARY CATALOGUING IN PUBLICATON DATA

Borodin, Leonid
Partings.
I. Title   II. Rasstavanie. *English*
891.73'44[F]   PG3479.4.0658
ISBN 0-00-271617-8

First published in Great Britain by Collins Harvill 1987
This edition first published by Collins Harvill 1988

© Possev Verlag, V. Gorachek KG 1984
© in the English translation William Collins Sons and Co Ltd and
Harcourt Brace Jovanovich Inc. 1987

Printed and bound in Great Britain by
Hartnolls Ltd, Bodmin, Cornwall

Introduction

The reader who begins by acquainting himself with Leonid Borodin's own tragic story may find *Partings* a surprising book. The distorting pressures of the Soviet state on the lives of its citizens are taken for granted and rarely mentioned, the dissidents here described include no-one of the intellectual and moral stature of Borodin himself. With very few exceptions *Partings* is populated by educated Muscovites intent on making the best of both worlds: ostentatiously accepting (with private reservations or special interpretations) the philosophy and the practices of the regime, or calculating (sometimes miscalculating) the risks of half-hearted dissent.

The hero of the book, Gennadi, is as Georgy Vladimov says, not a self-portrait of the author. Gennadi is "a mushroom poking up through the Moscow asphalt", an "homo esperantus", crippled by self-doubt and scepticism about the motivation of his fellows: Borodin is a Siberian (and so the most Russian of Russians) and above all a fighter, martyred for his beliefs. But we need not doubt that Borodin shares Gennadi's perception of the Moscow intelligentsia, and of the falsities and ambiguities so common in its outlook and its behaviour. Gennadi himself is rather more at home with his ostensibly ultraconformist father, a teacher of Marxism-Leninism and a masterly exponent of shoulder-shrugging pragmatism, than with the mother and sister who became modishly "madly dissident during a half-thaw": father is less intolerant of (harmless) dissent than mother and sister of (not conspicuously harmful) conformism. Gennadi, himself as honest as circumstances permit, is unshocked by his friend the intellectual spiv Poluëktov, who condemns all dissidents on the grounds that the Soviet regime has created ideal conditions for the businessman of talent. If he fails to condemn his father and Poluëktov, it is surely because his dissident and semi-dissident friends seem to him intellectually no more respectable. When his hysterical sister, betrayed by the lover who had converted her to dissidence, comes to grief, Gennadi is contemptuous of appeals invoking the "human rights guaranteed by the constitution": is this not playing into the hands of a regime which tolerates (encourages!) a modicum of controlled dissidence to prevent the emergence of true opposition? Gennadi's reactions to the intellectual audience (congregation would be an incongruous word) at a fashionable church are surely also those of the author: the eloquent priest and even his Jesus-haired bodyguard may be in danger, but for most of those present this is a risqué, rather than risky, experience.

Author and hero, then, both turn a sceptical gaze on emancipated Moscow. But for different reasons: Borodin is entitled to look ironically at facile or dishonest conformists and at those who play at dissidence. Gennadi's excuse must be that he is painfully conscious of his own inconsistencies and dishonesties. He is an escapist who could, he believes, have been happy as a minor official, cushioned by a cosy family life, in old Russia, of the sort so gratuitously (in his view) lampooned by 19th century Russian writers. As it is, he has fallen in love with Tosya, the daughter of a Siberian village priest, and plans to transport her, together with the freshness and simplicity of her life, to Moscow. First he must part with his old love, Irina – and with the bohemian circle to which they both belong. He will install his saintly village maiden in a flat paid for by morally ambiguous means: Poluëktov obtains for him a commission to ghost the memoirs of an indigent war hero, who will still be left with nothing but his one arm, his miserable pension and his memories . . . Drawn into the problems of his own family (collapse of his father's love affair with a "Marxoid" colleague, sister's betrayal by her lover and arrest), and of Irina (pregnant, and in danger of losing her job after producing an indiscreet television programme), reliant on further assistance from the dubious Poluëktov for his livelihood, Gennadi is inevitably reabsorbed by his natural milieu.

Perhaps he knew it from the first? Perhaps that is why there is a certain unreality, indeed farcicality, about some of the characters, as seen through Gennadi's eyes? It is one of the great merits of this rich and subtle novel that Borodin leaves us to make up our own minds about the motivations of his characters. He makes it possible for us to sympathise with many of them – and impossible for us to reject any of them as unlifelike or uninteresting.

HARRY WILLETTS
Oxford, 1987

Father Vasili, dear Father Vasili, what a holy man you are! Fancy carrying on like this – drinking with me, getting yourself drunk . . .

You like me? Well, you shouldn't. I ought to know! Take a closer look at me: I talk too much, use too many fancy words, and my face tells a lot of stories.

You shouldn't be drinking with me, Father Vasili. Somehow you don't seem the person you were a week ago, there in the village church: so impressive and saintly, so remote in your serenity, your voice deep and solemn, making me feel common and a nobody beside you. The feeling wasn't the result of some craven intellectual process within me: it came from outside, sweeping over me and knocking me over – when I've been so self-centred and easily hurt all my life . . . Suddenly I was just a worm, but it didn't hurt, it was pleasurable and, damn it, even enlightening! After all, what does – 'all my life' mean? It's always been the same, basically: fighting to keep my end up, first at one thing, then at something slightly better, then at something else again, and so on without any sense, the same thing all over again, not a spiral as it seemed at the beginning but round and round on the same level.

Then see what happened when I dropped in on one of your services . . . I felt as though I'd been catapulted back into my childhood and could start all over again, from childhood to adulthood, that I could grow up again and enjoy the growing . . . That experience keeps coming back to me like a present, a present from you.

I remember in my childhood a mysterious Father Christmas coming and leaving a present. He said something delightful to me, but then pulled off his beard and whiskers and blew his nose. I don't think I ever sat on the toy horse he brought me – it just stood in a corner for a couple of years and then disappeared somewhere . . .

You shouldn't be drinking with me, Father Vasili. You say such trite things about politics, like office-workers chatting over a cigarette. What can politics mean to you, who deal with the eternal? If I had faith like yours, wouldn't human vanity seem ridiculous to me? People must seem to you as if they were crawling on the ground, with their faces to the earth and the sun behind them. They claw at their own shadows all the while and call that objectivity! Isn't that it, Father Vasili? If a man truly has faith, then he sees life without it as blindness, as a joke by the depraved taking pride in their depravity. That's how you must see things.

No, if I believed as you believe I'd howl with rage at human stupidity. I'd twist people's self-satisfied mugs round towards the sky, hating them for the triviality of their passions, the pointlessness of their thoughts, and the insignificance of their deeds. But you are so serene. You drink vodka with me and you seem to like me – me, the lowest of the low. I have never done a good deed, ever, that was not to my advantage in some way. I just don't understand you, Father Vasili! There, in the church, I seemed to understand. There you were bigger than me, but now, at this table, you're getting smaller and smaller. Who knows, soon you may even drop below my worm's eye level, and then how shall I be able to look you in the face?

But the most important question is: why do you like me – so much that you are prepared to hand over your only daughter despite my vulgarity and depravity. I wouldn't let anyone like me go anywhere near a daughter of mine. Why are you doing it? Shall I ask you?

'Father Vasili, why are you handing your daughter over to me like this, without any fuss? After all, I'm not the right person for her, not by any criterion.'

I asked the question impudently, boorishly, cutting Father Vasili short in the middle of what he was saying – something about Africa. He stares at me; if only he would narrow his eyes and shame me, with a piercing look for my drunken tactlessness. But no, he only blinks.

'I am not handing her over to you; I'm making you a present of her. She is your future happiness, and happiness is my present to you.' And he smiles, wiggling his beard. 'I would willingly have presented you with the sun or the moon.'

'Have you really never met anyone better than me?'

'There have been others,' he says evasively, 'others, but whether better or worse, God knows.'

'So you're presenting her to me. And what are you offering as a dowry?'

'What would you like?' – he smiles again.

'I would like to be given faith . . .' I reply, not without malice.

He nods.

'That is not within my power to give. It is not for the giving.'

His confidence offends me in some way.

'Your daughter is a believer, and what am I?'

'You feel God's presence, but you don't understand. But you have a soul, and that means you will understand one day.'

I have become quarrelsome, wanting to shake him out of his complacency: 'Do you know how many sins I've got on my conscience?'

My tone is becoming more and more familiar: I am spinning downhill. But he just goes on smiling and wiggling his beard.

'Never mind your sins – they're more like outbursts of emotion. You've committed no sins to worry about. Don't try to frighten us.'

I find this insulting – what, have I lived my thirty years to no purpose, have I no sins on my conscience? Only our sins give us distinction: we construct a hierarchy according to the extent of our fall from grace. Sins are important: they are the reality, the spice of life. The seed of atheism is in them. He refuses to recognise my sins, does he? Does he take me for a bleating sheep? All right, I'll let him have it – I'll teach him to blink at me! What sin can I fling at him, that'll really make him stutter? But, my God, he's right! There's nothing to throw at him. My sins were all petty misdeeds – not a single shocker among them! Vasili the priest, my future father-in-law, has stripped me bare and exposed me for what I am. I have nothing to my name, whether good nor bad, so what have I lived these thirty years for? After all, I *have* lived, I *have had* certain passions and my nerves are in a mess – but for what? I can't remember anything of my life, it's as if nothing had ever happened, as if I had sat my life out somewhere in the shade. Oh Lord, how I regret my life!

. . . 'I often travel into town,' – listen to him, talking nonsense again – 'It's a long boring trip, and I have to stand all the way with people pushing and swearing all around me . . . But I have to go every week, or what would we have to eat? So I've invented a childish sort of game for myself. However crowded the bus is, and however much it swerves around the bends and over the pot-holes, I try not to bump into anybody throughout the journey. So what happens? Well, it's funny. I don't get pushed about either. Sometimes it lasts two hours, and no one pushes me about. It seems that there's this law: if you push your shoulder into the crowd, someone else will shove his shoulder into you. If you thrust your elbow into someone's ribs, somehow another elbow will end up smack in your own ribs. That's right, isn't it?'

I say nothing. That kind of philosophy is not to my taste.

'The moral of the story is this,' he says with a smile. 'Here are you, wanting to boast about your sins, but why? If you live modestly, and don't try to push people around, and they don't push you around too much, that's already pretty good. And as for Anastasia, she knows what she wants, too. How can I go against her wishes when I know she can stand on her own two feet?'

Aha! At last I'm beginning to understand. So the reason she and her father are so fond of me is because I am so innocent and gutless; they feel comfortable with me; because they'd be safe . . .

'Anastasia!' I shout out. I have never used her full first name like that before. She appears in the doorway and I am overcome by longing. What is it in her face that paralyses me every time I see her? She is somehow not of this world. Perhaps it is not love that I feel for her at all, perhaps I'm just affected by her other-worldliness?

'Anastasia,' my voice is hoarse, 'why do you love me?'

'Because *you* love *me*,' she replies.

She knows me better than I know myself.

'And what if I didn't love you? What then?'

'Nothing at all.'

'And simply to fall in love without being loved in return – aren't we capable of that?'

'I don't know. It's never happened to me.'

She stands leaning gently against the door with her hands locked together; her face is completely relaxed and almost expressionless, but I can tell she is happy. Father Vasili can feel it too, and he looks at me affectionately.

No, I don't like it at all. They are taking my personality away from me.

'I suppose you think,' – I address her very meaningfully – 'that I shall never hurt you?'

'But you will hurt me.'

'How do you know? Maybe I won't.'

She comes up to me, placing her hands on my shoulders from behind – I can feel her breathing and her lips are very close to me. Father Vasili is near to tears. Family of saints and fools! Had I made the two of them happy by turning up here? No, I know myself too well to be deceived: I couldn't make anybody happy. I didn't know how to give. I was too restless, too garrulous, a bearer of confusion and inconstancy. I was a destroyer; not a creator.

But they *were* happy, I *had* deceived them, and there was nothing I could do to convince either of them of it, neither the old man nor the young woman, she who was so strange to me and whom I needed so desperately.

As a rule, women like either to caress or to be caressed. She liked neither. Yet her hands were on my shoulders. They were giving me something, those hands of hers, what, I don't know, but now that I had experienced this new thing given to me by a woman I couldn't live without it. I wanted to grasp her hands and hold them so that they could not disappear whatever happened. But what was this new thing? Tranquillity? No, more than that.

She and I were already lovers, so how could I be so sure that the most important thing still lay ahead, that there was more in her that I had not yet discovered and made my own? It wasn't that I found her enigmatic. No, that wasn't it. She had something in her that was unchanging, something essential which I had always desired. It worried me and frightened me. I was rather afraid of her, the priest's daughter, and my fear was balm to my spirit.

She has such restful eyes: bright blue but not too blue, and devoid of mischief or cunning . . . A philosopher once said that one's soul not only looks out through the eyes, but is itself visible in them. I don't know exactly what the soul is, nor does anyone know, but I do know I can see something in her eyes which evokes answering feelings of joy and excitement in me;

if that was what is in her soul then I have been truly lucky. I want to marry this woman, to link my life with hers, of my own free will. I find it hard to credit the feeling, especially since I am not thinking of my own life: I'm thinking of her life, which I want to bind tightly to my own. It's not that I am surrendering to the institution of marriage; I'm simply making use of the institution for my own selfish purposes. I want to have this woman at my side for the rest of my life.

At the same time, there is something in me that resists everything I'm doing. I only hope that it is nothing but empty pride: I am so used to making the most of my feelings, I just can't ignore any one of them, because each one proves the complexity of my character, and what could be more important for an intellectual than complexity? Remove *that*, and the intellectual disappears, what's left is just an ordinary office-worker.

She ruffles my hair a little, and that simple gesture gives me such intoxicating pleasure that I turn to jelly . . .

No, so long as she is close it's no good trying to talk seriously about anything; but there is something I want very much to talk seriously about – I have only a vague idea what.

'I think, Tosya,' I said, catching my breath, 'I think we ought to have a talk.'

Her hands slide down from my shoulders and with my whole body I can feel them moving away. From the look on Father Vasili's face, I could guess that as she went away she was making signs to him behind my back not to let me drink any more, so on a childish impulse, I immediately grabbed the bottle and filled both our glasses. But actually I didn't want to drink any more, and the priest was clever enough to see that, so he didn't reach for his glass and pretended not to have noticed my childish reaction. I was about to assail his goodness again, but he spoke before I did:

'Do you understand the sin you have involved your future wife in?'

Taken by surprise, I could only blink at his smiling face. I felt myself blushing.

'Then you don't understand. But she does, you know. By sinning you wanted to put her love to the test. Will you help her expiate her sin?'

I remained silent, but the priest was in no hurry: he did not expect an answer from me. He had thrown a stone into the pond and was watching the circles spread out. What amounted to a 'sin' for the priest's daughter I could only guess. How was the account reckoned? If it was according to the Scriptures – 'thou shalt not covet', 'thou shalt not steal', 'thou shalt not commit murder', – then I certainly couldn't understand: I divided people into good and bad, that is to say good *for me* or bad *for me*, and talking about the sins of a good person struck me as the purest hypocrisy. Didn't the phrase 'a good person' say everything?

I tried to wriggle out of the situation by taking Father Vasili literally. 'Why do you say I have committed no sins, but that she has? Haven't we sinned together?'

'Do you think there is as much demanded of you as of her?' he replied with genuine astonishment.

'Demanded? Who is demanding?' I began to argue, glad to be getting away from a dangerous subject.

'People make demands of themselves. One person will be harder on himself, another easier. My daughter is very hard on herself.'

What I really wanted to say was that it was Tosya's and my business, after all; but I couldn't bring myself to. 'Everything will be all right, Father,' I said, almost affectionately, so that it sounded as if I was using the word 'father' in its usual sense. It sounded awkward, as though I was making myself a member of the family prematurely. Though actually, if anything, it was too late.

'Marry us, Father Vasili!' I burst out.

He shook his head. 'Are you really alone in the world? You must have parents somewhere.'

'What about my parents? I could have been a parent myself long ago, and in any case they don't care about me.'

Again he shook his head. 'You're in too much of a hurry. Go back home to Moscow. Take a look at all this from a distance. Make sure of yourself.'

'That's nonsense!'

'It may be nonsense to you; for you, getting married is just a formality. But what does it mean to her, to Anastasia?'

Suddenly I realised that I really would have to go back to Moscow. I couldn't get married with only a rucksack to my name, and I would have to think about where we could live. And, God, there were so many other things to worry about! But that wasn't the most important thing. I would have to leave Tosya here, and that was something I just couldn't imagine.

'Tosya!' I shouted.

And there she was, in the room again, looking a little sleepy. Apparently she had been dozing next door. I leapt up from my chair, seized her in my arms and began kissing her all over her face. She looked so beautiful, now, that it hurt. Her response was restrained, but I knew what it concealed. It made me tremble, and I said, my voice thick with drink:

'Tosya, you know, I must go away!' Then quickly added, defensively, 'but not for long.'

'Of course,' she replied, so calmly that I exploded.

'Doesn't it worry you at all?'

'No,' she said and frowned in the direction of Father Vasili, who was chuckling away at us from under the chandelier.

'But, for goodness sake . . . how do you know I haven't got a woman in Moscow that I have to see?'

'Then, you must go and see her and explain everything,' she said quietly, tickling my face with a lock of her hair.

Actually, I *did* have someone in Moscow whom I would have to have things out with, but Tosya was the most self-assured of women, she simply glowed with self-confidence, she behaved as though she had already crept around all the dusty corners of my rubbish-ridden soul. I dragged her by the hand to Father Vasili.

'Tell her she shouldn't be so confident!'

He shrugged his shoulders, stroked his beard, and chuckled happily. I embraced him and gave him a noisy kiss on the cheek.

'You're both saints!' I shouted in his ear. 'It's wonderful being with you! But will it always be like this?'

'There's no such thing as always,' he replied. 'But it could happen quite often.'

I dashed into Tosya's room, snatched up her tape recorder and turned it on full blast, then swung the priest's daughter by the hand, pushing her away from me, meanwhile performing the sort of convulsions that pass for dancing nowadays. I could tell she could feel the rhythm, but she did no more than sway gently in time, scarcely moving her shoulders and holding her hands chin-high. And all the time with that sleepy, happy smile on her face.

'Well, Father,' I yelled above the sound of the machine, 'in the Middle Ages they'd have burnt the three of us at the stake! For even witnessing such music and dancing, let alone for arranging it! Isn't that right?'

Tosya raised her eyebrows, as if to ask what it had to do with her. But I knew what those slight movements of hers meant: there was real wickedness in them – for them you would sell your soul to the Devil.

'And you'd have been roasted over a slow fire!' I shouted at her. 'With the greenest of logs!'

I looked down at her little feet in their soft slippers trimmed with cheap fur and was struck with horror at the thought that things like that really happened once, they really had burned people . . . I saw tongues of flame licking the soles of her slippers. They reached the ankles, the calves, the knees . . . Oh, God! I was convulsed by shivers, then froze in the middle of the room like a statue. Tosya too stood stock still and looked down at her feet, was there anything wrong with them? Then she came up to me and with a touch, calmed my runaway imagination. I sat down on a chair facing Father Vasili and she sat on my knee.

'If mankind could be regarded historically as a whole, then that whole would be worthy of contempt. I threw this out to Father Vasili as a challenge.

But he did not accept the challenge. He simply did not take me seriously. And in general in conversation with him my aggressive manner of arguing did not work. The priest just smiled to himself: it's all clean fun, he was saying. I was better educated than he was: he did not have a hundredth part of my knowledge of the world; he had never read Dostoyevsky, so we could not talk on equal terms. Either he was caught up in some deep conspiracy remote from everyday life, or else he really was in a state of blissful ignorance, and that can't be classified as a state of mind – not of my mind at any rate.

The tape recorder was still playing. I frowned in its direction. Tosya jumped up from my knees and switched it off.

'It's getting late,' she hinted.

Father Vasili's eyes were bloodshot. He always rose early, hardly leaving me time to jump out of Tosya's window and scramble back up into the attic.

Now all that seemed silly and cheap. He knew about our meetings. So what were we going to do today? I simply had to go to her . . . Yet I had pangs of conscience about the distasteful situation I had created by bringing such immoral behaviour into a world of blissfully happy people. There was something about it that I could not grasp.

In the world I had lived in till now I had not only felt quite at home, I had also been fairly popular. But *those* women were careful not to love me too much. All my affairs had been short-lived, and the feelings of the women who paid me any attention had turned out to be even shorter-lived. As a rule they soon found I didn't suit them, and they discovered in me a mass of shortcomings, the most important of which, as I now realised, was my inner confusion and my happy-go-lucky attitude to the future. All of which, come to think of it, might have attracted a certain type of woman, but the trouble was that for some reason women like that did not suit me.

Only here, in this heavenly little retreat, had I, who was dissolute and rotten to the last cell of my miserable being, suddenly discovered for the first time how a woman could love a person like me and how I could love in return.

No, I would have to leave the next day and clear up the situation with the new insight gained by the long time I had spent away. In short, tomorrow I would begin a new life. I had already made so many new starts – every Monday, every first day of a new month, every New Year – that I hadn't much faith in the idea of making a new life, but this time I really had to try!

'I will come to you.' I whispered in Tosya's ear as I accompanied her to the door of her room. Her silence was of acceptance. In the clasp of her hand there was both joy and shyness, and something else that I could only guess at, and I didn't really want to try. She regarded *that* as a sin. But such subtleties did not really reach me, meant nothing to me, and I could allow myself not to worry my head over them.

I went back to the table. Father Vasili was nearly asleep. I said goodnight to him and went outside but didn't feel like clambering up into the attic, so I walked out through the gate. It was a bright night; the moon, in a ring of cloud, was suspended over the lake, and I could hear the water faintly lapping the shore. I went down to the shore to sit for a while on an upturned boat, but saw that someone was already sitting there. After some hesitation I decided to approach him. The person either hadn't seen me or was pretending not to notice me. I made myself comfortable at the other end of the boat – and at practically the same moment I heard him say:

'You don't believe in God and therefore you don't realise that destroying a person's soul is just as much of a crime as destroying his body. Worse!'

Now I knew who it was: It was the young deacon from

Father Vasili's church. I remembered him. He had an amazing singing voice. He could have been an opera singer. His beard was neatly trimmed, his hair, straight and plentiful, was shoulder length. He was handsome and, no doubt, also a saint.

A love triangle, then. I was pleased with the speed at which my mind worked. From the boat, Father Vasili's house looked like a stage set. Tosya's little window, which I used to climb through at night, was there, lit up by the moon. My priest's daughter – Aphrodite – bathed in this pale yellow light; I used to leave my watch on the window-sill on purpose, and then make her get it, and I would hold my breath as she dived hurriedly into the moonlight. And all the time the unfortunate deacon must have been sitting on the crumbling boat and suffering . . .

'So you saw?'

'I saw,' he replied, without stirring.

'And you told Father Vasili?'

'Yes, I told him.'

'And what did he say?'

'He asked me to pray for you.'

'For me or for both of us?'

'For both of you.' He dropped his head.

'I suppose it didn't work very well in my case?'

He sighed and nodded.

'It was difficult.'

I sat down beside him. What could I tell him? Normal people would have punched each other in the face. But this fellow had been praying for me. It had been difficult, of course, but he had prayed. How deeply suppressed were his natural, human feelings? Supposing I were to pull his beard or to drag him by his whiskers, would some ordinary human emotion awake in him then? Would he hit me? What a difficult and complicated part he had to play in life! He was only a boy, yet he had taken on the part. Was it healthy, when someone stole a woman from a man, that the man should pray for the thief? No, it was a distortion of morality, a form of schizophrenia, although it was a very convenient illness for other people. For me, for example.

'You realise, of course,' I said to him, 'that according to all the rules, a priest's daughter ought to become the wife of the deacon. Isn't that right?'

'Now I shall have to become a monk,' he said quietly. 'But, you know, I'm not ready for it.'

'She's not the only woman in the world, you know.'

He cut me off abruptly: 'She's the only one for me.'

'For me, too,' I replied. 'What are we going to do?'

He remained silent, and I knew what he would have said if he had been of this world. He would have said that my world was full of beautiful women who were right for me, as I was right for them. But for him in his world there was only Tosya, brought up to be the wife of a priest. In my world she would be out of place, she would stick out like a sore thumb, unless I transformed her completely, in other words, 'destroyed her soul'. I was just an outsider, an intruder, who, to get what he wanted had used tricks that were unheard of in this saintly world. I had seduced an innocent soul and lit her with the fire of her passion. No, it wasn't hard to kindle passion in a provincial maiden, to introduce her to the beating of another heart, to a different way of life, luring her, captivating her, until the prize was firmly in one's hands.

I was unprincipled, the devil incarnate, the anti-Christ in action, the personification of evil in mankind.

All this was true, but it was quite untrue at the same time.

I was finding it difficult to choose my words, and to talk to the lovelorn deacon – we spoke such different languages. But I tried to find a common language, a sort of Esperanto:

'Listen, you're are as pure as a newborn babe and as straight as a die. You understand the most important things in this world, but can only guess at the rest. You've had the good fortune to find true faith and all you need for complete happiness is this woman. But what about me? What am I? A dirty, crooked thing, like a dried up worm! I don't know the truth, and I don't even believe in the truth; I possess neither peace of mind nor well-being. I have no chance of salvation except one thing – except her. Who needs her more, then? Your faith enables you to turn the other cheek and rejoice in the knowledge of your own humility. But if I were slapped in the face, I would hang myself. So which of us finds it easier to give way? And as for Tosya herself . . . I may be seducing her with the attractions of another life, but with you she will never know temptation and will never be able to test herself. It may be also that her mission in life is to save me.'

The deacon looked me in the face, trying to see into my soul. The naïvety of it! Even in sunlight you can't see inside a person, let alone in moonlight.

'I'm not sure,' he said, shaking his head, 'whether you're talking seriously or mocking me. If you're mocking me, that's not very nice.'

'I'm not mocking you.'

'You're better educated and cleverer than I am. You can dress your mind up any way you like – I mean you can understand and imitate anything. I used to be able to do that too. But in the end the result is emptiness.'

Aha, I thought, the young man's not as simple as he seems. Surely he was a former intellectual? I was utterly convinced that an intellectual could never be anything but an intellectual, was simply not capable of being anything else, that his intellectuality would, sooner or later, erode his faith like rust or erode whatever he'd masked it with . . . For example, intellectuals like to dress themselves up as peasants . . . but it never works. The intellectual's constitution is impervious to such things – it permits only one object of worship – oneself. Generally speaking, an intellectual in the contemporary version is an exceptionally resourceful and, essentially, pitiful being. In this cruel world of ours, which is forced to obey the demands of society down to the last detail, is it easy to preserve the pose of an independent thinking person? Today's intellectual has to carry his head high, whilst wagging his tail happily. Not everybody is capable of this, and sometimes one of them will decide to adopt a pose – religion, for example. I have met people like that. I just can't bear them!

But was the deacon one of those? Not very likely.

We were both silent. I would have liked to say something more, something weighty and clever, but the trouble was that I felt no guilt and no sympathy for the deacon. I was far too happy myself to pity anybody or repent of anything.

'Forgive me,' I said to him, 'but there's no way I can help you.'

'Are you really a complete unbeliever?'

So that was what he was after! But I didn't talk even to myself on that subject, and I certainly wasn't going to discuss it with the first deacon that came along.

'Let's not talk about that,' I said firmly, and the young man hastened to apologise.

'It's getting cold . . . and there are mosquitoes . . . I'm going, but . . .'

'Let's go,' I agreed.

'Goodbye. The Lord preserve you!'

He walked away with his rather peculiar gait, leaning slightly forward but at the same time straight-backed, moving very steadily and without swinging his arms or even bending his knees.

All the same, the budding priest had injected something into my mind that made me feel depressed and unsure of myself. I continued to sit with my back to Father Vasili's house and to the window behind which Tosya was waiting for me. I did not hurry; I delayed that turn of my head which would result in my seeing nothing but that window. What exactly was this uneasiness that this righteous man, the deacon, had instilled in me? I had no regrets . . . Or was I just trying to have no regrets? Or would it be better not to remain true to myself, to look more closely at the world into which I had landed by chance and submit to its laws, so that everything would be washed clean?

Before I realised it myself, I was standing at the window, opening it and climbing up onto the sill. I felt for her hands and met her lips. I whispered straight into her ear: 'The deacon sits down there. On the boat. Every night he sits there. You gave him something to hope for, didn't you?'

'I promised to be his wife,' she replied, also in a whisper.

I jerked away, nearly lost my foothold and had to hang on to the window-sill by my hands.

'You did?'

'He's a very good man,' she said, but did not try to excuse herself. 'We were supposed to get married next year.'

'Listen, Tosya,' I said in a loud, hoarse whisper, my chest squashed against the window-sill. 'Don't you regret what you've done? Could you really live the sort of life I lead? I'm a completely different kind of person; I can't see even a day ahead in my life.'

'But can you see me?'

Her hands were on my neck. But no, I was sober, and I wanted to talk, and for her to dispel my doubts, absolve my sins, and I wouldn't even object if she took those sins on herself. What could I do? It was my reflexes at work. I didn't want to defend myself – let other people do that – but I would struggle and writhe so much that not a single cell in my body would remain undefended. I was a bad man – let them prove that I was no worse than the others; I played dirty tricks on people – let them convince me that I could not behave otherwise, that anyone in my place would have done the same; I am a liar – so demonstrate, damn it, that my lie was objectively necessary and that there's no need to be a fool.

'Forgive me, Tosya!' I whispered with sincerity and passion. 'I should have behaved differently. None of this should have happened.' I banged my fist on the window-sill. 'Forgive me!'

Of course she would forgive me. I had no doubt of that.

But she had already taken me in her arms and was kissing me, persuading me that everything was as it should be, that she had wanted everything that had passed between us, and that she knew better than I what sort of person I really was. Well, thank God! I calmed down. With the very slightest movement of her hands she beckoned me into the room. I climbed over the window-sill.

'Tosya,' I said quite calmly, 'I'm going away tomorrow and I won't be back back until I have everything ready and all my business is taken care of. I love you. I'm going, now, and I shall set out in the morning, while you're still asleep, and I shall return early in the morning when you will be asleep too . . . And then everything will be different for us both. Is that right? It was no accident that we came together . . .'

'Of course, of course!' she whispered. 'That's how God decreed it for you. And for me.'

'I promise that I'll try to understand what I do not understand now. After all, I'm made out of the same material!'

I sat on the window-sill, squeezed her tight till it hurt, kissed her face, unlinked her hands, jumped to the ground and ran off, then ran up the outside steps to the attic, fell on the bed and wept silently. Later, tomorrow or after, I would reflect on all this and analyse its parts, but for the moment I was experiencing a rare happy moment of honest emotion, and I was so glad of it that I believed the moment might be extended, that it might last for ever.

I

My father is what I would call a good man. That's why I live with him and not with my mother. I get on well with him, so he is a good man as far as I am concerned.

His health is remarkable: he has double-bass strings instead of nerves. Nothing upsets him. The more I study my father the more I am impressed by his uniqueness. He regards the whole world, all the people around him and all his affairs both personal and professional as though he himself was the only reality in the whole world and all the rest was just cinema. Of course, he permits himself certain emotions, but he would find the very idea of giving in to them seriously laughable.

I have never met anybody else who could shrug his shoulders the way my father does. In that inimitable gesture there is more philosophy than in the discourses of any of the Stoics. I spent a long time teaching myself to copy that shrug of the shoulders, but I could never get it right.

Towards the end of their life together my mother would have hysterics every time she saw that gesture, and all she would get in reply to her hysterics would be the same gesture over again.

My father's indifference to the world and to mankind often permitted him to express very sober and reasonable ideas which gave me food for thought. And when I was approaching twenty my mother began to eye me with alienation and even overt hostility. Lyuska, my younger sister and my mother's accomplice and helper in everything, would squint in scorn and pass judgement on me: 'Daddy's little boy! Just as thick-skinned!' My mother would defend me half-heartedly, and I did not take offence. My mother's lack of equanimity in her view of life also struck me as false; I knew that I was thin-skinned and that unless I made myself less sensitive it was going to be difficult for me in this world, where everyone tried to tread on your toes, to jab you with their elbows, or to wound you with their tongue.

In the period of the 'Thaw' my mother and Lyuska got desperately involved in the dissident movement. Their one-room flat on Novoslobodskaya hummed with voices and was cluttered up with underground publications. Say what you like, it really was a happy time! You could smell the ozone, and how people loved it! The machines rattled away producing copy after copy of the human word rescued from the depths of silence. I, too, was caught up in the dissident stream. My father's flat was turned into a staging post for the distribution of hastily typed sheets. My father read everything I brought in and would comment: 'Curious' or 'Interesting' or sometimes briefly: 'Rubbish' and, as it appeared to me, a minute later would have forgotten what he had read. There was nothing to disturb his peace of mind. He didn't even express any concern that he might experience difficulties because of all this paper circulating, though my activities and his own involvement with the dissidents was only indirect. After all, it was his typewriter on which I used to tap out, with one finger, copies of uncensored poems, appeals and manifestoes.

As for my mother and Lyuska, that was another matter. They tore around Moscow like ones possessed, meeting somebody here, driving somebody else there, spending their evenings gasping over pages of *samizdat* signed by free-thinking physicists and poets.

Meanwhile Lyuska was keeping up with her studies at the faculty of journalism, my mother went on working at the institute of social science, and my father was teaching Marxism-Leninism at a technical college. And I was coming to the end of a training course in historical archiving and was already looking out for a cushy job in some big museum. It was a wonderful and very strange time to live through!

Eventually it all came to an end. The authorities came to their senses. The dissidents retreated into their own circles. The activists disappeared: some went West, some went East. In my mother's flat all that remained of the whole iconostasis of free-thinkers were the photographs of Akhmatova and Pasternak. Once again my father's bookshelves displayed only the sober bindings of the Russian classics.

Lyuska, the only one to suffer, now manages by doing odd jobs and hack work. Her relationship with our mother has cooled somewhat, but they get along all right. It seems to me that what keeps them together is their scorn for my father and me, although my relationship with my mother is more complex. We love each other, but are utterly different by nature. However, one's mother is one's mother. I miss her, but I couldn't stand living with her for a single day. My mother is aggressive, and it suits me better to be with my father, who is generous. Lyuska and my mother refuse on principle to accept any help from him. I don't refuse, and thereby even give him some pleasure. I don't take much from him, but the little I take makes all the difference between life and death.

My father has a woman friend, also a kind of Marxoid, from the same college. But he doesn't bring her home. He goes to her flat, or maybe they meet somewhere else – it's none of my business. He's often away from home, and the flat can be at my disposal for weeks on end. I have to admit it's a great set-up, but here I am, almost thirty, and it still seems that life hasn't yet begun, that it's on the point of starting, but, like the horizon, the beginning keeps retreating from me in proportion to the number of paces I take in its direction, and I am still not living, still only preparing to live . . .

That's the way it was until I made this last trip into the provinces.

I'm returning to Moscow a new man, or at any rate that is what I tell myself. I sense novelty in everything, in all my impressions and all my intentions. No, so far I am not aware of anything new about myself: where could it come from, the newness? It's a readiness, rather, for something new, a pleasant anticipation . . . I feel fine!

Today I like Moscow. I am not annoyed by the crush in the Metro, I smile at pretty women and at the less pretty ones too, and I probably look idiotic, but I am not to blame if the smile won't leave my face.

It's two months since I was in Moscow, but could I say, hand on heart, that I have longed to return to it? Not really. We are strange people, we city-dwellers. When we seek solitude, we leave our over-populated flats and dive into the crowd and contrive to see no one, to hear nothing and to think despite the screech of brakes: we know how to be alone with our egos while elbowing our way through crowds, dodging the onslaught of cars and being dazzled by advertisements. The whole of our way of life is abnormal, but if you agree to live that life, then it becomes the norm.

It is only when you return to Moscow that you realise how differently from the people in the provinces we native Moscovites regard the capital. We don't think of it as the capital of the country or the state. For us, Moscow is a political centre. What exactly it is the centre of is difficult to say. But in Moscow even a sneeze is a political event – there just aren't any non-political events. We can smell the politics, and we cut ourselves off from it in the little worlds that we create and destroy and re-create, and, for a true Moscovite, Moscow is a few flats where there is unlimited talk, excessive eating and wild drinking – a sort of mini-revolt against the universal involvement in politics. It is there that we liberate ourselves from serfdom, spread malicious stories, gossip about people, improvise, vulgarise, turn ourselves inside out, and it is really only this that we call living, not doing our jobs.

There are other lines of communication in our way of life, in our personal life which exists underground – the telephone wires. This telephone of ours is our inalienable, untouchable right, our freedom. A telephone in the entrance hall, on a window-sill or on a shelf, is not a telephone and any flat where there is a telephone like that can't belong to a real Moscovite. A Moscovite has his telephone next to a sofa or couch on a little table, so that he doesn't have to reach very far for it or strain into an awkward position. Your Moscovite enjoys telephoning in comfort, and there is only one good position: stretched out on a couch (divan or ottoman), a cigarette between his lips, a cup of black coffee with no sugar on the little table, and so, half lying, half sitting, he stretches out his free hand to take the receiver, dials the number without hurrying, and in a tired voice, taking his time, starts to gossip with whoever is on the other end, who is also in no hurry. It is an entirely new art form, a product of the second half of the twentieth century.

Every true Moscovite is sure, or at least hopes, that his telephone is being tapped – otherwise it would mean he would not be a person of any importance! But he also hopes, is even sure, that the secret police realise that he is not a dangerous person, well – a little irony perhaps, a little free-thinking, but thank God we have real dissidents, whom the police can easily distinguish from intellectuals who must have a little licence if they are to raise the productivity of their labour. After all, the secret police today are no longer made up of grave-diggers and executioners as in Stalin's day – they no longer grab every complainer by the throat, they just give him a gentle reprimand.

The true Moscovite's public persona is a little further to the left than his private self; deep down he believes that if it is possible to abuse any system a little, then one can make a life in it. That is, one can feel that one is living one's life in one's own way, free enough to respect oneself and despise whomever one wants to.

Moscow itself, for a true Moscovite, is a few blocks of buildings, streets or houses, perhaps a theatre, a few artists, poets, actors and exceptional personalities – that is what makes Moscow Moscow – not Moscow the capital but Moscow the micro-world of the elite, which excludes the political busy-bodies and the goggle-eyed provincials.

'Ah, Arbat, my Arbat!' The provincial won't understand what these words mean. They don't refer to a district of Moscow in which, maybe, he grew up, but to an illusory micro-world created by that simple song to counterbalance the slogans, the huge portraits and the skyscrapers. For a Moscov-ite 'our Moscow' is not the hero-city or the source of socialist power, heaven forbid! You have to make an effort to under-stand what 'our Moscow' is.

It makes no difference to the Moscovite that tomorrow he will be out on the street with a flag, and on full pay, on awful Kalinin Avenue to greet representatives of some hostile-friendly state; no difference that the next day at a Party meeting he will make a speech about the readiness of his department to accept bigger socialist obligations to mark the forthcoming congress; none of that matters, because on his shelf at home he has a copy of *The Master and Margarita*, and last year a dissident left a typewriter in his care, and the year before that he donated part of his fee for an article, believe it or not, to the fund for aid to . . . 'Ah, Arbat, my Arbat!'

Well, and what do I feel about Moscow? Love or hate? A bond, that's the word, precise and objective. You can be bonded to anything – and I am bonded to Moscow.

With my very first step off the train, I fell again into the ritual of my Moscow life. At the entrance to the Metro on Kropotkinskaya I dived into a telephone kiosk and phoned home. This was a rule. When my father returned from his trips he would also telephone the flat. After all, I might have a woman there. And he too might have one – less likely, perhaps, but he might, and so I phoned. No-one at home, fortunately. I practically ran down my street and only glanced briefly into the letter box as I entered the building. Nothing. Which meant that my father had been there that day. I unlocked the door and I was home: I looked into my father's room – everything in order as usual. The refrigerator was full. Only then did I go into my own room.

Dust everywhere. My father never touches any of my papers. He's the right sort of father! I unpacked my suitcase, threw the stuff gathered on my trip onto the table, put my washing in the bathroom, or rather under the bath, and my case under the couch. I collapsed onto the couch myself, with the telephone close to hand. Should I call someone? No, somehow I didn't want to. The altered circumstances of my private life had dragged me out of my rut. My much-loved room was private, all sixteen metres square of it, full of books and hung with a lot of reproductions and even a few originals, with a window looking on to the square and the area beyond. But today it felt sort of empty. I tried to imagine the priest's daughter in my room and tried to look with her eyes at every detail and at myself, stretched out on the couch by the telephone.

A nineteenth-century icon hangs alongside a photograph of Solzhenitsyn – that's a Moscow banality, but I take the icon in my hands as Tosya would and glance at the corner where there's a reproduction of Picasso's *Don Quixote*. With delicate, Tosya-like fingers I remove the Knight of the Sorrowful Countenance and put the icon in his place. I then take the Bible from a shelf full of old books in antique bindings and hold it in my hands, pressed to my chest; there's nowhere to put it so that it's separate from the other objects and books: and I need a little shelf for the icon, but I can't make it with these Tosya hands. To tell the truth I'm scarcely capable of doing it even with my own. So I borrow the exceptionally competent hands of one of my friends to fix up a shelf in the corner and the

Bible has a place. But then the table for papers and magazines is wrong so I move it right up to the writing desk, pull the table towards the bookshelves, remove the hanging shelves and put them up in other places; then down onto the floor come the pictures, reproductions and photographs. Now the couch is in the way of the door, and the telephone is completely hidden. Tired and annoyed by now, I turf the priest's daughter out of the room, put everything back in its place, and so recover a measure of tranquillity, but only a measure, because the priest's daughter is just outside the door and that isn't the place for her; her place is beside me, and so back she comes into the room with delicate steps, surveys the whole room until her gaze settles on the icon that was next to Solzhenitsyn, and she stretches out her hands to take it . . . starting the whole business all over again! I picked up the receiver and rang my mother.

'So you're back?' she asked.

'Yes, my trip is over.'

'How are you?'

'Fine!'

'Are you coming round?'

'Of course.'

'Is anything wrong?'

'Why should there be anything wrong?'

'If you are coming round *of course*, it means something must have happened.'

My mother loved to display her intuition.

'I suppose something has happened. I'm getting married.'

'When?'

'Not when, Mother, who. It's not Irina.'

'You've met someone in the country?'

'Yes.'

'When are you coming round?'

I could tell that my mother was worried about me, and I was grateful to her for it. 'She isn't in Moscow, and she won't be here for some time yet. How's Lyuska?'

My mother didn't reply, and I felt uneasy at once.

'What's up with her?'

'Not what you think . . . Come on round.'

'This evening. All right?'

Mother was glad that I was going to see her the same day. There must be something wrong with Lyuska. But, as far as I could make out, it was not because of her dissident connections. Something always had to happen with Lyuska. She lived on her nerves. Even as a child her lips were always bleeding because she'd bitten them. She breathed anxiety, she was always exposing or denouncing someone, always utterly devoted to someone else. When she was little I used to make fun of her and didn't notice when she'd ceased to be a little girl; on one occasion I earned a slap in the face for my mockery – probably well deserved. That slap upset our early relationship and nothing replaced it; and I began to be afraid of her, while she developed a certain contempt for me. But you can't suppress family feelings, and I got used to loving my sister at a distance. Which may be the most genuine kind of love, anyway, or the only kind. I keep everyone at a distance. To judge when to allow a little cold to enter into a relationship – there's a lot of wisdom in that.

I suppose it's not so much my style as my father's. But while I do it consciously, sometimes having to force myself, in my father's case it happens unforcedly, naturally: for him, passion simply does enter into a relationship. Passion in another person makes him detached enough so he can take advantage of the heat of that fire without getting burnt.

I'm indebted to my father for a great deal. He was my first love. I worshipped him as a child, he was so calm, serious, industrious and self-assured. But it was he who first made me feel slighted. Sensing my excessive attachment to him, he pushed me away on one occasion with the cold palm of his hand – gently, but it was impossible for me not to understand what the gesture meant. After that I was always aware of the space that he had created between the two of us. I have never forgotten the way I suffered, and decided even as a child never again to expose myself to such pain. Later in life, when I pushed others away from myself and saw how hurt they were, I would say to myself: let that be a lesson to you, my friend, that's life; once bitten, twice shy!

There was the sound of a key turning in a lock and the door opening quietly. My father was back.

'Gena, you home?'

I went out to greet him with a welcoming gesture. That was all we permitted ourselves on meeting. My father's hair was, as always, carefully trimmed and he was smartly dressed in grey, a colour that suited him. He was good-looking and clean-shaven; in his eyes were intelligence and repose, in his movements restraint and in his speech precision and maximum economy.

'All well?' he asks, and it is not an empty question but meant seriously, because things do not always go well, and then I reply accordingly and we have a useful and businesslike conversation. But on this occasion I reply:

'All's well. But I must have a talk with you.'

He nodded understandingly. 'Have you eaten or shall we eat together?'

'Together.'

'Put the kettle on, then, and warm up the meat-balls. I'll go and change.'

I could, of course, imitate my father, but it would never be more than an imitation. My character, alas, has been diluted by my mother's emotional nature. I only play the accompaniment to my father, and for all our similarity on the surface – we seem to use the same words and share the same principles – the things that he does so easily and unselfconsciously demand in my case an effort of will. I have to force myself.

I knew, for example, the sort of conversation we would now have – not the conversation that I really wanted.

I switched on the hot-plate, banged the frying pan and kettle about, clattered the crockery, and sat down to wait for my father. Well, there was the difference. Would I ever learn to change my clothes so pedantically when I got home, to hang my things up in the wardrobe, to put my shoes together beneath the coats, or even not to batter my slippers so mercilessly?

My father appeared in what he wore at home, no less smart, his hair carefully brushed, creases in his trousers. What was the use of having creases in the trousers he wore at home? I envied him, but my envy did not affect my conduct.

I distributed the meat-balls and poured the tea. For some time we ate in silence. Finally I asked him: 'How are things with you?'

'No change.'

That was not an evasion of the question. It meant that there really had been no changes in his life for better or worse.

'I'm going to get married,' I said.

He stopped eating and regarded at me seriously.

'Not to Irina,' I continued, anticipating his question. 'Not to anyone in Moscow.'

He looked at me for a good half minute, which was enough for him to take in the situation.

'You'll need a flat.'

Does anyone else have a father like that?

'A single-roomed flat built by a cooperative costs four thousand. I can let you have two thousand.'

That means he really can't produce more. I had not counted on anything like that! But why did I feel so sad? *He* would part from me without any regrets, and *I* would have liked the three of us to live together – Tosya, me and my father – and I would even have liked to have all four of us there – Father Vasili as well. Or even five of us together – my mother and even Lyuska too, so long as her room was well away from mine. We could live as one big family, the whole clan. We'd get on so well together! Who wouldn't Tosya get along with?

All this flashed quickly through my mind. But my father saw much further ahead than I did. Children! I wanted to

have them. Tosya too, of course. Father didn't need anybody.
Even me.

'Who is she?' Father asked.

I can't lie to my father. I told him the truth: 'She's a priest's
daughter.'

Father was surprised: 'That's original,' he said. 'And, probably, a good thing. It could have been one of these dissidents.
In any case, it's out of the ordinary. Does your mother know?'

'I talked to her on the phone. I'm going to see her today.
What's happened to Lyuska?'

Father didn't know. Lyuska could be dying and she wouldn't
let Father know. This seems cruel to me, but it obviously
doesn't seem to bother him. Our father will probably live to
be a hundred.

He answered my question with another question: 'I gather
she's still hanging around with dissidents?'

I shrugged my shoulders. 'She'll end up marrying a Jew and
going to Israel.'

I tried to detect the slightest nuance in his voice, but there
was none; it was just a calm, controlled statement. That really
was what could happen to Lyuska. And Father was ready for
it.

'And you? How are you going to come to terms with your
wife concerning God?'

'I'll try to understand the idea.' I shrugged my shoulders in
almost the same way as my father did.

'Your generation certainly loves complications.' He speaks
without condemnation or envy, he's simply stating a fact. 'But
she ought to make a good wife.'

Again, he was right. Tosya *would* be a good wife. But in
what way had my mother been bad for my father? I longed to
ask him that, but he answered my question without it being
asked: 'A woman's intellect is not measured in terms of edu-
cation, but by her ability to be a wife and mother, to create a
family and to hold it together . . . Who needs her degrees and
titles?'

Those remarks would have sounded trite if they had not referred to my mother. It was true – who needed *her* academic degrees, obtained by out-and-out hack-work? My father's degree had been obtained in the same way, and it was no use to anybody but him. I couldn't tell him that. But then again, why shouldn't I?

'Well, and what about your Marxism, Dad?'

It wasn't the first time this subject had come up between us. He poured himself some more tea. I refused more.

'It all depends what you mean by the truth. Is Marxism really only Marx and Lenin? It is the theory of socialism. And the socialist ideal is as old as mankind. A portion of mankind has longed for and still longs for a socialist way of life, and can one really deny the truth of something that has existed for thousands of years? What exists is reasonable. If it is reasonable, it follows that it is true, that is to say it is a real element of being. There are some people who do not find this element to their taste, but so what? Every truth of Marxism put forward separately may sound questionable – like, incidentally, any other truth – but taken together Marxism, or socialism, is a reality, towards which millions of people are striving even today. And where? There, in the West, at what might seem the opposite pole. In a certain sense, socialism is a biological attraction for a person against which facts and arguments are powerless and, consequently, it contains the real truth of existence. Take nationalisation, for example – is it a good thing? The fact is that it is inevitable; it is what mankind is moving towards, drawn on by instinct. That means it is also true.'

My father looked at me. I knew he never imposed his views on me and would say not another word if he saw that I was not listening or was not listening properly.

'But you are making a career out of Marxism in a country in which Marxism has compromised itself.'

My father's eyebrows shot up in amazement. 'Compromised itself? Not in the least. On the contrary, it is in this country

that socialism has triumphed completely through having transformed the human psyche without leaving a single cell free for
any alternative.'

My father smiled, and I knew that smile, which meant that
he was about to deliver some painful truth.

'One of the reasons that socialism triumphed was because it
was able to defuse the opposition. Take yourself, for example,
do you really represent a danger to socialism? Yet you are in
opposition to it. But you are not dangerous because your
opposition is not directed at the essence of the system but is
essentially self-centred.'

'And you don't count the dissidents either?'

'No,' he replied, 'and for the same reasons. Their dissidence
does not affect the essence of socialism, and their egoism is
extremely clannish.'

'Does that mean you think that people who go to prison are
motivated by egoism?'

My father was listening closely to my tone of voice. If he
felt that I was not being serious the conversation would end.

'No, what I believe is different,' he said. He chose his words
carefully. 'The Populists who were opposed to Tsarism were
ready to fight it to the death, that is, they promised death to
their enemies and were ready to die themselves. But *our*
dissidents bend over backwards to demonstrate that they are
not anti-Soviet, that they are not engaged in political activity,
and they themselves are quite convinced that there is no reason
that they should be imprisoned. You don't have to look far for
an example – your own sister is convinced that the authorities
ought to pay attention to everything she says; which is often
pretty confused, but they must heed her words because, you
see, she, your little sister, wishes the authorities well! Now,
honestly, isn't it ridiculous to imagine that a regime that rests
on the support of millions, even if the support is silent . . .'

At that point he caught the grin on my face. 'Ah, you're
thinking about the bayonets. But bayonets are used to put
down a revolt; there are no bayonets that can prevent one if

the situation is ripe for it. The dissidents aren't in revolt, are they? So isn't it ridiculous to suggest that the authorities must take heed and change their ways every time a few over-excited girls demand it? All right, granted it's not only girls. But these are people who have neither a programme nor even a clear idea of what they are fighting. The Soviet system is the product of a whole epoch, the sum of a thousand years of history, and a dozen intellectuals at odds with each other present no danger to it. I personally admire the political system we have: it is magnificent and grandiose . . .'

'And do you admire the prison camps as well?' I interjected gloomily.

'You're making me sound like a monster,' said my father calmly. 'As as a political system that has reached the stage of optimal stability, socialism cannot fail to command respect. History proves that bluffing never works: it is only what is unique and essential that succeeds, and always according to the desire of the people themselves. We have got what we asked for.'

'And you personally – do you like the thing you serve?'

He gave the familiar shrug of the shoulders.

'I am fifty. Is that good, what do you think, you, at thirty? There's probably very little that's good about it, and that makes me rather sad. But I find there are certain advantages in being my age. My age is just as unalterable a fact as the socialist system I serve. I don't propose to squeeze myself into jeans and wear shirts with parrots on them and I don't run after eighteen-year-old girls. Have you got your answer?'

'Yes, I suppose so,' but I asked him one more question. 'Do you recognise that Lyuska and the others have a moral right to act as they do?'

Another shrug of the shoulders. 'Why not? But can you,' – said my father, smiling, – 'can you argue that the mouse has a greater moral right to live than the cat has to eat it?'

'Father, this is no more than cynicism.'

'No,' he objected vigorously. 'It's realism, adult realism.

And it's serious. If only Lyuska's friends would understand that they are not dealing with a 'police dictatorship', to use that cliché of the nineteenth century, but with the harsh reality of a political system which contains its own justification in the fact of its very existence; if they could understand that, they would be more serious opponents. But the whole point is that they are not opponents, only dissidents, and their presence can easily be regulated by the system.'

My father looked at me with his bright Marxist eyes, and I so envied his confidence, a confidence which was so alien to me, envied his ability to lean assuredly on something more stable than himself. I was like a sapling with weak roots; always trying to assume a pose of firmness, but always being pushed in all directions, bending with the wind, like a mime artiste. The unnaturalness of my movements some superficial observers took for originality; of course I hastened to assure them of the correctness of their impression – but anyone who has been through that knows how tired you can get of striking poses and trying to be original . . .

My father was looking at me with his bright, disinterested eyes. I knew that I had the same eyes. I was, after all, my father's son, only mine were somewhat bluer, while his had lost some of their brightness because of his passion for Marxism. Here we were eyeing each other, fusing our gaze into something united, related at least in the flesh; we stared at each other, as if each of us were studying his own likeness in a mirror, and then our eyes broke away, each of us returned to his own thoughts, to his own world. Our worlds were alien, between them there was no family resemblance, only a mutually advantageous tolerance.

'How's your work going?' he asked.

'It's under control,' I replied.

For me that 'under control' might mean a lot of things, for my father it meant one thing only: moderation in effort that provided you with a means of livelihood.

'Will you clear away?' he asked, rising from the table.

I nodded. In our flat everything had long ago been agreed once and for all. If I cleared the table today, that meant he would do it the next time.

'When should I give you the money?' He was already in the hall when he asked.

'Not just yet.'

'Let me know.'

He went off to his own room, and it was time for me to think about some things which I had to resolve straight away. The money, for example. I would have to get at least another four thousand. That meant I had to get myself some odd jobs straight away. In my mind, I went through all my acquaintances and settled on Yevgeni Poluëktov, a bespectacled owlish-looking extremely shrewd operator who had been doing literary hack-work for years. Some jobs had already come my way through him; he would pass one on to me if he'd been offered two at once. I'd met him through Irina. For a long time I'd had my suspicions that it wasn't only work I shared with him, but Irina dismissed any such suggestions with indignation, and in any case it was immaterial, given the style of relationship that had formed between me and Irina from our first meeting.

Oh, yes, Irina, too. It wasn't going to be easy to deal with her either.

I wanted to see her. Just to see her – nothing more. No feelings ever vanish without trace, and what I feared most of all was that I would start pitying her when the time came to have it out with her. I ought to have learnt from my father how to part from people.

I phoned Zhenka Poluëktov's flat. A woman's voice cheerfully gave me the phone number where Zhenka could be reached in the next hour. I rang the number and asked in a cool and businesslike voice for Yevgeni Vladislavovich to be called to the telephone: I was keeping up appearances on Zhenka's behalf. We agreed to meet at eight o'clock in his flat, which meant that I could spend till seven in the evening with my mother. It was already after three.

I didn't tell my father that I was going out or when I would
be back. It didn't matter to him. If anything had happened to
either of us when we were out of the flat neither would
have missed the other for months on end. It was an ideal
relationship. But from time to time I was drawn away from
that ideal to visit my mother. I didn't much like her flat: there
were always people there talking about their problems, and
every time I appeared they would for some reason all start
complaining, as though they wanted to underline how difficult
their lives were, and how compared with them I was nothing
but a dreary philistine. Lyuska was especially aggressive. She
would start praising somebody for his courage as a citizen,
someone else for a skilful piece of conspiracy, a third person
for his reaction to a dissident event. If I tried to enter into the
conversation Lyuska would ignore me, or interrupt me, or,
frowning with scorn, she might ask: 'Why did you come along?'

My mother would annoy me in her own way: she would ask
me about my affairs, and if I gave way under her questioning
she would start telling me how to run my life, abusing my
father, and explaining what a bad influence he was on me.

This time I was in luck. Even as Lyuska opened the door I
realised that there were no visitors in the flat. But I was worried
by something else – Lyuska's face, always drawn and thin, was
now no more than skin and bone. Her eyes were feverish. Her
bones stuck out under her dressing-gown. Her lips were blue.
She looked a real mess.

Lyuska opened the door without saying a word, pushed
some slippers towards me and went off to the kitchen.

'Come in here, Gena!' my mother called from her room. So
I realised that mother and daughter had just been quarrelling,
and that my arrival was very opportune because through me
they could make peace with each other: in the end their joint
attitude to me would re-unite them.

My mother also looked strained, but well. Whenever I saw
her again after a long break the same illusion came over me:
that everything was now going to be different, we would now

find a common language once and for all – what was there for us to quarrel about? – and I would be overcome by a sudden tenderness towards her. Perhaps it was mutual.

'You're looking very well,' she said.

That was what she always said.

'So are you,' I always said this, sometimes when it was not true, as on this occasion.

'Would you like coffee?'

I said I would.

'Lyuska!' my mother called. 'Make us some coffee, please.'

A step, this, towards the reconciliation that both of them desperately needed. My sister did not reply, but made a lot of noise with the cups and saucers, a way of saying that she was still cross but was ready to make it up.

'This trip was to somewhere very far away, wasn't it?'

'Very far. To Siberia.'

'It must have been very interesting . . .' My mother said uncertainly.

'For me, yes.'

'How's your father?'

At this point Lyuska came in with a jar of instant coffee. Whenever there was talk about our father she couldn't restrain herself, she had to take part.

'Yes, how *is* Daddy getting on?'

'You could always ask him yourself,' I replied. Lyuska's cheeks flushed and tears of rage came into her eyes.

'Surely something must happen to him sometime?' she hissed, but our mother stopped her:

'That's enough, you really shouldn't talk like that.'

I know something my mother doesn't know. Lyuska hates Father, she hates him just as passionately as she loved him in childhood – and she suffers because of that hate. Three years ago she phoned him early one morning and asked him to wait at home until she arrived. Throughout the night she had prepared what she wanted to tell him, after which they were to be friends again. But, arriving in a taxi, she could do no more than howl: 'Daddy, I love you!' and burst into tears. Her father calmed her down and then scolded her for making him late for work.

After he left, Lyuska made a terrible scene in the flat, so bad I could hardly cope. She hurled every insult she could at me, tried to scratch my face, and as she left she shouted from the outside landing: 'You're both inhuman monsters!' When I told my father later how Lyuska's visit had ended he just shrugged his shoulders.

'So how are things?' Lyuska was *still* trying to get at me. 'Does our father still shave twice a day?'

I tried to reply quietly: 'Your friend Shurik never shaves, but that doesn't seem to bother you.'

They were both suddenly silent.

'He's been shaved already, no doubt you'll be delighted to hear,' Lyuska said maliciously.

I glanced at my mother.

'They sent him to prison a month ago.'

Lyuska had been in love for many years with Shurik – I didn't know his surname. At the beginning it had been a one-sided affair – Shurik was married. In the end Lyuska had got her own way, but they'd never got married. I don't really know why. It was through Shurik that my mother and Lyuska had got involved in the dissident movement.

Lyuska pursed her lips, and her eyes filled with tears.

'What happened was . . .' my mother began, but Lyuska screamed:

'Don't you dare! You know it will only give him pleasure!'

'Why are you so sure of that?' my mother asked timidly.

I shrugged my shoulders, and I could tell by Lyuska's fierce look that at last I had succeeded in reproducing my father's favourite gesture.

'They're not capable of understanding anything!' Lyuska hissed. 'They' meant my father and me. 'They're robots!'

'Stop it,' said my mother sharply. 'Do you want Gena to hear about it from other people?'

With a quick jerk of her shoulders Lyuska ran out of the room.

'The truth of the matter is,' my mother said quietly, 'that Shurik has been providing them with evidence. About Lyuska, too. It's so unexpected . . .'

I just didn't know what to say. It was the first time for many years such an active and dedicated dissident should suddenly . . .

'Lyuska was called in for questioning. She told them nothing, she was trying to protect Shurik, but then they organised a face-to-face confrontation and he, in the presence of the interrogator, tried to persuade Lyuska to conceal nothing because, as he put it, he had come to understand a great many things *in there*, had seen his mistakes and was making a clean breast of it all. We can't understand his recanting. He always spoke with such passion and conviction . . . Maybe they put something in his food . . . or maybe they used hypnosis . . . what do you think? You knew him, after all.'

Yes, I had known him and I had listened to him and read his articles, which were always outspoken and well-argued.

'What can I tell you, Mother? Maybe he panicked. I might do the same. I'm afraid of prison. Perhaps he is too –'

When Lyuska reappeared in the doorway, I didn't notice her.

'Listen to him – he's actually comparing *Shurik* to *himself!*' She gave me a withering look. 'You! Did you ever have any convictions, anything you really believed in? Any feelings, apart from a desire to conform?'

My mother hastened to intervene.

'Lyuska thinks they're keeping him on drugs, injecting him with something . . . After all, in his day Bukharin also confessed to God knows what, and so did others . . .'

'Perhaps,' I replied, doubtfully, 'but in my opinion – of course I'm not a fighter like you – in my opinion fear of prison is perfectly normal in anybody, and anybody can be intimidated . . .'

'Rubbish,' Lyuska shouted. '*I'm* not afraid of going to prison! I tell you, I'm not afraid. Are you capable of understanding that, you moron?'

Without giving me a chance to reply my mother spoke softly, obviously confused by what had happened:

'You're right – prison is a terrible thing . . . But then there are one's convictions . . . and there's elementary decency . . . And he did love Lyuska.'

'But maybe he actully *has* repented?'

'Of what?' the two of them exclaimed.

'Well, maybe he realised that it's all useless.'

Lyuska clutched her forehead and shook her head. 'I can't stand this! Stop it at once! At once! Mother, *please!*'

'All right, all right, we won't talk about it. Let's have some coffee.'

'Mother,' I enquired, 'have you got anything a little stronger to drink?'

In her confusion she passed on my question to Lyuska: 'Do we have anything?'

'I wouldn't mind a drink myself,' Lyuska muttered.

At last she'd managed to utter at least a couple of normal words, after all the repulsive things she had said. I wanted simultaneously to embrace her and box her ears. But how could I do such a thing given the present state of our relationship?

She produced an opened bottle of vermouth and my mother brought out some glasses.

'Do you want something to eat?'

I didn't want to eat, I wanted to drink. I felt rather sick, and also depressed. I was rather sorry for everybody, myself included.

'So you're going to get married,' my mother said.

I drank down the wine at a gulp and without asking poured myself another glass and did the same with that. Mother eyed me with surprise.

'This is something new! Are you taking to drink?'

I waved the remark away. Lyuska held her glass for some time between the palms of her hands, as though she was warming the wine, then drank it carefully in little sips, as if it were boiled water, then held the glass for a while between her palms again.

'So who is she, your future wife?'

'She's the daughter of a priest,' I replied in a normal voice.

'You're joking!'

'No, Mother, she really is a priest's daughter, that is, the daughter of a clergyman.'

'And does she . . . believe? . . . Is she a believer?'

'Yes, she believes in God.'

Mother was about to ask a stream of awkward questions, but paused, undecided.

'That means it's all over with Irina?'

'That's it.'

'Forgive me, but I can't tell whether this is serious or just goes under the category of originality. I mean, it somehow doesn't make sense.'

'Come on, of course you can understand, Mother,' Lyuska exploded again. 'Gena simply doesn't want to be behind the times. Every revolutionary decline is accompanied by a boom in religion. Religion is safe and original. This is the right time to marry priests' daughters. It may even become the fashion among deserters!'

'Thanks, deserter,' I replied. 'Come to think of it, I still have Solzhenitsyn hanging on my wall, but I don't see anything on yours.'

'Why should you take Solzhenitsyn down?' Lyuska was going to scratch my face any minute. 'He's a Russian patriot now. He's already pining for totalitarianism. You just wait and see – he'll be back here, your Solzhenitsyn.'

'*My* Solzhenitsyn?' I nearly fell over in surprise. 'Wasn't it you . . .'

'What, me! . . .' Lyuska shouted. 'Cowards and traitors! People are dying in prison cells and camps while you rush to marry priests' daughters! I hope you drown in your lust, you Judas!'

My patience was at an end, and I banged on the table with the palm of my hand. Mother just managed to grab her glass with one hand and hold the bottle with the other. My glass had fallen to the floor. Lyuska cringed as I approached her.

'Bitch!' I said, losing control of myself.

'Gennadi!' my mother cried out.

'Yes, a bitch, that's what you are. Your Shurik isn't the first person ever to be sent to prison. Plenty of people have been through it before. And when you slept with him, what were' you doing together – summarising *Gulag*? And what about your abortions – were they the fruit of revolutionary zeal?'

'Gennadi, please,' my mother begged.

But no, now I had started, I was going to finish saying what I had to say to this hysterical ninny.

'Your hero turned out to be a phoney and a coward. That's the truth! But it's not the point. The point is that you, with your hysterical ways, managed to choose a phoney and a coward of all people. After all, up to now he's the only one who's broken down. You are a hysterical fool!'

I bent over her, and she shrank down into the chair – more out of shock than fear.

'Your way of life revolts me. Playing at being heroes! Revolutionary love! The very language you use is revolting. It's so out of date. And it's so cheap. I'm scared of prison, yes, but I wouldn't have let you down the way your Shurik has done. OK, I might have slapped your face – but that would have done some good, if only from a medical point of view.'

Mother jumped up from her chair and grabbed me by the shoulders.

'Gennadi, get out of here at once! At once! I didn't know you could be such a brute.'

I swallowed hard and said quietly:

'I'm not a brute, Mother, but I'm not like my father either. I won't come to see you again. You aren't normal people. What did I ever do to you to make you hate me? But you hate anyone who isn't one of you, who doesn't live and think as you do. I'm no hero and no fighter, but you'll never achieve anything either, because you're choking with hatred.'

'Gennadi!'

'I'm going, I'm going.'

'Wait, Mother!' Lyuska cried, jumping up and standing in the passageway.

What on earth did she want now! Her hands resting on the door-frame were white, she was shaking all over, the veins in her neck stood out; my God, she looked hideous!

I stood there, waiting. She said nothing, but her lips were twitching.

'Mother,' she said at last, 'leave us two alone.'

'Fine! All we need is a fight. Gennadi, please go.

I took a step towards the door, but Lyuska cried out: 'No, he's staying here. Mother, leave us alone. Do you hear, Mother? Otherwise you and I will quarrel.'

'As far as I can see,' said my mother wearily, 'that's about all you and I have been doing today.' She made a gesture with her hand and left the room, hanging her head.

Lyuska took a step towards me. I was slightly tipsy but on my guard.

'Genka, help me,' she said suddenly with a sob. 'Save me, I'm at the end of my tether. I don't want to live any more, Genka!'

She took another step, and I rushed to take her in my arms, kissed her gaunt cheeks and forehead and stroked her tangled hair.

'Help me, Genka!' she whispered and went on crying.

'Of course, of course, we'll think of something.' I was having trouble with my eyes, too.

'What am I to do, Genka?'

'I don't know, but I'll think of something, I promise.'

I was sure there must be some way out: I felt confident and reassured her with a clear conscience. At such moments our differences seemed so unimportant that I started to dream vaguely again of a large, happy family, and I whispered to Lyuska: 'We must all live together, all of us . . .'

She moved away, still sobbing, her shoulders shaking.

'What are you talking about? That's impossible!'

I could hardly hear her, she spoke so quietly, but I knew that nothing had changed, that I was not going to be able to think of anything that could help my sister, and that she realised that I was powerless . . . You could see that she too was fed up with our fighting, that she had wanted for a moment to stand in that embrace as though we had always been friendly and close; now I thought she was about to start shouting and cursing but she only whispered: 'What am I to do?' She was no longer whispering to me but to herself.

'Maybe go away somewhere,' I said.

'Where to?'

'I know one place where you could relax, where you would be looked after and where you would be at peace.'

'You mean with your priest's daughter?' She guessed at once and shook her head. 'That wouldn't suit me at all.'

'But you've no idea what sort of people they are!' I argued.

'What's more, I don't have the money to get there.'

'I'll give you money . . .'

'And where will you get it from?' There was already suspicion in her voice. 'From Father?'

'Why from him?' I mumbled. 'I was on an assignment, and I got a bonus.'

She didn't believe me: she knew me too well.

'Genka,' she said, turning away to the window, 'do you really think he just got scared?'

I said nothing. But silence was also a reply.

'You know, he had a foreboding, shortly before it happened he said: come on, let's go away. He'd been sent an invitation to go to Israel, a real one, he has relations there. Does that mean he was afraid? Afraid he wouldn't hold up?'

I still said nothing. But now it was pretty clear to me. Her

Shurik had planned to make himself scarce as soon as he smelt danger, but he had miscalculated and in his disappointment he had broken down. He'd had no intention of going to prison and he hadn't prepared himself for it.

'When he told me to conceal nothing from the police I looked him straight in the eye. I was already thinking, thinking that maybe everything we had done was actually a mistake and I hadn't realised it. If you see what I mean – I can admit that might be true in my case, but surely he . . . he couldn't have been mistaken.'

I interrupted her, I hadn't the patience to listen to her any longer: 'You aren't concentrating on what matters. The only important thing now is whether you love him or not. That's the question.'

She simply brushed my remark aside. 'I'm not seventeen, to love a man for no reason. Even at seventeen that doesn't happen.'

'Lyuska, I'll get the money. Go there – believe me, you'll come back a different person.'

She gave a nervous laugh. 'Thanks, but that treatment isn't for me. I can't go away now, don't you understand? That would mean deserting him. So you see – you can't help me at all . . . Mother!'

My mother reappeared and it was clear she'd been crying. Lyuska sat her down next to her and beckoned me to sit at my mother's other side. Lyuska filled our glasses.

'Right! We've shouted ourselves hoarse and cried our eyes out, and now we have to go on living. Give Mother a hug, idiot!'

I put my arm round my mother, crossing over Lyuska's arm too. My mother wiped her eyes with a handkerchief and placed her hands on our knees. An idyllic picture! We drank without clinking glasses and without any toasts. What would be the point of toasts! I was sniffing and tears were welling into my eyes which I no longer attempted to conceal.

*

By the time I left my mother it was half past seven. I was going to be late at Zhenka's, so I hailed a taxi.

It was pathetic: thirty years old, and still no real character of my own. With my father I behaved like my father; with my mother and Lyuska, I was just as crazy and hysterical as they were. And in general, I adapted myself to situations, I blended in. It was time to figure out which style was natural to me: where I began and imitation left off.

I was sorry for Lyuska, but there was nothing I could do to help her. The most important thing for her now was to be left alone, and for some reason I had a feeling she would be. I couldn't imagine Lyuska in prison. I personally had a pathological fear of prison. From the stories told by the *zaks* under Stalin, and by today's political prisoners as well, I had a good idea of the inhumanity there and could not imagine anything so important that I would voluntarily condemn myself to all the humiliation and restrictions that prison meant for its sake. No matter how horrible our life might be, it still retained a certain degree of pleasure or simply normality. Consequently, whenever I heard that someone had been sent to prison I shuddered and I sympathised with him, whoever he might be. And when I heard people say about the latest person to disappear something to the effect that he had brought it on himself, that he had asked for it, I eyed them with suspicion. They seemed to me to be bigger cowards than I was. The fear in their hearts overwhelmed them and clouded their power of reasoning – how could anyone really want to go to prison?

And yet how often I'd had occasion to listen to the reminiscences of former prison camp inmates and to see their eyes shine with sheer joy and even, incredibly, happiness! Recalling the 'old times', they would always find bright moments in them; to hear them talk you would think that they had experienced their moments of greatest happiness in the camps. I feel ill when I hear that sort of talk: I see it as a sort of moral perversion. I don't understand people like that; I don't want to understand them, and I even find it impossible to respect them – everything in me cries out against them. It makes me shudder and I think that is quite natural and normal. I am simply unable to imagine that one can experience happy or even merely pleasant moments in prison. I'm prepared to accept that, at the animal level to which a person can be reduced in prison, it may be possible to experience happiness, say, when one gets an extra ration of food, but for that kind of dog's happiness to be recalled as real happiness by someone enjoying his freedom . . . I also don't believe that people conceive great ideas or undergo moral purification in prison either. Perhaps I'm too down-to-earth, but if I were prevented from seeing the face of the woman I love no ideology could ease my pain, and my whole life would be one of hopeless suffering without prospect of renewal.

I sat back in the comfortable seat of the taxi and sped round the Sadovoye ring-road, with Moscow flashing past. It doesn't matter whether I like Moscow or not; it is my life and today I had enough money to indulge in the luxury of riding alone through the city. There were a thousand problems ahead of me; I might be exhausted by them and feel bogged down in trivia, but I wouldn't exchange them for any kind of prison heroism.

Another thing I disliked in Lyuska's world was their crude way of repeating the past. Thousands, if not millions, of people had exchanged life for the negation of life simply so that someone like me could have the pleasure of riding in a taxi. And now thousands more were throwing away their lives in order to try and eliminate global suffering, and they didn't see the senselessness of that, though it screamed out from every page of history and from every street-corner; in the scream you could hear the universal lack of order and lack of satisfaction and all the other shortcomings which were in fact the very essence of life – remove them, do away with them, and what would be left?

Sometimes, when I managed to look at life as a whole, I would find a legitimate place for Lyuska and her friends in that whole. They may not have been an important element in the grand scheme; but added to the flavouring . . . But I tried not to follow this line of thought through to the end, because from the word 'flavouring' to the word 'salt' was but one logical step. There was no way I could regard Lyuska's furious activity as the salt of the earth. In general, thoughts unpursued seem more significant, and I see myself as a quiet thinker with Rodinesque lines across my forehead, a wise man speeding in a taxi above the many-coloured bustle of life.

I have to justify myself because I love myself and that self-love – that alone – makes it possible for me to love those close to me. Even if I despise myself for everything I know about myself, are those around me any different, any better than I? But I love myself as I am, which means that I am obliged to love my neighbour out of a sense of justice, and if I don't always succeed it is only because it can be rather difficult, sometimes, not to despise oneself.

That's why I try to understand everybody, not to agree with them but actually to understand them, and I think that's probably the only approach to people that will stem feelings of hatred or even revulsion. There is only one problem: the more you understand people the less you like them and the more inevitable solitude becomes; isn't it better to believe what a person thinks about himself? After all, we still don't know what's more genuine in a person – his actions or his intentions. If I am judged by my intentions I seem a pretty fine fellow; to be frank, it is because of my very intentions that I admire myself. Am I really to blame if things work out differently in life? A person exists both in the pure state – as the sum of his intentions – and in real life – that is, in interaction with everything around him. The really bad person has bad intentions.

'Here?' the taxi-driver asked.

It's no accident that I like riding in taxis. If I could spend even two hours a day in a travelling nest like this I'd turn into an Immanuel Kant and would create a philosophy of my very own, called something like 'The New Humanist'. But my journeys in taxis are too short to allow me to arrive at any important conclusions – you can't do a lot of philosophising for three roubles!

I went up in the lift to the sixteenth floor, where my prospective source of income Zhenka Poluëktov lived at the very top of the building. For each of us, a flat is a different thing: for my father it was a study; for my mother a passage-way; for me it was a lair. Zhenka's flat was a sort of advertisement. The amount of money that had been spent on all the special wallpaper, special parquet floors and special tiles was beyond belief. A visitor was bound to realise that the owner of such a flat was a person in a secure position and with unlimited connections. Everything was intended to overwhelm a guest with the owner's intellectual qualities. Eighteenth-century icons and vast paintings by masters of abstract art, bookshelves with valuable first editions, contemporary works inscribed by the authors scattered carelessly around the room, an imported foreign typewriter, piles of good quality paper, and manu-scripts everywhere – the appealing disorder of a working author but with everything in its place. And then the owner himself, an impressive figure with beard and moustache, a luxurious ankle-length dressing-gown with a Marlboro or a Camel cigarette in his mouth. He spoke in a soft baritone, with a hint of fatigue or langour, a voice incapable of expressing surprise. That was Zhenka Poluëktov. True, he never put on a performance for me – we had known each other too long for that.

'Gena, my friend, I've been waiting for you,' he said as he opened the door to me. 'Just a minute while I see my guest out.'

While I was removing my shoes he sailed into the room and returned with a man who looked like a Tungus or a Nanai from Siberia, smartly dressed and freshly barbered.

'My dear fellow,' Zhenka was saying in a silky voice, 'rest assured, everything will be done in the best possible way. You are lucky to be dealing with someone who's no beginner in these matters.'

The man cast a not very trusting glance at Zhenka, thanked him in a rather perfunctory way, and left, without bothering to look in my direction. When the foreign lock on the door had clicked shut Zhenka sighed with relief and said, this time without the silken intonation:

'That younger brother in our family of nations has upset my profoundly internationalist sentiments for a moment. Come on in.'

'Who was it?'

'He's the goose that laid the golden egg. They are preparing to publish an anthology of poetry written by the peoples of the North. It's the cave of the forty thieves for an intellectual. I have been offered – please note – offered, I didn't ask for it myself – the chance to enrich world poetry by translating the work of some children of the polar night. I'll tell you about it and then you'll see what I mean . . .'

He threw off his luxurious dressing-gown and revealed a splendid track-suit beneath it. Then he got busy with the coffee machine.

'A word-for-word translation of this groom of Pegasus reads' – he snatched up a page from the desk as follows: '"When I was but a little puppy, and my mother cleaned up my shit behind me . . ." You don't believe me? Take a look. For a whole hour I tried to obtain his permission to delete the excrement at least, but he only shook his head and demanded an exact translation. Neither could we agree about the word "puppy". I tried in vain to explain to him that in Russian the word "puppy" applied to a child has a rather pejorative meaning; for him a puppy is a beautiful creature that could not possibly evoke any negative feelings in a reader. So you see, old boy, the sort of conditions I have to work in. There is no safety net.'

'Is it worth it?'

'Need you ask!'

I looked around the room.

'A new acquisition?'

Zhenka spread out his arms, as if to say: what can I do, I am fond of art. On my last visit, something different had been hanging there.

'Where have you hidden it?'

'The Sinitsky? The bastard's offended my most sacred feelings. He's made off to the West. I can have no fellow-feeling for traitors to the cause of socialism.'

'You sold it?'

'Well, I'm hardly going to give pseudo art away to my friends, am I? The traitor switched his allegiance to the imperialist intelligence services, and the picture doubled in price in the meantime. Sugar?'

'No.'

'I'm not offering you any grub, I haven't got any. Did you hear the dreadful things Irina's been up to?'

'Irina? I haven't seen her yet.'

Zhenka gave me an odd look.

'You haven't seen her?'

We were half-sitting half-lying, in deep armchairs next to a low occasional table. Elegant lamps cast a pleasant blue light on the table. We sat in shadow whilst our hands holding bowl-shaped china cups moved from time to time into the light and out again. The rest of the room was also in semi-darkness and Zhenka's face opposite mine looked like one of the exhibits in an agreeable mini-museum of rarities. It was all so cosy in fact that I didn't want to talk.

'Well, so now I'll tell you what our Irina's been up to.'

I didn't like the familiar tone he adopted with regard to Irina; I'd even had a row about it with him once. Fair enough, I had no grounds for jealousy now; all the same it annoyed me for some reason. That's human nature, alas . . .

'She took a cameraman and burst in on some top official in the city council, stuck the camera in his face and then asked him in all seriousness: "Ivan Ivanovich, a year ago you promised the public that such and such a building would be completed in a certain time. The year has passed and nothing's changed, so would you kindly tell us when – and for what reason –" and so forth. You can imagine Ivan Ivanovich, a well-fed Party official, blinking stupidly at the lens and making a scissors movement with his fingers, meaning "cut that bit out afterwards". Irina replied that nothing was going to be cut out. "Then I've nothing to say to you!" said the official, and he took out his pen and started drawing something on a piece of paper. Irina winked to the cameraman, who moved right in and shot the drawings in close-up. And it all went out in a programme. Result: Irina was suddenly put on leave, the official had a heart attack, and housewives and pensioners are roaring with laughter in the suburbs. How do you like that?'

'She went too far,' I said. 'She won't get away with it.'

'She will,' Zhenka said smugly, 'though not unscathed. I took steps.'

He gave me a meaningful wink. One of the miracles of our way of life is that, although the local policemen treat Zhenka with contempt and on two occasions have even tried to arrest him for 'parasitism', he really does have influence with the bosses of the television service. I have only the vaguest idea of his complex network of acquaintances and back-door operators but I could only admire him for it. There wasn't much benevolence in my admiration, generally, but all power to his elbow at the moment. Irina mustn't be left to screw things up for herself. I was powerless, but Zhenka might be able to help.

'So you haven't seen her yet?' he asked again, which bothered me.

'No, why?'

Zhenka avoided replying.

'And how's your family?'

'They've sent Lyuska's fancy man to prison,' I said and immediately regretted having said it. I knew in advance what Zhenka's reaction would be.

'Quite right!' said Zhenka maliciously. 'All those troublemakers should be put away. It'll stop them stirring up trouble. In any case, even without them stirring it up, the water's too muddy to let a smart guy go quietly fishing in it.'

I had promised myself not to get involved in any more quarrels, but here I was caught up in one again.

'What harm do they do to you?'

'They can't do me any harm,' Zhenka said condescendingly, 'they're no better than puppies, even the most respected of them. They're fools, that's all. All right, I'm just going to answer you: don't sit there grinding your teeth. I consider that the Soviet Union, just as it is today, is the ideal country for a person of initiative and intellect. Especially for a person of intellect. Forget about the masses; let's take my case. Gena, I'm completely satisfied with my life. I've enough energy and brains to get hold of everything my very demanding nature wants. Our system hasn't got itself bogged down in economics as the West has done; a person's economic situation isn't the decisive factor in assessing him. Between ourselves, what am I? An opportunist. Many think that the West is the place for an opportunist. Rubbish! What score is there for a businessman on that well trodden path? But our state, old boy, is sufficiently ideological to let business initiative be exercised behind the façade of ideology. The state focuses on ideology and is so appreciative of ideological support that it's willing to overlook economic pranks played by those who fundamentally conform to its ideology. In this state it's only the stupid and the lazy who can't succeed. If I'd been attracted by a Party career I'd have been a member of the Central Committee by now. You have to like the game and know how to play it. Who are the ones who oppose our system? People who haven't got sufficient ability to play some variation of the game of self-advancement. They talk about human rights. But who, apart from them, needs those rights? Not me, thank God! With those rights the windbags would come to power and screw up this whole beautifully-tuned machine. You think the masses need those rights? Believe me, it's the rights-campaigners' good luck to be judged by the courts and not by the politically conscious masses. Tell me, honestly, do you need those rights? Do you really need them to be happy?'

I shrugged.

'Happiness, Gena, is an illusion, and in that case what the hell use are your rights! All these campaigners are just suffering nut cases.'

'The scientists as well?'

'Why not? Anyway there aren't that many of them: they're a statistical fluctuation, to use a scientific term, or in everyday language an exception. A person's degree of learning doesn't define his personality. But to go back to the Soviet Union: I'll go even further. I have an interest in it. I find it interesting to work one's way through its prohibitions and conditions, even to bamboozle it, though it's a mighty state and you are just a tiny grain of sand, quivering in the wind and making as much noise as you like. There's real interest in that – a healthy rivalry between the structure and one of its elements. I admit I regret not having lived in Stalin's time. To survive then you really had to make an effort, use your head and be on your toes every minute of the day. But nowdays? Sometimes I get fed up, and even start to hate it.'

I was rather shocked by what he was saying. 'You do talk a lot of nonsense. I suppose you don't really believe what you say.'

'I'm sorry!' Zhenka swung round in his chair and bent over so that the shadow from his beard lengthened and spread out in a strange shape from one corner of the table to the other. 'I'm sorry – I do believe it. I consider myself a real person because I face up to this state and don't start whining that it has offended me – this poor little, weak little me. I face it on equal terms. Sometimes it puts pressure on me, sometimes I hit back but on the whole I maintain a businesslike relationship with it. It insists on laying down the ideology, and I vote with both hands for the Soviet regime and for every Marxist axiom. I will not fail it. I am genuinely interested in the prosperity of this state – and precisely in its present ideological, Marxist form – because I understand everything about it. The state in its turn appreciates this compromise of mine – it knows that it *is* a compromise, that an intellectual person cannot take seriously all that ideological clap-trap, which is intended to fill a mental vacuum – and it silently thanks me. Then it is up to me whether or not I take advantage of its gratitude.'

'I thought my father was a cynic, but compared to you he's nothing . . . You're the very apostle of cynicism.'

Zhenka smiled condescendingly. 'You've been hanging around too long with the freedom-fighters and picked up the habit of sticking labels on people from them. I don't mind – but let me tell you that if you fail, if you're broken, it won't be the state's fault. The state will break you – that's its sacred duty – if you are too weak. I see the tragedy of our intelligentsia in an abundance of ambition, but insufficient strength to achieve it. The disproportion is enormous. Take you, for example . . .'

'Zhenka,' I interrupted him. 'I don't disagree with you – in principle. But I'm here on business.'

He gave me a look of amazement. 'And I was just thinking that you were going to grab me by the beard. By the way, what do you think of my beard? A few people have said I look like Vladimir Solovyev. More coffee?'

'It's cold.'

Zhenka seized the coffee machine with both hands.

'It'll do. So what do you need, old boy?'

'A job. Right away.'

'What sort of money?'

'Around four thousand.'

'Oho!' said Zhenka with respect. 'Now let's think why, let's guess. You must want to buy a flat. Is that it? Which means you're getting married.'

'Yes, I'm getting married,' I replied reluctantly.

'So that's it.'

Oddly enough, this seemed to make Zhenka nervous: I

knew the signs – he started twitching his whiskers like a cockroach.

'So you're going to get married. But why don't you want to live in Irina's flat?'

I said nothing. I still had to see Irina, and tell her everything myself. If I told Zhenka, he would phone her right away. I was silent.

'You're right,' – and he grimaced – 'it's dishwater, not coffee. Shall we do without it? I don't want to make any more. So, you need a job . . .'

He looked at me as though he was either trying to remember something or was making a decision; it was a strange look.

'You know, old boy,' – he was now talking with unusual seriousness – 'it looks as though I've lost a bet. Lost it to myself. But no matter . . . You can thank me already. I'll let you have a job I wanted for myself.'

He reached across the table and patted me on the back, and I felt a weight lift off my shoulders – Zhenka could be trusted in matters of business.

'Do you like fishing?' he asked suddenly.

'I can't bear it.'

'You'll have to learn to like it, starting tomorrow morning. Stay there: I'll be back in a minute.'

From the sound of chairs being moved and doors banging, I realised he had scrambled into the attic. I couldn't imagine what fishing had to do with it, but if Zhenka said so he meant business. He reappeared with a foldable fishing rod and a tightly packed rucksack.

'You will go tomorrow instead of me. It's been fixed for ages – you'd better appreciate it. I've even got some fresh bait here. The meeting place is the pond in the Tsaritsyn Park on the side opposite the entrance. You'll recognise the man you want by the fact that he has only one arm and may be drunk. Open the rucksack.'

Inside, I found a bottle of vodka.

'That's the password,' said Zhenka. 'Take it from there – play it by ear. That's all.'

'You couldn't be a little more precise?'

Zhenka flopped down in the chair so that his feet shot up in the air.

'You *are* dim, Gena. Don't you remember what great event is happening in the near future?'

I remained patiently silent.

'Well, you ought to. We always have some great event or other coming up. Last year it was the Party congress. At this moment, you blockhead, we are preparing for the round-figure anniversary of Victory over the raving Fascist Beast. So what does that mean?' He pointed upward. 'It means that this year the subject of war is especially in demand. The fee which I am passing on to you, out of the kindness of my heart, should be well in excess of your miserable four thousand. If you're smart, you'll take ten. I guarantee the deal. I've already had a word with the editor of *Molodaya Gvardia*.'

Amazed at Zhenka's generosity, I asked him, not without a touch of suspicion: 'And what about you – don't you need the ten thousand?'

'Alas,' he sighed. 'There is no such thing as unwanted money, but right now I'm up to my eyes in prestige work. Spreading myself thin. So get on with it! An outline is due in a couple of weeks. Then you'll get a contract, and an advance – a lump sum.'

It was clear to me now. I'd been lucky – if I really wanted to I could do this job in a couple of months. I'd hand in the results of my trip, resign from my job, then do two months of furious work – I was quite capable of this – and my first problem would be solved. The ubiquitous Poluëktov would help me to find another job.

'Why do they call you "Poluëtot"?' I asked out of the blue.

Zhenka's eyes narrowed.

'Who did you hear that from?'

'From Irina.'

'And what does she think it means?'

'She doesn't know either.'

'I'll tell you. It's simple. I'm a half-breed, or, as they say nowadays, a ha'penny. I'm half Jewish, in other words.'

It was the first I had heard of it.

'It's what our anti-Semites call me. But I don't mind.'

I felt rather awkward, as if I ought to say something.

'Personally,' Zhenka went on, 'I recognise the right of anti-Semitism, but I also reserve the right to make fools of the anti-Semites. I love the struggle for survival! But the Jews, you know, aren't so marvellous either, so when I outwit some Jewish twister I take pleasure in that, too. Being "half-blooded" is an advantage – it means freedom from any obligations at all towards either of the ingredients in my blood. The future of mankind, if it has a future, will belong to people like me. Presence of mind and objectivity – that's what the hybrids will give to mankind. I hope I'm not offending your racially pure sensibilities?'

I shrugged my shoulders. What a marvellous gesture that is – it gets you out of so many difficult situations.

'So when are you going to see Irina?' Zhenka said, suddenly changing the subject.

'Probably tomorrow . . .'

'If she phones shall I tell her you're back?'

'Does she phone often?'

The question shot out of its own accord. In my mind I kept repeating: 'I don't care. It's none of my business.'

'Now and again. You're not jealous?'

Every time the subject of Irina came up, I began really to dislike Zhenka. Something strange, unintelligible and very disagreeable came into his voice. I wasn't jealous – after all, that would be rather silly now. It was just unpleasant. But I did my best not to show it.

'So we can cobble together a book?' I said, dodging the awkward subject.

'It's quite straightforward. The one-armed guy is a godsend. The main thing is not to let him talk too much.'

'He's a great talker?'

'Yes. Lap it up, but look it up afterwards.'

We had said all we had to say and it was time for me to leave. When I got up from my chair Zhenka did not object. We usually bore each other at about the same speed. Zhenka was too complicated a character for me, and I was too simple for him.

Again the bother of changing footwear which has been made a custom by Moscow's fastidious flat-dwellers. I carefully replaced the slippers and laced up my boots laboriously, while Zhenka stood over me puffing at a Marlboro cigarette, and I could tell that he very much wanted to say something else. I even guessed it was about Irina, but I did everything to prevent him opening his mouth – cursing the bootlaces and the Russian footwear industry, I hastily took my leave and breathed a great sigh of relief when I heard the click of the lock behind me.

Once outside I hopped into the first phone box and called Irina. She was obviously glad to hear from me, though her voice was deliberately weary and indifferent.

'Take a taxi, I'll pay,' Irina said. Previously, when I had no money, I would have done that. But now the offer touched my pride. I still had about five roubles in my pocket, so I replied coldly that I was quite credit-worthy, but wasn't it rather late? I could tell that I'd put her on her guard.

'I suppose it is,' she replied, and I began to feel sorry for her. Anyway, it would be better to get it all over today.

'I'll be with you in forty minutes,' I said as matter-of-factly as possible, but my heart sank. How could I calm myself, prepare myself for this confrontation? I could only rely on the fact that we had no special feeling for each other. I was too vague and undecided for her, she too businesslike for me. We had been together for nearly three years, and I had more than once suggested that we make the relationship official, but she had always brushed the idea aside with a laugh – perhaps in the hope that something better would turn up. Oddly enough, this didn't offend me; I just assumed that we were not that serious.

Over the years, though, we had grown together into a sort of unit, and separation was going to be painful for both of us. I would have to be brutal about it. But it made me all the more anxious that she should not feel abandoned. That could happen even when two people separated by mutual agreement, or even when they loathed each other. And things never turned out for me as they did for anyone else: there were always complications and misery. I could, of course, have had it out with her by phone or by letter – better by letter because then you could choose your words carefully and say precisely what you wanted to say: in a letter there was no chance of hearing someone's voice or looking into their eyes. But I couldn't behave like that with Irina. It was frightening to realise how much life there still was in the bond I was about to sever.

'Going fishing?' asked the taxi-driver, seeing me collapse into the seat clutching the fishing-rod.

'Tomorrow.'

'They say there are carp weighing half a kilogram down at Avtozavodskaya, only you can't eat them because they stink of kerosene.'

Hell hath no fury like a talkative taxi driver.

I lay back in the seat and pretended to doze off.

I had to settle all my affairs by the end of the day, I told myself – but actually what other affairs did I have apart from Irina? I couldn't put off seeing her any longer. Zhenka and Lyuska would phone her, so she would know I was back. I tried to persuade myself that I was doing the right thing, so as not to get cold feet at the last moment and put it off.

We were now in Irina's district, where everything reminded me of her: the cinema, and the cafe, and the little squares, all the streets and houses were connected with the life that had ended with my last trip out of Moscow.

*

I had only to glance at her in the entrance hall to know that she suspected, she sensed that something was wrong. We didn't kiss, though that was not my fault – I went to embrace her, but without pausing to think she stepped back and waved me away.

'I've got make-up on.'

She never used to bother with that before I arrived.

'Have you been fishing?'

'I'm going tomorrow. Zhenka's fixed me up with some work.'

I looked closely at her, but without letting her feel my gaze. As I looked, I was overcome by pity. She wasn't simply less attractive than Tosya: there was no comparison at all. I felt terribly sorry for Irina – and ashamed to be comparing her with someone else whose only virtue was that she was younger. What had Irina done to deserve being compared with anybody?

Her tinted hair was untidy, as usual. She did her hair 'straight', that is she did nothing to it, in fact, just combed it out over her shoulders. She ought to have had her hair done properly; it was nice hair and something could have been made of it. But Irina didn't have time to go to the hairdresser; the tempo of her life was not like Tosya's. Tosya had time for everything, time flowed around her slowly and smoothly. Whirlpools and tornadoes raged round Irina, on the other hand – once I would have said a great deal of unnecessary fuss and bother, but now I did not wish to utter a single word of criticism of her. I could see the wrinkles around her eyes and mouth and a certain weariness in the way she walked, as well as that air of efficiency which deprived her of half of her femininity. It would have been better for me not to see this!

'Do you want something to eat?' she asked. In the past she'd always said: 'I'll give you something to eat right away!' It seemed to me she had sensed something and was preparing herself for it, and this made my task even more difficult. I found myself wanting to persuade her that nothing had happened and became entangled in the net of my own indecision.

'What were you up to in the studio? Zhenka didn't tell me much . . .'

It was shoddy to talk about trivial things, leaving the most important till later. It felt like stabbing her in the back. She made it clear that she could tell I was evading the issue. 'It doesn't matter, it's silly to talk about that when we haven't seen each other for so long.' And she repeated her question more insistently: 'Will you have something to eat?'

I was faint with hunger, as it happened. But how could I possibly eat at a moment like that? Then again, to refuse would be a pathetic ploy.

'Coffee, I suppose,' I said uncertainly, though I really didn't want any. I was getting more and more confused and cross with myself.

Irina might as well have been my wife. A tiny thing now made this clear:

'When were you at Zhenka's?'

'Just now.'

'Did you drink coffee there?'

'I did.'

'Then that's enough for today. So will you eat or not?'

It was a sort of rebuke. Don't dither, be a man, I told myself. I said more decisively:

'No, I don't want to eat.'

For a moment her face turned to stone, but she was herself again immediately.

'Well, let's go into the sitting room.'

She put out the light in the kitchen and we went through into the room. I restrained myself from sprawling on the couch; I sat down quietly in an armchair. I needed to concentrate, but this room in which I had been so happy with Irina distracted me. What I needed to do was to half-close my eyes for a minute and get a clear picture of Tosya. I could see her, dancing dreamily with me to the wail of the tape recorder, her slightly sleepy face fixed in an innocent half-smile, and her hands pressed to her breast.

'Let's talk,' – Irina, not I, began suddenly, sitting down facing me on the edge of the couch. I couldn't allow her to take the initiative – and didn't want to lose her respect. But I lost my chance. 'It's like this, Genochka,' she said, looking me straight in the eye. 'While you have been away on your long trip certain things have happened.'

So I gave in: 'What sort of things?'

She grinned, aware that she had the upper hand.

'I've been seeing another man.'

I lowered my eyes in regret and embarrassment that Irina had been forced to put on this act. 'We're not going to have a row about it, I hope?' she continued, still grinning as before.

I lifted my head and looked into her wary eyes, eyes that were so dear to me, and I wanted to fall on my knees before her and beg her forgiveness. And after she'd forgiven me as she surely would, I'd ask her blessing on my happiness with another woman!

'I also have something to tell you . . .' I mumbled.

'What, you too?' she asked, with obviously affected surprise.

'Ira . . .' I muttered, distractedly, jumping up from the chair and taking a step towards her. She stared at me, and I, wounded by her look, felt a rush of . . . of what? Love for her? But that would be ridiculous! Or was I simply under the influence of those three years we had had together? Habit (I hoped it was only habit), had become part of me like a living thing that didn't want to die, it was threshing about and struggling and hurting me.

'But that's all for the best, Gena!' she said. 'We'll remain friends. After all, there was never anything serious between us. Especially,' – and she hung her head – 'since it seems I'm going to have a child.'

'Whose child?' I asked in a voice that had suddenly gone hoarse.

'I told you – I've met another man.'

'Ira,' I said threateningly, 'enough play-acting.'

She opened her eyes wide. 'It all took me by surprise, not like with us, and I was just careless. But I don't regret it.'

I ceased to understand anything at all. I settled down deep in the armchair. I had to get over the shock, collect my thoughts and absorb Irina's astonishing news.

'Who is he? I mean, whose child is it?'

'I don't see why you're interested, Gena,' she said insinuatingly. 'From what you say, things have changed for you, too!'

'You know perfectly well that it concerns me, whose child you're carrying, because . . . I . . . because if what you say is true, the child could be mine.'

She was about to say something, but I cut her off with an entreaty:

'Ira, don't lie to me! I shan't believe you anyway!'

'And when I have the child – will you believe me then?' she said, quite coldly and even maliciously. 'Relax, you know the man. But I'm not going to name him yet because I haven't told him yet and anyway I'm not entirely sure. I'm going to see the doctor on Monday.'

What was going on? Had Irina been unfaithful to me, and with one of my friends, too? I tried to look at this woman afresh, and gradually the word 'catastrophe' formed in my mind. If this was all true then I really did not know Irina. She'd remained an utterly unknown quantity for me. I tried to recall the last days before my departure, how she had ordered a taxi for me to go to the station and the taxi had come rather sooner than we had expected, and how annoyed we had both been because of it. True, she had not accompanied me as she usually did, but then I'd left at night . . . At that point I suddenly came to my senses and reminded myself that the fact that we had parted on good terms hadn't prevented me from falling in love with Tosya. Damn it all, though, Irina wasn't in love, and there was no one among my acquaintances who could cause me to be jealous.

Zhenka? But they had been friends for ages. There couldn't be anything new between them.

'Ira, if you've made all this up . . .'

'That's enough, Gena,' she cut me off with a grimace of weariness and pain. 'That's enough. I've told you everything. I'm not asking *you* any questions, because for me it's completely irrelevant now. And it's already late . . .'

I was overcome by a feeling of spitefulness – I was no longer concerned with justice – I simply couldn't swallow this insult.

'You're right. There have been changes with me, too. I have fallen in love like a schoolboy. In love! But you? Are you going to tell me that you're in love? Have you any idea what you are?'

'I'm the future mother of a child which is not yours. You're an intelligent person; is that what you were going to say?'

I could see that she was on the verge of tears and I knew that she'd cry when I'd gone – the only thing I didn't know was what on earth she was crying about. It was time to go: the Metro would soon be closed, and I had no more money for a taxi, but I couldn't make myself move.

'I'm not going till you've told me everything.'

'Suit yourself.'

She tidied her hair and turned away, but I guessed that there were tears on her face.

'You can stay here,' – she'd made up her mind now – 'here on the couch.'

She dashed into her bedroom and immediately closed the door behind her. I ran in after her.

'Don't you dare come in,' she said quietly but firmly. Her face was already tear-stained – the tears had streamed forth the very moment she closed the door behind her.

I was brimming over with pity and repentance. I forgot everything and squeezed her shoulders.

'Don't you dare touch me,' she whispered.

'Are you really pregnant?' I asked, also in a whisper.

She nodded.

'But it's my child, isn't it? Isn't it?'

'No,' she said, even more quietly. 'It's not yours.'

'Then tell me who he is! *Please* tell me!'

She extricated herself cautiously from my grasp and moved over to the divan above which hung a painting in a makeshift frame by a young and well-known artist about whom Irina had once written a feature article. I remembered the rage with which I had greeted the arrival of this gift with its dedication: 'To the most fascinating of women' . . . That was in the spring of our romance. I had criticised the artist very severely, but she only laughed. Maybe that's who it was?

There was a cupboard next to Irina's bed. She opened it and handed me a rug.

'Go in there – I'll bring the bedding.'

How I would have liked to be in my own room! I was worn out guessing, worn out in general – it hadn't been the easiest of days. But to take money off her for a taxi . . . I was tired. I wanted to sleep. Overwhelming depression.

*

My love!

I received your letter and it made me cry. Such different words, and everything different, and I can't hear your voice! If I receive another letter like that it will mean that everything that happened was just a dream. Father says that it is hard for a man to put his thoughts on paper. Father sometimes thinks up such wonderful sermons in his head; if he could only deliver them in the church, people would do less evil! But when he tries to write them down, he can't.

But that's a very different matter, isn't it? A clever sermon comes mainly from the head. If one speaks from the heart, can the paper really get in the way?

I am praying that you should succeed in everything you are doing, though I can't understand why we need so much money! But you know best. Only I beg you – no more letters like that! I'm afraid of them.

It's still warm down here, but they say on the television that it's raining in Moscow. They show Moscow, the streets, and I look closely to see if you will suddenly appear.
I love you! I pray for you, my love!
I am already tired of being without you!
Your Tosya.

II

II

For a whole week I worked like a man possessed. At the museum they had let me go without any sign of regret. I hadn't expected anything else, but I was hurt, just the same.

It occurred to me now for the first time that being inessential in such a basic sense must actually be the result of a lack of will-power. I had always found the 'superfluous men' of literature flat and vulgar. I think that only in our own time has the simple truth emerged that there is nothing original and certainly nothing outstanding in opposing one's own personality to the age one is living in. It all begins to look so hackneyed – the same pose, the same words – and I have a strong suspicion that all those 'superfluous' people, about whom there has been so much discussion, so many theories developed and so many words written were actually very much like me – and I know exactly what *I* amount to! I'm just a very irresolute person with too many feelings for any one of them to dominate my will. But I want everything that other people – those who are not 'superfluous' – want; a measure of success, and some respect and love. In that order. At least, that's how it had been up to now.

Now I was putting my money on love: I needed a stable and dependable retreat into which I could disappear, if need be, out of the real world when I tired of it. The knowledge that there was somewhere to retreat to should lend a certain ease to my words and deeds and introduce an element of fun into my life. Life's failures were people who took too serious a view of what they were doing, of their actions and how others reacted to them. Real success was always a little theatrical; it was only in one's private retreat, amongst one's family, that things were solid and natural. So I was betting on love. I was counting on Tosya, the priest's daughter. And this last job would provide me with the material basis for building my little nest.

The job turned out in fact to be rather more serious than I had thought, and I was afraid of getting too involved with it. Each morning before I started work on it I told myself that I was only out to make a bit of money, that it was the fee I was after, and that I ought not to get too involved in the subject matter because the people I was doing it for didn't expect a masterpiece. But nonetheless the thing was taking hold of me . . .

It all began quite straightforwardly, just as Zhenka had planned. I met the one-armed man. We sat side by side and fortunately the fish weren't biting. I took out the vodka and offered it to him. Then I asked him a few questions and in no time had the material for a best-seller. Andrei Semyonich had been a divisional intelligence officer during the war. When he started recounting his exploits I thought he was rather exaggerating, but at home he showed me a whole iconostasis of decorations. His wife, Polina Mikhailovna, wasn't impressed by her husband's achievements and didn't approve of his passion for fishing which put him in hospital every autumn.

When I suggested writing a book about him he replied quite seriously and with dignity: 'And why not? I see films and I read books about the war, but what happened to me was a lot more exciting. Go ahead!'

The Press at the time was full of stories about the war. The first war story I'd ever read was by Remarque. What really interested me in all the accounts was people's attitude to death. In the evenings, working through the tape-recordings, I would suddenly detect in some phrase or even in the tone of voice of my hero something profoundly, unfathomably philosophical; I would be confronted with a psychological reaction that was beyond my knowledge or understanding. Take, for example, a passage like this: 'The Armenian and I crawled as far as the hillock, and there was a burst of machine-gun fire. We flattened ourselves on the ground. But we had only seconds left! I poked him in the side with my elbow. We had to move on. But he was already dead. So I crawled on alone.'

I listened over and over again to that phrase. 'So I crawled on alone', unable to understand why it sent a shiver down my spine. I wasn't sure whether it was because there had been some Armenian and seconds later he had ceased to exist, or because a moment after his death someone else had crawled on as though nothing had happened. I tried to understand this familiarity with death. There was presumably no heroism here, no exercise of the will to overcome fear. I believe there are millions of people who are unable to be heroes and that the term 'mass heroism' is just as nonsensical as to speak of genius on a mass scale. But to call it familiarity or habit is not right either; the fear of death hasn't disappeared. I fear death; that is why I could not walk along a parapet on the ninth floor of a building, no matter what, because fear would totally supplant my will. But what had happened psychologically to those people in the war, if fear did not paralyse their will? Perhaps there was some other, more powerful, will at work? A mixture, probably, composed of hatred, obedience to commands and the inevitability of the situation. Also faith in success. And professional training.

When I was with Andrei Semyonich I would study his face and the photographs of him in wartime and try to understand or to guess at what had made possible his acceptance of death, his own and others'. It was useless to ask him.

He had twelve decorations for his part in military operations, for feats of heroism, and I divided them into different categories. Two were a matter of luck that could have happened to anyone. Five were the result of first-class professionalism. But the remaining five were for taking risks, for dicing with death, and I had no hesitation in calling them acts of heroism, (that is, actions running directly counter to the instinct of self-preservation, the most powerful instinct in any living being). It was these deeds about which I questioned him particularly carefully and insistently, forcing him to dig into his memory and even annoying him with my repeated questions. He could not understand what I wanted from him, and I wasn't that sure myself what I was reaching for in someone else's memory. It was as though there was something here which concerned me personally as if I wanted to understand myself, not him, the former soldier . . . but what had the war to do with me? I had never been in a war. Then doubt suddenly crept in – was it really like that?'

In short, I was getting too closely involved. So I kept on drumming it into myself: I'm only a hack, I'm only in this for the fee, and I ought to keep my eye on the ball – that is to say, on the business side. The deal demanded only that I should produce a tolerable account of the battle exploits of a divisional intelligence officer on behalf of his socialist motherland. I was sorry to be doing the work just for the money when a subject had come my way which I could really have put my heart into. But who needed my efforts?

Meanwhile, Andrei Semyonich seemed to be changing before my very eyes. Previously, his fatuous buffoonery and weariness had been apparent in everything – his bearing, his gait, his voice – but now it had vanished. He stood up straighter; his watery eyes, which only yesterday had blinked shyly and filled with tears, seemed today to have recovered their colour and brightness and gave a look so piercing, that I could hardly recognise the garrulous boozer whom I had fished with in the Tsaritsyn Park. Incidentally, only the day before

I had gone fishing with him again and it was amazing how he chatted with the other fishermen and with me in their presence, how he handled his fishing rod and how he removed the carp from the hook without any fuss or boasting.

Yesterday he floored me with yet another of his stories, or rather with a confession. Before that I had been digging in the archives, to which my father had got me access, and had found some minor inaccuracies in the dates in Andrei Semyonich's account. When I told him this he took offence and started to clam up.

'So you've been checking, to see if I'm telling lies?'

I explained as tactfully as possible that if he mixed up September and December it was not very serious, but that if I permitted such a mistake to appear in the book it would be a serious fault and it would be embarrassing for me when it was pointed out. Andrei Semyonich remained gloomily silent for some time, then said with a sigh:

'There *is* one bit of fiction that I have fed you. God knows what is in those archives, what they've kept there about us. I didn't lose my arm on a mine. It was quite a different story.'

And this is the story he told me. He was crawling through the ruins of a house overgrown with weeds, not daring to raise himself an inch off the ground, when suddenly he felt a piercing pain in his arm. He saw something slimy slithering along close to him, then another sharp pain. He couldn't cry out – that would have meant death! So he crawled on with two snake-bites in his arm, feeling it go numb and swelling before his eyes. 'Since then I haven't been able to look at a snake. Even if they hadn't taken my arm off I wouldn't have been able to go on fighting. I am afraid of the soil, the grass; it'll stay with me all my life. I see snakes everywhere. If I see a snake in a film I begin to tremble. I moved out of the village where I grew up. I can't stand the country, and only feel safe when I'm on asphalt. But you can't live on a pension, so my wife and I grow potatoes just beyond Vostryakov. I don't mind planting them out, but lifting them . . . There's always something crawling in the bushes. That's the truth.'

Andrei Semyonich had no idea what a superb couple of pages this account would make in the book. Here was human interest at last. What extraordinary things happen in war – making a peasant hate the soil! But the editors would surely cut it. I had to get on with the job. I was beginning to feel ashamed.

All my hopes were centred on my father. He could tell me how to turn my compulsory hack-work into something worthwhile. I knocked on his door and heard him say: 'Come in!' That meant he wasn't working and was willing to talk to me. He was sitting on the divan holding a book and invited me with a wave of the hand to sit in his working chair. This was so comfortable that I would never have been able to do any work in it.

'Tell me about the war,' I said abruptly.

My father raised his eyebrows in surprise, then silently pointed to the bookshelf where there was a row of military memoirs and other books about war.

'No,' I said. 'Tell me about *your* war. What was the war like for you?'

'What's the point of this?' he asked in surprise.

'I've got a bit of writing to do on a wartime subject.'

My father could see nothing wrong in that: he was a realist.

'But you know perfectly well – my war doesn't count. I've only got one medal – the "Victory" medal. Everyone got that.'

'But you applied several times to be sent to the front. Why?'

He shrugged his shoulders.

'I was only nineteen years old. I was surrounded by men from the front in their uniforms and medals, looking very fine and talking a lot. But I was very small fry, back behind the lines, away from the fighting. Girls weren't interested. I was even disappointed when the war came to an end. I was still just a boy.'

It didn't look as if my father was going to be much use.

'Tell me, why is it that, so many years later, our peace-loving socialist society still keeps on playing war games: student exercises, detachments, soldiers, commanders, nothing but explosions or epaulettes, gunfire even in films? Why can't we forget any of it? Why doesn't a normal peaceful life inspire us, why do we have to keep exploiting war?'

My father thought this over for a time. Usually he has an answer ready. So I asked him: 'Is that a difficult question?'

'I suppose so,' he agreed. 'I don't know on what level to reply to you.'

'On your own, of course.'

'You know, our political system is a closed one, closed, so to speak, by definition, that is to say being closed is essential to its perfection. In a sense my enemy is my friend. The clearer the faces of our enemies, the more firmly we can stand on our own feet. Do you follow me?'

'Are you trying to say the détente is not in our interests?'

My father's bright eyes sparkled with irony. 'Your generation scorns dialectic, and that's a mistake. Dialectic trains you to think and teaches you to look at things from various angles. Détente is to the advantage of the socialist camp, but international tension, for its part, cements the socialist structure. Consequently socialism is inconquerable. Do you understand?'

I stared uncomprehendingly at my father. There was laughter in his eyes, and I had the impression that I was being mocked by something strange, something tremendous and powerful which was quite out of my reach.

'Détente provides our economic system with prospects and the possibility of growth, but it tends to upset the socialist structure, and the regular periods of cold war – launched, of course, not by us but by those who are annoyed by the advantages we derive from détente – brings centripetal tend-encies into operation. And all the flowers of socialism,' – my father pointed upwards – 'all the flowers grow new blooms, while all that we have acquired in the period of détente remains with us. History is on the side of socialism. Do you think that the young idiots who snort at the greatest reality in history understand what they're doing?'

By now my father was laughing openly. I wasn't.

'Even so, what's the point of all this military symbolism?'

'The point is that socialism triumphs when it defends its own achievements.'

'Can't you put it more simply?'

'One can only talk more simply, Gena, about something that is itself simple. If military subjects are on our agenda, then I would compare the socialist advance to a bullet fired from a rifle. The force and the distance covered by such a bullet depends upon the speed at which it revolves which in turn is determined by the rifling in the gun-barrel. The triumph of socialism depends upon the degree of orthodoxy in its structure. Don't forget that our political system enjoyed its greatest popularity in the world at the very time when it was, let us say, unattractive – I refer to the Stalin period.'

'Are you trying to say that Stalinism is the orthodox . . .'

'By no means,' my father hastened to interrupt me. 'All those prison camps were just part of the cost of the socialist process.'

'The chips that fly when you chop wood?'

'No, the cost that has to be counted,' he insisted. 'The orthodoxy of socialism has many sides to it. But in that period the aims were drawn more clearly and more precisely. Unwillingness to compromise – that is the most attractive aspect of the socialist ideal. Your Solzhenitsyn, no doubt, thinks that it was he with his scribblings who turned the West against us. Nothing of the sort. It was Khrushchev who compromised our socialism, because he violated the principle that the path to socialism must not be criticised.'

I leapt out of my chair. 'Listen. Father, why don't you say all this in your lectures?'

I had broken the unwritten law governing our relationship

– never to get personal. In a flash it was as though my father had pulled a mask over his face.

'I was trying to talk to you man to man.'

'And what, in your opinion, do I need to be a man?'

'Courage,' he said, and I felt a pain, as though he had struck me on an old wound. I tried to return to the original subject of our conversation.

'So you think that playing at war is a way of strengthening the structure? Is that it?'

'Yes,' my father agreed reluctantly, 'to put it very simply.'

But I knew that already. So what was it I wanted to hear? Something, I suppose, that I *didn't* already know, because sometimes you think that everything would be all right if you only knew the one thing you don't know.

'It's possible that what you say is true – the facts, at any rate.' I rubbed my forehead vigorously. 'But what if I don't like that truth, if I object to it?'

'That doesn't affect the truth.'

'Then how ought I to live so as to respect myself?'

He eyed me as though he were assessing my ability to take in the ultimate, bitter truths.

'Fighting against the world of objective reality is a task for madmen!'

'What alternative is there?'

'To leave this world, I suppose.'

God, what sort of a man was my father? To say such a thing to his own son without winking an eye, without flinching.

'And if I follow your advice will you not suffer any pangs of conscience?'

'No,' he said calmly. 'If a person chooses death voluntarily that means that he finds life worse than death.'

I very much wanted to shout: 'You're not a human being! You're a monument, a Marxist tablet in marble!' But I didn't. I made for the door, but my father called me back.

'I've got something to put to you, as well.'

My father was embarrassed – he pulled at the hair at his temples, a sure sign of agitation. I sat down again in his armchair and he stood facing me.

'I would like to introduce you to Valentina.'

'Is that absolutely necessary, Father?' I asked as gently as possible. I hadn't the slightest desire to meet this woman. My father pulled at his hair and it was strange to see him standing there: I felt really awkward on his account.

'It's not necessary, of course, but I just haven't been able to explain to her why it isn't necessary.'

Now everything was clear. If she wanted to get to know me, it meant that she had some far-reaching plans involving my father. Did he realise that?

'One question, please.'

'Go ahead.'

'Does your relationship have a future, or . . .'

'I understand.' Again he replied hastily. 'I can only ask you once again if you will agree to meet her.'

In my naïve way I had hoped to exploit the situation – to make my father open up just a little. Some hope!

'Of course, Father, we just need to fix a date – I'm working like a horse at the moment.'

'I'll let you know in a couple of days.'

'Fine.'

I left the room, my head quite empty and quite incapable of work. I cast a tired glance over the papers on my desk, then threw them down and my hand reached involuntarily for the telephone. I thought I could even feel the receiver trembling with pleasure – I hadn't touched it for a week.

What first came into my head was Irina. But no, I was not going to call her, I didn't have the strength at the moment. Zhenka? I dialled his number, but there was no reply. Should I phone my mother? That was also rather complicated. What on earth was the matter? Was there no one I could have a good gossip with, just to relax? I opened my notebook at random. There the answer was – Oleg Skurikhin, professional telephone chatterbox, a hack-writer from Irina's former circle of friends, out of which I had snatched her.

'So you're back?' he cried with delight. 'At last! Where is Irina?'

'At home, probably.' The last thing I wanted to talk about was Irina.

'At home? Haven't you seen her? And don't you know what's happened? They've thrown her out of the TV – she produced a feature there.'

'I heard about the programme. When did they sack her?'

'Yesterday. Listen, come round to my place, the whole gang is here – we'll work out what to do. We can't leave her at their mercy.'

'I'm on my way,' I replied, and hung up.

*

The 'whole gang' consisted in the first place of Oleg himself. He was beginning to run to fat, his dark, shiny hair was receding, and his round face usually bore an expression of playfulness. But he was a very competent journalist with a lively turn of phrase and he was highly thought of. His wife Maria, who had some rather undefined duties in an animated film studio, could also not be described as having a good figure, and she had a despotic nature and an imperious voice. Maria liked to intervene in other people's conversations and was very fond of bringing a discussion to an end with a would-be profound remark. I thought her as stupid as any woman who makes a big effort to appear intelligent.

Felix Rokhman, Irina's regular cameraman, was a busy, talkative, long-limbed Jew always bursting with information about what was going on in the Bohemian world of the cinema.

Anatoli Dmitrievich Zhukov, Irina's producer, was the eldest member of the 'gang' – slow-moving but ostentatious like the foreign briefcase with the combination lock that he carried.

Lena Khudova was skin and bone. A very sweet girl of indeterminate age and curious position: she was always with

Zhukov. He introduced her as his assistant, but I fear she did not appear in the staff list of the TV studio.

Finally, there was Yura Lepchenko, who said little and looked a bit sad and tired, but who was an exceptionally kind person and who managed to make a very good living though he was a pretty bad poet.

All in all we formed a very pleasant and undemanding company, which had scarcely changed over the years, if you didn't count Zhenka and myself. It was only now and then that we two took a swim in this pond of pleasant time-passing. Zhenka was not a frequent visitor because of the difference in social levels, he being a genius and a businessman, while I, having snatched Irina from this group three years before, tended to avoid turning up there with her, because I liked her less when she was with the others.

Oleg had an excellent three-roomed flat, and his children spent all their time with their grandparents. I found everyone in the principal room, which was furnished as a living-room. The furniture had been pushed back to the corners of the room, leaving a table stranded in the middle, laden with plates, glasses and bottles. There was soft music or a stereo. An enormous black cat known as Snorter was moving with dignity from one chair to another.

Upon my arrival they all gathered around the table and the glasses were quickly filled. I greedily gulped down a glass of vodka. My throat and eyes paid for my greed, but I soon recovered.

'It's like this, then,' said Maria, gesticulating with her chubby little hand. 'We have discussed the matter and have come to the conclusion that it is a clear breach of the law. We must take steps.'

'How was the notice worded?' I asked Zhukov.

Maria didn't give him time to answer: 'The wording? "At her own request", of course.'

'Ah, so she herself . . .'

'What do you mean, "she herself"?'

'The trouble is,' Zhukov intervened, 'that we can't find her, she's simply vanished. And it's important to have the details.'

'What other details do we need?' Maria shouted at him.

Oleg reminded her that she had a glass in her hand, and while she drank, screwing up her face, and ate a canapé, we hastily exchanged views.

Felix shook his curls and leant across the table. 'We know that she was in her boss's office for over an hour.'

'But after all there's the censor; it's *his* responsibility . . .'

Felix hastened to explain to me what had happened: 'He was new to the job and he slipped up. Irina said at the preview that the Party committee passed it. The censor will be carpetted too, don't you worry.'

'The fat bureaucrat receives foreign delegations on behalf of the city council, and we have exposed him for what he is,' Zhukov added.

'But why the hell did she have to do it?' I asked, looking at the bridge of Zhukov's nose, on which his silver-framed glasses were perched.

He was surprised by my question, and expressed his surprise in mine. Then Lenochka Khudova made herself heard, as behoves an assistant:

'Oh, come on, Gena! It had to be done! We must make them fear public opinion and realise that they are accountable to people.'

Without turning round to face her, Zhukov added: 'We're not concerned with them really; we're concerned with ourselves. We must at least sometimes make use of the weapon we've been given.'

I was sure that 'we' had really done nothing, that it had all been Irina's doing – the producer and cameraman were secondary figures. Neither Zhukov nor Felix would make a move independently: Irina had involved them in the affair, and they were perfectly happy to have risked nothing.

I realised suddenly that I was not thinking about her as a stranger and I recalled the new development that had so complicated our parting. If she really were pregnant then they could not have sacked her. She had agreed to be dismissed, meant either that she had not wanted to take advantage of her condition, or that there was no such condition.

'Anyway, we have decided to send a telegram to the Central Committee,' Oleg said, summing up, and Maria immediately butted in:

'Will *you* sign it?'

I didn't turn my head in her direction. 'We ought to know what Irina thinks about it and whether she wants us to take up her defence.'

'Listen,' – Felix put in, 'maybe we ought to let the Jews have the story?'

'What Jews?' asked Maria, cautiously.

'The dissidents. By tomorrow the Western radio stations would spread it everywhere!'

Felix, I knew, was terribly proud of the fact that there were many Jews among the dissidents, even though he was himself a perfectly contented Moscovite without any desire to leave Moscow).

At this point the reticent Yura Lepchenko put in a word: 'Your Jews can't be bothered with us just now – they've got their own troubles.'

They all turned to me. I was the one closest to the dissidents, because Lyuska was actively involved.

'I don't think Irina would approve,' I said.

I could see that nearly all of them, including Felix, agreed with me, although they said nothing. It was only Maria who couldn't drop the subject.

'That's all we need – for Irka to be considered a dissident!'

Snorter the cat leapt on to my lap and reached for the table with his paws. Maria gave him a slap and he vanished quickly under the chairs.

'He's getting far too cheeky!'

'And so,' I summed up, 'we need to hear from Irina herself. Until then there's no sense in doing anything.'

Again they all gladly agreed, which meant that I was left with everything to do – to meet Irina, discuss it all with her and reach a decision. That was why I had been invited.

Yet another unopened bottle appeared.

'Who's come into money?' I enquired.

Oleg pointed to Yura Lepchenko.

'I've actually been paid a fee! I hit on a wonderful rhyme. Knocked Voznesensky flat – pinched it from under his nose.'

Yura's poems were a constant target for jokes. But he never took offence. Either he recognised the poor quality of his verses, or else he thought of himself as a misunderstood genius.

'So what's it like there, in the backwoods of Russia?' Zhukov asked me.

I got out of replying with a shrug of the shoulders.

'Did you ever come across the town of Uryupinsk?' This was Oleg, and it meant he had a joke to tell:

'Students are being examined on the history of the Communist Party of the Soviet Union:

'"Tell me something about the decisions taken at the Twenty-third Congress," says the teacher.

'"*What* congress?" the student asks in surprise.

'"Where on earth do you come from?"

'"I'm from Uryupinsk."

'The teacher clutches his head and says: "Shall I fail him, or shall I chuck up everything and move to Uryupinsk?"'

We all had a good laugh.

'My friends!' exclaimed Oleg. 'Surely somewhere in this country there must be a place called Uryupinsk. I want to go to Uryupinsk! Maria, shall we go to Uryupinsk?'

His wife looked at him scornfully – she knew that her Oleg would not move anywhere and that none of us would exchange Moscow for any Uryupinsk even if it did exist somewhere. We were all children of the age and we lived in it like fish in water.

Lenochka Khudova was a little drunk. She wanted to sing, but was waiting patiently for someone to ask her. So I said:

'Lenochka!'

She cast a swift glance at her producer. Zhukov indicated with a movement of his eyebrows that he approved and she rushed across to the piano. She only sang Russian love songs; she chose her repertoire carefully and always had a surprise for us. As the first chords were played I could tell it was indeed something new – that is to say something old, from the first half of the nineteenth century, perhaps even the first quarter of it. The lyrics were very unsophisticated in style and the melody was sweet and simple; in both lyrics and melody there was a certain reluctance to innovate, but the feelings were stated frankly, each given its proper name. No evasion, no concealment, no double-talk. I longed to be able to speak in the same uncomplicated tongue, so that sorrow would be sorrow, love would be love and jealousy jealousy.

When Lenochka sang, I always fell in love with her; in fact I always fall in love with any woman who sings well. I jumped up from my chair, went up to Lenochka and kissed her on the cheek, knowing that everyone would understand my action for what it was.

I collapsed on a chair behind her and, as soon as the sound of her voice had died away, I whispered with my lips touching her hair:

'Lenochka, I love you!'

From behind me came the tired voice of Yura Lepchenko: 'You appear to be loving her today a little earlier than usual.'

I swung round and said with all the venom I could muster: 'Shut up, you bloody versifier. Do not besmirch the purity of my feelings with your cynicism. I have been slaving away the whole week producing high quality stuff. I've got callouses on my fingers from using that fascist Olympia typewriter.'

'Olympia is an East German firm,' Felix Rokhman corrected me.

'It's easy for you,' I told Felix, 'you've got your historic homeland, your Auntie Golda and Uncle Dayan, and your Wailing Wall. We miserable chauvinists, though, with our imperial outlook, where can we lay our heads, who can we cry on? We have only our past. You were not a part of that past, but I was, and deep down inside me I remember it all, and Lenochka does too. You do remember, don't you, Lenochka? As a young, mustachioed hussar I wrote that song in your honour and it was not so long ago, no more than a hundred and fifty years back.'

'I remember!' Lenochka replied, with a kiss, and I felt a little tear on my cheek. 'I remember – it was autumn and you had just proposed to me, but I loved another. Yet I pitied you and I wrote down the words of your song in my album and decorated the page with sad little vignettes of tiny hearts.'

'You see!' I cried triumphantly. 'That *is* how it was! We really lived!'

'And amused yourselves now and again by flogging a few peasants,' Felix interjected.

'I don't recall that!' I objected firmly.

'But maybe *he* remembers!' Felix poked his finger into the back of Yura Lepchenko's neck. 'Deep down inside, no doubt.'

I broke away from Lenochka, went up to Yura and dropped down on my knees before him.

'If you remember that, can you forgive? I have also been flogged by history, cruelly flogged. All our backs are in shreds. So will you forgive us?'

He held out his hand.

'I forgive you. Rise, brother.'

'You see!' I called out to Felix. 'Do you know what this means? It's our chance to have a common future!'

'What's the matter with you today, Gena?' enquired Zhukov in surprise. 'You never went in for Slavophilism. That's an exceptionally boring occupation.'

'But fashionable,' added Felix.

I went back to Lenochka who was not quite sure now whether she should sing or not, since the menfolk had begun to discuss serious matters.

'I didn't know it was called "Slavophilism",' I replied,

looking at Lenochka. 'It's just that I'm beginning a new life and, what is more, not on a Monday. So come on, Lenochka, sing – sing, my love, don't be shy. There is more wisdom in your voice than in all our male heads.'

But something had upset our hostess, Maria. 'Sing for him, Lenochka! Men sometimes want to have a good cry and tear their shirts open so they can show their chests.'

Lenochka sang again; but now the melody and her voice seemed to be in conflict and the music seemed to emphasise every word.

There was a noise going on behind me, not loud, but apparently deliberate. It was Maria, who just couldn't keep quiet. I seemed to have annoyed her in some way. Lenochka glanced at me enquiringly several times – perhaps she should stop? – but I encouraged her with a nod of the head, and she continued. We had won the day! When Lenochka finished singing everybody applauded in genuine appreciation. I could see how Zhukov's eyes were shining – he was now very much in love with his extra-curricular assistant – Felix remained silent, and even Maria at that moment was in a better mood and seemed quite attractive. Oleg and Yura the poet both extended a hand to Lenochka at the same time as she went to the table, but she looked across at Zhukov and there was a reproach in her look.

'Lenka, if that fancy boy of yours,' – I nodded in Zhukov's direction – 'doesn't marry you within the year, just remember that you have another proposal in reserve.'

'And what about Irka?' asked Maria, perking up again.

'Irka won't get lost,' commented Oleg. 'She's always got Zhenka "Poluëtot" in reserve.'

'Zhenka?' I sobered up in a flash. 'What's Zhenka got to do with it?'

Oleg looked across at his wife, and Maria took over the job of explaining.

'Unlike certain people' – she fixed me with her little round eyes, then glanced at Zhukov, – 'who value their freedom,

Zhenka "Poluëtot" values Irina. Moreover, if you had not turned up in her life Irka would not now be sweating over scenarios; she'd be bearing him children.'

I recalled the careful but insistent questions that Zhenka had put to me about Irina, and my suspicions were renewed. I suppose I must have still been a bit drunk, because I immediately grabbed the telephone and dialled Zhenka's number. There was no answer. Every one was watching my every move. Then I dialled Irina's number. Again no answer. I felt the blood rushing to my head. So I tried to repeat over and over again in my mind the sentence: 'What has it all got to do with me now?' But I just couldn't get it out – it moved around in my brain, like a stick, jabbing me in the temple first with one end then with the other, and I wanted to twist it into a spiral, into a coil, to fit it into the convolutions of my brain, and then everything would become quite straightforward and easy – after all, what had it really got to do with me? So now I had said it, and my thoughts now flowed smoothly, without interruptions, following logically one upon the other. If Zhenka suited Irina, that would simplify everything, and it would release me from the sense of guilt of my own indecision. I was free. So what the devil was I doing here? I ought to be in my own room, with my tape-recorder on my left and my typewriter on my right, and I ought to be writing steadily, because Tosya was waiting for me, and that was more wonderful than any freedom.

I turned to the whole company, who had now dispersed to different parts of the room.

'I need a flat in a cooperative,' I said solemnly. 'Does anybody know a reliable fixer?'

They all took it that I had decided to marry Irina at last and that it was they, the whole gang, who had pushed me into this decision, and Maria was beaming more than anyone because it was her remark that had done the trick. Everyone talked at once, and it was Yura Lepchenko, the quiet Soviet poet, who was pushed to the fore.

'I've got the very man for you,' he said proudly. 'A representative of the old Russian intelligentsia, a philosopher, a student of Berdyaev, who, as a mark of protest, has taken up the business of organising people's happiness. Charges very little for his services, too. Shall I phone him? If he's home we can drop in on him.'

'Go ahead,' I said decisively. 'A fixer and an intellectual too – that's an interesting combination. And if he can help me out he's a real godsend.'

Without putting the telephone down, Yura continued to persuade me:

'You'll see – he's not a crook. He's unique! . . . Vitali Leopoldovich? Hello!' Yura winked slyly at me. 'Even his patronymic – what class! It's Yura Lepchenko here. Greetings! – Could we pop in to have a word with you? – Now? – Sure!' he shouted happily into the receiver. 'We'll be with you in about forty minutes.'

I bade everybody a warm farewell, especially Lenochka, into whose ear I whispered so that Zhukov could hear:

'You're lovely! If that donkey keeps dragging things out, just let me know . . .'

Lenochka, full of gratitude, kissed me on the cheek. Maria's kiss was like a mother's blessing.

Yura and I crossed the road, jumped on a bus, travelled two stops standing and shaking, hopped off, dived into the Metro and just managed to squeeze into the last carriage.

'Incidentally,' said Yura, 'I'm also thinking of doing a bit of business.'

'What kind of business?'

'Flats. It's very profitable. It can even be interesting, almost like mathematics – an equation with a lot of unknowns. Leopoldovich makes an art of it!'

Had my friend the poet really acquired a taste for property dealing? It seemed unlikely. Perhaps he, too, wanted to start a new life; speculation in flats was probably better than selling rhymes. I took the chance of asking him.

'What about your poetry?' I said, above the clatter of the train.

'I may be no Pushkin, but I'm no worse than the others.'

I thought Yura wrote dreadful verse, but why should I tell him so? We were all hack-writers – our professional life was one big piece of hack work. We all understood certain things and had certain feelings, but we kept them under wraps. When the time came we would show what was in us. We pretended to believe in such a turn of events, but in our present way of life there seemed to be no genuine business – everything was phoney. We realised that too, but, alas, our wisdom did not lead to anything. The only thing we were capable of was understanding everything, or at least having a guess, and meanwhile building up within ourselves an unprecedented spiritual strength. The pride of self-disparagement was an almost demonic, devilish form of pride.

Yura understood exactly what his poetry was worth, but he didn't let that knowledge torture him – he was proud of it. Unlike other hack-writers he knew his own value and therefore did not condemn others.

I was also one of those who understood and did not condemn. Whenever I heard one artist criticising another for doing hack work I considered him not plain-spoken but a fool. But if he said of another: 'The man has something', he was one of us.

So I said to Yura: 'You sometimes write some pretty good lines.'

Yura changed his position, took hold of the strap hanging above his head with the other hand and cast a glance at me that was full of gratitude. If the need ever arose, he would not let me down.

Nevertheless I know these poets! Praise one a little and he begins to think: 'Maybe I really have got something.' So he spends the whole night going over what he has written and stored away through the years, sorting out what may be something worthwhile after all from those in which there's certainly nothing. But even the pieces that are no good at all don't get torn up or flushed down the lavatory: they are put carefully aside in a folder, tied up with string and put away in some secret place.

The life going on around us was full of falsity: words with double meaning, ideas disguised in masks, every action ambiguous. If it were just our wonderful society of 'advancing socialism' that inspired these reactions in me – then everything would be easy! I could become a fighter, a passionate dissident like Lyuska: after all, it wasn't that I was a dispassionate person – it had merely never occurred to me till now to concentrate my emotions on something worthy of passion.

But no. I found the same falseness, the same cheapness, in the world on the other side of the Iron Curtain, which we call the alternative, out of laziness and lack of imagination. Yet maybe it *was* a different kind of falseness; but was it worthwhile experimenting only to replace one kind of shoddy existence by another? It wasn't worth even my tears, let alone the tears of a child, to embark on an experiment that could change nothing in human nature and consequently in human fate. Inequality, for example, might be intrinsic in human beings.

'Let's go,' said Yura, taking me by the elbow.

How annoying – another couple of stops and I would have reached some very profound conclusions. As we went up on the escalator I managed to return to my original thought: the world of Father Vasili and Tosya was drawing me into itself because there was no falsity about it. I got my foot caught in the gap as I stepped off the escalator and was brought up short, shaking my brain to the core. And what if I were to find falsity there too, in the last refuge of my degenerate but suffering soul?

I recalled my father's argument: if insincerity is inherent everywhere in the real world, then it is not false. All you need do is look at things differently, and that corrosive negative particle 'in' would disappear and dissolve into thin air. For my father life was as simple as breathing. His mind was balanced and at peace, and he looked like a real man in comparison with people like me.

What would Father Vasili think of my line of thought? I recalled his generous smile, the way his eyes kept blinking, his awkward gestures; I could hear his rather timid voice, but I couldn't make out what he was saying.

*

It was one of those old Moscow houses that have miraculously survived amid rows of modern concrete boxes. It stood slightly at an angle to the main avenue, half turning its back on it, so to speak, as if to indicate both acceptance of its fate and a certain stubborn resentment.

The wide, shallow-stepped stone staircase had been built for people who were not in a hurry. As your hand slid along the smooth curve of the bannister you felt an invitation to take things slowly. The doors were tall and solid, not the sort you could shove with your shoulder or slip through quickly; they were doors to be approached with decorum and respect, because behind them was more than a mere habitation; it was an entire world of its own, unique and inimitable.

The appearance of the entrance hall prepared me for my meeting with the grey-haired elderly man who was the occupant of the flat on the third floor. I shook his hand with a slight bow, feeling like a member of the landed gentry at the very least. I passed through one room, then another, without letting my eyes dwell on the bureaux and secretaires and stacks of books, and sat down in an antique armchair that was offered to me, as coolly as if I'd never sat in anything else. But after one glance at my host's slippers which showed beneath his jeans and his jacket with its threadbare cuffs I realised how impossible it was for me to make myself part of such surroundings, and I shrank back into the chair under the gaze of our host – the kindly, attentive gaze of a man brought up in the old way.

Yura wasn't very comfortable either – he just couldn't adopt a relaxed pose and look at ease.

'Well, how are things on Parnassus?' our host asked Yura.

'He's getting married,' Yura said instead of replying, and poked me with his finger. 'He can put in a two-roomed flat, with adjoining rooms . . . How many square metres is it?'

I shook my head. 'None at all. I've got nothing to exchange. I need a cooperative flat with one or two rooms.'

Yura was completely baffled. 'Then what are you going to do with Irina's flat?'

Vitali Leopoldovich looked at me, then at Yura, then back at me. He was in no hurry – he would wait for us to explain.

'Yura isn't up to date. I need a cooperative flat . . . to buy . . . without anything in exchange.'

Our host smiled at me in a fatherly way. I didn't understand what his smile meant, but smiled back at him. I had been well brought up, too.

'Apparently,' he said quietly, 'our mutual friend . . .' and he inclined his head in Yura's direction '. . . has not informed you quite accurately as to the nature of my business, and there is nothing for it but for me to enlighten you.'

He rose from his chair, and walked round behind Yura. The doors of a mahogany cupboard, heavily carved and gilded, opened with a pleasant squeak to reveal a set of little drawers each with a number and some letters on it.

With a well-rehearsed, rather theatrical gesture he touched a concealed mechanism and one of the drawers slid slowly open and stopped. I almost expected index cards to rise up automatically.

Vitali Leopoldovich removed a card with his finger and thumb and, scarcely glancing at it, said:

'For example, here's one possibility. There is a three-roomed flat in Kuzminki and a one-roomed flat near the Water-sport Stadium. The people are seeking a two-roomer in the Zamoskvorechye district and another two-roomer, in the centre maybe. In this section there are a hundred and fifty cards – that's the file on the example I quoted. Really, it's a job for a computer, except that a computer is powerless to cope with people's whims and tastes: which floor the flat is on, whether it is on the sunny side, how much privacy there is, the lay-out, whether it has a telephone, the arrangement of the lavatory and bathroom, the sound insulation, what the neighbours are like, and if there is a lift. So you see, young man, the sort of problems I handle. And what exactly do you want from me?'

A scarcely noticeable movement of the fingers and the little drawer slid back in, with an almost melodious squeak of the door. Vitali Leopoldovich walked back around Yura again, who had a look of delight on his face, and sat back in his chair.

'What you want me to do, instead, is to find some scoundrel who could be bribed so that you can jump the queue and buy a cooperative flat.'

He looked at me in such a way as to make me feel ashamed of asking him any favour. Nevertheless I quickly started thinking up some sharp plan, wondering how I could describe my needs to this grey-haired snob so as to interest him. For example, we could exchange my father's flat for a bigger one, then exchange that for two flats, and then exchange mine, the smaller one, for a two-roomer. Would the fixer see the artificiality of my plan and be able to reduce the complicated formula to its original very simple form?

'Listen,' Yura butted in at last, 'I just don't understand what on earth you intend doing with Irina's flat!'

'And who said I was intending to marry Irina?'

Yura was struck dumb, and I took advantage of this to disguise the futility of our visit a little.

'Have you been handling these flat problems for long?'

Our host allowed his beard to pass through his fingers and let it flow out again leaving every hair in place.

'Over thirty years,' Vitali Leopoldovich replied, not without pride. 'And believe me I have derived real satisfaction from the business. Are you, for example, satisfied with your profession? Does it bring you many minutes of happiness?'

I dismissed this with a wave of the hand.

'Although,' he went on, 'if I had my life over again I would probably become a doctor or a surgeon.'

'Yura told me you were once a pupil of Berdyaev.'

'Well, that's not quite true.' He fingered his beard again and grinned at me, but only with his eyes. 'I didn't study under him. But I knew him well and even argued with him. I once stood beside him at the same counter in the writers' shop – do you know what I mean?'

'Berdyaev is very much in fashion now,' I said.

'So I've heard, and I'm surprised. It won't last. Nowadays everybody seems to want to think in a programmed way, if I may put it like that; but Nikolai Aleksandrovich was – I mean his ideas were – no more than the thoughts of a man passionately seeking, though expressed somewhat didactically. Nonetheless, he had the most wonderful insights.'

He had said this facing me; now he turned to Yura. 'What about you, Yura, what have you read of Berdyaev?'

'*Self-Knowledge*,' Yura squeaked happily.

Vitali Leopoldovich gave him a condescending smile.

'I've heard that reply more times than I can remember. And you . . .' he turned to me with the same smile, 'I suppose you've read it too?'

I had in fact read two or three other books of Berdyaev's as well, but as I'd rather listen than talk, I nodded, as if to say: Yes, that's it, only *Self-Knowledge*.

'A pity. I am personally indebted to Nikolai Aleksandrovich for a great deal. I'm going on for seventy-six now, so I can say with confidence that I am a survivor. You young people cannot possibly understand what it means for someone to have survived if the Cheka already had him on their files in 1920, if he refused to join the Party in 1930, and if in 1940 there was a reference to him in the memoirs of a well-known counter-revolutionary. I am indebted to the blessed memory of Nikolai Aleksandrovich Berdyaev for the fact that I understood from the very beginning what the new Russian regime was going to develop into. And I'm lucky!' There were tears in his eyes. 'I have lived out my life in Russia, or at least in the place where Russia used to be. And I haven't dirtied my hands!'

He held out his hands out to me, extending them far beyond his cuffs. I could only see that they were the hands of a very old man.

'Do you think it was easy to survive in Russia and not dirty your hands? And, above all, I remember one remark of Nikolai Aleksandrovich's . . .'

With an elegant movement he swept away a tear and pulled out a handkerchief.

'I was one of the people who saw him off. There was a minute to go, and he said to me: "If you want to live your life in Russia you must regard that as your most important goal in life, and then, perhaps, you will be successful . . . But avoid illusions; who knows, perhaps the life you have led so far is regrettable?" He did not avoid illusions himself.'

He sighed, and, following his gaze, I saw in a glass-fronted bookcase a row of books by his famous teacher. I had the feeling that he was ready to withdraw into himself and guessed that such 'withdrawals' were a frequent occurrence, so I hastened to continue the conversation:

'You mentioned his insights. What did you have in mind?'

He looked searchingly first at me and then at Yura, who was obviously bored.

'Since you ask, I will try to reply.' It was a well-known tactic meaning that the speaker was absolving himself of responsibility for what he was about to say. 'Nikolai Aleksandrovich was the first to observe that socialism was not an alternative to bourgeois society but rather an alternative to Christianity. Conversely there is only one alternative to socialism.'

His look implied more than he said and it was clear that his words had an underlying meaning. I found it slightly amusing to imagine the importance that this pupil of Berdyaev attached to this statement; and I could guess how it had helped him to survive – it had armed him with the right to be inactive, and that right had developed into a moral category and had become the foundation of a theory of survival. It was sinful to laugh at this. Yet this mastodon was, for all his charm, a ridiculous figure evoking neither admiration nor sympathy. I pitied the man. Perhaps it would have been better for him if he had left Russia and died of longing for his native land – then at least he would have suffered real *Weltschmerz*. I recalled the lines of Rainis:

> But your pain will become a great pain,
> And your longing will become Weltschmerz.

When one tried to survive in this country, to survive and nothing more, how could one not become indifferent to everything that had happened to and was still happening to its people, about whom it could be said, only by stretching the meaning of the word, that they had 'survived'. And we who had been born later, who had emerged from this country and been shaped by it – could one say we had all survived?

We took our leave formally in the entrance hall; it was bigger than the room I lived in and so such formality was possible. Just try bowing your way out of the average Soviet citizen's entry hall – you would only bump your head.

As we were walking away from the building I looked around and saw clearly how it had turned away from us and was standing, awkwardly and offended, like the stump of a tree amidst the glass and concrete. It hadn't been demolished; they had taken pity on it. But there's an art to pity too. To pity without artistry might only offend. I wouldn't have risked it.

Yura jumped on me with all sorts of questions. I didn't want to explain, but I could see that he was genuinely concerned about Irina, and that pleased me, almost as if he'd been concerned for me. But I wasn't going to tell him about the priest's daughter, in fact I was beginning to want to change my relationship with the majority of my friends and acquaintances radically. True, it would be difficult to find the resources to limit my circle of friends; basically, I was a gregarious creature. But my new life would be built on different values, have different coordinates, and so my socialism must be reduced to a minimum. I pictured myself, warmed by happiness, in need of no one, acquiring higher wisdom in the comfort of family life, inaccessible to the victims of the hustle and bustle of the capital.

Before diving into the Metro again, I told Yura, underlining every word: 'It's not Irina I'm marrying. We have parted amicably. That's the way it is, Yura.'

But then Yura, the hack poet, suddenly gave me a penetrating look and said with surprising bluntness: 'You've chosen the right time to dump Irina. Because of certain circumstances she's not too eligible at the moment.'

I wasn't angry: his defence of Irina was so unexpected. But I couldn't leave his challenge unanswered, because then I would have offended him, and I didn't want to do that.

'There is one circumstance which all poets are very familiar with – love. Have I answered you?'

Yura was not satisfied: love was all very well, but what about decent behaviour? That could be seen in his look, and I was glad, damned glad, because it was good to discover in people qualities you didn't know they had. Though this was a special case. Everybody liked Irina. Why, I didn't know. Of course her friends loved her, with a different kind of love from the love I'd had for her, and I saw no grounds for that *other* love. Was it her involvement in television scandals? Her devotion to her work? I was the only one who could really appreciate her work, although it had robbed me of her, robbed us of our evenings together, even of our nights. I had no use for Irina the go-getter. But she was probably the only person among my acquaintances I would not call a hack.

In the Metro carriage I shouted into the ear of the sulky, frowning Yura: 'Tell me, why does everybody love Irina?'

Strangely enough, he was not surprised. 'She doesn't mix people with business,' Yura replied. 'She treats a person as a human being, that's all.'

'I don't understand you,' I said right into his ear.

'Well, for example, she doesn't give a damn what sort of poetry I write. I am important to her for myself. I could just as well not write any poems at all.'

I nodded to show I understood and then tried to recall Irina in some situation where it might have been possible to observe this quality in her. The idea seemed doubtful – how could you separate a person from his or her occupation? But maybe a woman could?

Yes, I had noticed something like that in Irina: she defended people who weren't really worth defending.

So there: everybody loved Irina, and here was Yura the hack poet giving me to understand that I was a bastard for thinking of marrying someone else. I wanted to explain to Yura, yet I couldn't talk, not in the Metro or on the street to Yura the poet or to anyone else about that other, strange world inhabited by Father Vasili and his daughter Tosya and the virtuous deacon who was hopelessly in love with my – yes, *my* – priest's daughter, and that other world where God was present. It seemed to me that His presence was there only. Where else could He be? Not in our world of empty gesturing: it was too well defended against Him – we were living in a cleverly constructed God-shelter! I remember once reading in a children's book about a fencer who wielded his sword so skilfully that no drop of rain could fall on him. We too fenced so artfully with our words and actions that God could not get through to our souls; we were well protected against the human idea somewhere above our heads, leaving only tiny little islands in the sea of the world, like Father Vasili's home, occasional holes in the dome of the common God-shelter; it was only there that
what had been intended for the whole of humanity could be realised.

Father Vasili's world was too serious for me to discuss with Yura. But while we were changing trains, on the escalator, for some reason I asked him:

'Have you been baptised?'

I had clearly caught Yura unawares and immediately regretted having put the question. He eyed me suspiciously – something had put him on his guard.

'Let's say I was,' he replied, and I had to turn away, to hide my smile. I could tell from his tone of voice that Yura, in addition to everything else, was also dabbling in religion.

'Which church do you attend?' I asked him straight out.

Yura hesitated, but I had a certain reputation; everyone knew I rubbed elbows with dissidents, so he replied: 'At Sokolniki.'

'And is it serious?'

It was a superfluous question. Yura the hack poet could never be serious. He tried to compensate for his social inadequacy. Yura played about, toyed with things, was looking for excitement in the intolerable flatness of his life. I understood him, in fact I understood him very well and it wouldn't have surprised me even if he fasted from time to time; in Moscow, after all, you can find substitutes for forbidden food. We're lucky, it's not the Siberian backwoods.

'Take me along with you sometime,' I said to Yura, but I wasn't able to judge by his face how he'd taken my request.

We were hurrying to catch trains in different directions; I shouted to him as we parted: 'I'll give you a ring tomorrow – we can fix it then!'

Again I couldn't make out his reaction. I got a glimpse of Yura's face through the glass, before the carriage sped off along the platform into the tunnel, above which a clock was ticking off the seconds.

On my desk at home I found a thick folder of papers waiting for me. When I had finished this job I would be done with hack work for the rest of my life. Never before had I been so aware of the possibility, the necessity of a different life. I could see that other life in my mind so clearly that I became excited and impatient. But I forced myself to go to bed and sleep, so that I could wake up early next day and settle down to work. So far the job was the only real guarantee I had of my new life in the future. I wished myself sweet dreams.

*

Thank you, my love, thank you for your letter! It was just the kind I was waiting for! I knew I would get one. It was almost like seeing you, but not quite, because only yesterday I found it harder to remember your face, and today it was harder still, which frightens me a little. When I start trying to recall you in detail everything dissolves before my eyes, and you say in your letter that you're not coming back soon . . . But, my love, what do we need so much money for? Papa says he's got two and a half thousand and maybe there's no need at all for you to work so much. Every morning it's harder to remember how you laughed or lost your temper, yet I can still see just the outline of you as it was when you stood at the window that night with the lake behind you and the moon overhead.

I must tell you what happened here three days ago at church on Sunday. I was singing in the choir when I saw a quite elderly stranger come in – he'd come in a car, I learnt later. For a long time he simply stood there, so I thought he had just come to look. But then he called Papa over and discussed something with him, and then Papa led him to the confessional and showed him how to cross himself and kiss the Bible. The man spent a long time at confession, and when I glanced later at Papa he was quite pale and his hands shook when he gave communion to the man, and when the man left the church Papa stood there as if he'd been turned to stone, and he had such a frightened look in his eyes that I really was afraid for him. Even today he's not himself somehow. I don't ask him about it – he wouldn't tell me anyhow, but yesterday evening I cried because Papa sat the whole evening at the window saying nothing, and when I went to bed he prayed for a

*long time in a whisper. I keep on wondering what that
man had said about himself to make Papa ill – because
Papa already knows so much about people that if I knew
what he knows I would go out of my mind! The man was
an ordinary person – there was nothing special about his
face – I had a good look at him. Volodya the deacon says
the stranger must have confessed something terrible to
Papa. But, as you know, my father is a very good man,
and I believe that, if he had to absolve the man of some
great sin, he is now tormenting himself because deep down
he couldn't really forgive the man for what he had done.
Actually, this isn't what I think at all, it's Volodya's idea.*

*It is so hard for me without you, my love! I know it has
to be, but why do we need so much money? I just want
you here!*

*I pray for you every day – maybe my prayers don't
mean much to you, but just remember that I think of you
every day; that means something, doesn't it?*

*So I'll write: the Lord preserve you! That means that I
want everything to go well for you, and I know that
everything will go well because I want it so much!*

I am waiting for you.

Your Tosya.

III

III

I know no-one more reliable than Zhenka Poluëktov. He isn't just reliable: he's a very paragon of reliability. Where on earth do people like him spring from? In Russia they represent a new anthropological type; it is unthinkable for an ordinary Russian to be so businesslike. The Poluëktovs of this world have invented a new profession – wheeling and dealing their way round our strictly controlled and grim system and have found a golden key to make it work for them. I am full of admiration for people like this and really sorry for our poor Russian lay-abouts who are doomed to extinction in the new climate of efficiency created by the Poluëktovs. Some of these good-for-nothings wanted to get their noses in the trough too, but they used such primitive methods to butt their way in that they ended up covered in scorn – they didn't know how to disguise themselves or how to force their way through using other people's elbows. And they all operate as individuals or as pathetic little groups, and if one of them succeeds on his own he kicks all the others out of the way. More often than not such success is the result of the efforts of the Poluëktovs of this world anyway. *They* know how to step out of the way at the right moment and let the freshly promoted big-shot through, and then they quietly make a circle round him and perform a Russian dance, singing: 'We've sown the seeds and our new man is here!'

No, I don't condemn Zhenka. What is the right way to live in this society? To fight it? What's the point? So there's only one way: milk the damned thing, milk it dry, turn the whole lot of it into one willing, many-nippled udder.

You don't like the idea? You object? Well, then, marry a priest's daughter and live in the exalted world of the spirit.

Personally I don't believe that there will ever be anything to rejoice about in this country or for that matter in mankind as a whole. A new civilisation is being created and none of the old concepts will be applicable; it may possibly permit the existence of special reservations for sentimental fools, for priests and priests' daughters, but it will develop such over-whelming irony and condescension towards the exceptions and the eccentrics that it will not have to fight them: on the contrary, they will be entered in the Red Books and protected by law, like marsupial bears or viviparous herons. Those whose inferiority complex turns out to be insuperable in conditions of hourly changing reality, who are out of step with the times, who fail to keep up in the race for the good things of life, or who do not hold on to what the good Lord sends will have to find satisfaction in their rarity. As throwbacks.

I know I'm a throwback. Of course, I'll defend my reputation to the world at large and put a good face on my poor perform-ance. But privately I envy my contemporaries whose life is just one mad steeplechase, just as now with a tiny part of myself I envy Zhenka Poluëktov. My envy is pointless, not only because I could never perform Zhenka's role but also because I do not have the slightest desire to do so. No desire, but envy, and that sums me up.

Zhenka is really terrific. For a whole week he vanished completely, but then he reappeared at the very moment when I was beginning to have doubts about him. 'Hello, Gena, old man!' he yelled over the telephone. I couldn't stand that mode of address, but I was greatly relieved.

The publishing house he had got the money from was the most patriotic in existence. But even there Zhenka had his own man, another 'half-breed' – apparently even a flag-waving publisher can't do without them. So there I was – in one pocket, a contract, and in the other, a fat advance. It occurred to me that I could have done it all myself: I'd written the chapters conscientiously, and I could have managed without Zhenka's connections. But there again, I also knew that in that case I wouldn't have had either the advance or the contract by now. That was the obvious advantage of Zhenka's system. The person he dealt with was always insured by Zhenka himself, and if anything went wrong, Zhenka and his friends would find him another job, no less important and privileged. Consequently he was freer to make decisions and therefore better able to produce results. This wasn't just a closed circle, it was the death-sentence of idealism.

All this would have been very sad had it not been a reality. Reality demands respect and recognition.

I met Zhenka at the Kashirskaya Metro station and we set off to visit the hero of the book I was writing. We were going to celebrate our success, so I had a bag in each hand. Respectable Soviet citizens eyed the bags with interest as they passed: unfamiliar bottles of Western spirits were sticking out of them, as did French salami in fancy wrapping paper. I feared that the contrast between the contents of my bags and my person, dressed in the usual Soviet style from head to foot, might very well make people suspicious. I felt like a black-marketeer dealing in Indian condoms.

But Zhenka was with me, reliable and unpretentious. He had on expensive glasses, but had carefully chosen subdued clothes for the occasion. We were about to call on an ordinary Soviet citizen; the latest Paris fashions would have been out of place. Better to exhibit our intellectual qualities and our important connections, so that he would feel he was dealing with 'writers'.

Zhenka was cheerful; his eyes shone and he was more than usually vigorous and sweeping in his movements.

'So, Gena, you're going off to live with real people, are you?'

Zhenka's eyes peering through his glasses seemed to be coming through the slits of a concrete bunker; they reflected confidence and sharpness.

I waited for him to explain what he was getting at. We were standing at the end of a queue ten yards long for the bus.

'Frankly, Gena, I've always thought that Irina wasn't right for you.'

'And who *is* she right for?'

'For me!' replied Zhenka. I tried in vain to look into his eyes; the sky was reflected in his lenses and concealed them. 'She and I – the deals we could have pulled off together! Irka isn't just energetic – she's a power-house. You're a dead weight alongside her. But a priest's daughter now – that's the very thing for you. I don't mean to disparage you, you understand, and you have many fine qualities.'

I nodded, undecided as to when to shut Zhenka up.

'At least religion will cure you of your dissident tendencies. Paradoxical it may seem, but religion always contains an element of healthy realism, and that's just what you lack.'

'And Irina?' I asked provocatively. But Zhenka was carried away and didn't catch the tone of my voice.

'Ira is a fighter who hasn't found the right battlefield yet; that explains her skirmishes in the television studio. You know, I could have cleared the whole thing up without any trouble, but she didn't want me to – she seems to have realised at last that she is not cut out for that sort of work.'

'So what is she cut out for?' I asked casually, as I shuffled along to get on the bus.

When Zhenka, looking pretty crushed and rumpled, finally fought his way through to where I was standing in the bus he muttered crossly: 'I told you – we should have taken a taxi.'

I was really enjoying seeing him taken down a peg or two; his individuality was extinguished in the crowd, and there was a hurt look in the bright eyes behind his glasses. His carefully trimmed beard looked out of place in the crush. I wanted to say something about submitting oneself to objective reality, but I couldn't think of anything witty enough. I hadn't yet had time to reflect why Zhenka had been pleased on learning of my break with Irina. In fact everything connected with Irina had faded into the background in the last few days and I seemed to have ceased to be aware of everything that ought to have required my attention. I'd even forbidden myself to think about Irina or about the child . . . whose child? An obstacle, that, in the way of my new life. I cherished a secret hope that everything would somehow resolve itself on its own, leaving the way to the little world of Father Vasili wide open. I felt that everything around me was purely temporary, almost as a mirage; it was only when the mirage was over that something real would begin.

I led Zhenka through side-streets and courtyards to the peeling five-storied block in which the hero of my book lived. We were expected: he'd glimpsed me from the window at the flat, and on the second floor of a filthy stairwell smelling of cats a door padded with artificial leather swung open to admit us. We were greeted by my hero's wife, Polina Mikhailovna, in her best clothes. She was a tall slender woman, already in her sixties, but energetic, quick in her movements and, I thought, unattractive only because of the permanent worried look on her face. There was one peculiar movement of her arms and shoulders that was like a heavy sigh of weariness and despair: it was probably just an old habit, but it immediately endeared her to you and made you sorry for her. The woman's whole appearance – the wrinkles on her face, her ponderous masculine way of moving, her big mannish hands – were a sad reflection of an unenviable life.

She was used to me – by now I was practically one of the family – but when she saw Zhenka behind me she became flustered and her expression turned wooden. I understood: Zhenka was the great man, and I was small fry compared to him! At that moment our hero appeared in the hall – in full dress uniform with a whole iconastasis of decorations right down to his waist and an expression on his face of triumph, dignity and complete sobriety – he had obviously not touched a single drop prior to our arrival.

I had some difficulty in persuading Polina Mikhailovna to take the shopping bags with food and drink from me. We were invited into the living room where we found the table already laid and sitting at it were Andrei Semyonich's elder daughter with her husband and three other men, one of whom I recognised as a regular angler at the pond in Tsaritsyn Park. Smiling, he stretched out his hand with the air of an old acquaintance. To everyone present I introduced Zhenka as a member of the staff of the publishing house and we sat down at the table. Zhenka ostentatiously refused to take the seat of honour at the head of the table and almost used force to make the real cause of the celebrations sit there. Our hero beamed, eyes twinkling, and his medals rattling on his chest, and I who now knew how he had won each of those decorations suddenly felt a completely new respect for him. Zhenka began playing the role of a representative of the grateful generation of children paying homage to the valiant deeds of their fathers. He played the part poorly on the whole but at about the level demanded, and within five minutes was the centre of attention. Meanwhile our hostess was hastily replacing the drinks, the sausages and the cheese, so that Zhenka's act had to compete with the appearance of the imported salami and whisky in fancy bottles.

The happiest of all was the hero's daughter, who was glowing with pleasure at the sudden opportunity to be proud of her father. Her happiness almost made me happy too. Of course, I never forgot that I was simply out to make some money – but the people in this home were happy, and it was my doing.

Now Zhenka was on his feet, glass in hand, and everybody literally held their breath out of respect for him.

'Friends!' he began somewhat emotionally. 'Before this year is out yet another just cause will come to fruition in our country. Shortly our country will learn of a hitherto unsung hero whose name should be, and will be, written into the history of the Great Patriotic War. Our dear Andrei Semyonich!'

At any moment, it seemed, tears would come to Zhenka's eyes. His voice was trembling. Was this objectionable or not? I wasn't sure. As a partner in the enterprise I had no moral right to dissociate myself from Zhenka; but if he had not been there I would probably have fallen in with the general mood of the company – without this bitter sense of cynicism and duplicity.

'Dear Andrei Semyonich! Your life is a text-book for us, the generation that has not known war, on how to live. By your deeds of heroism in the defence of our Soviet system you have provided an example . . .'

There was actually a great deal of truth in Zhenka's oratory. The men who had laid down their lives at the Front had indeed defended the Soviet system *for Zhenka* and for all the Zhenkas who were now benefiting from of the system. Everybody else was dissatisfied for some reason or in some way, but I knew just how much that was worth. It was the sort of ineffective grumbling that accompanies all periods and all systems and amounts to nothing. Zhenka, though, was content!

'We wish you long life, dear Andrei Semyonich! And to your wife and children happiness and every success!'

They all rose to their feet and clinked their glasses together. In his embarrassment our hero spilt whisky over the table, then, looking each one in the eyes, thanked everyone. Following Zhenka's toast, joy and pride were in everyone's eyes, and also a certain bewilderment.

On my left I had Andrei Semyonich's son-in-law. In the course of the evening I learnt that he was a high-ranking official and I guessed that he was now going through a pleasant transformation in his relationship to his father-in-law: his left, less controlled hand still indicated a casual attitude, but the right one had already been reoriented and was reaching eagerly, clutching a glass, towards the hero of the day. His eyes had already cultivated a new expression – a mixture of encouragement and reproach, as if to say: shame on you, concealing such heroic deeds from us – we would have known how to appreciate them! He treated me in a rather patronising manner, patting me on the back in the Party way, because after all he was present not only as son-in-law but also as representative of . . . so to speak, on behalf of . . . because by virtue of his position he was always representing or acting on behalf of somebody.

The fisherman from the Tsaritsyn pond followed the proceedings with eyes wide with enthusiasm, flattered at being drawn into such an important gathering. I concluded that he also was a war veteran and that he was envious of his friend, but his envy pleased me, because he saw in Andrei Semyonich's sudden rise in the world the triumph of justice for the vanishing generation of men who had fought in the last war.

I felt like Gogol's Khlestakov, but only a little, damn it, and I also felt like a writer. To feel like a writer means to feel uplifted, specially and actively remote from reality. Anyway, there's something other-worldly about the experience, at least at moments like this.

It fell to my lot to propose the third toast. I didn't find it easy. Zhenka's presence was disruptive; it prevented me from saying what I sincerely thought and I finished with banalities:

'Once in a lifetime a man is tested in all his qualities. For you, dear Andrei Semyonich, that test was the war with Nazi Germany. God grant that each of us should pass his test as you did!'

I knew very well that these were just well-tried clichés which had as much to do with real life as I had to do with being a writer. I very much wanted to speak to my hero sincerely, but instead of saying anything – in any case, I couldn't find the words – I rose from my seat, went up to Andrei Semyonich and embraced him. We clinked our glasses and downed our drinks in one gulp. Everyone applauded and shouted. He put his only arm around me. There were tears in the eyes of his wife and daughter. I cast a glance at Zhenka – he was looking happy too, and I wanted to believe that his happiness was genuine – why shouldn't it be – was he made of steel, after all?

It wasn't long before I knew everybody's names and professions and family relationship. Soon we were all singing old Russian songs about Stenka Razin and the last war. More than one glass had been spilt over the table-cloth and more than one fork had fallen beneath the table.

I was beginning to feel a bit tipsy so I looked enquiringly at Zhenka and he, the wretch, pointed to his watch.

But then the fisherman, 'Mishka' (as he insisted I call him, though he was older than my father) leaned across the table to me.

'Tell me, lad, when you finish the book, I suppose you'll get pretty well paid for it?'

Not realising the danger of the subject, I nodded complacently.

'How much, if it's no secret?'

I was immediately on my guard, but the fisherman's look indicated only straightforward curiosity. I hesitated, then turned to Zhenka. I became aware of the silence that had fallen on the company. Everybody was interested, even the high official, the hero's son-in-law. And the hero himself and his wife. I felt rather awkward, because the subject didn't seem to fit the situation, but I found a way out – I pointed out Zhenka:

'He knows better than I do. Whatever they pay, that's what I shall get.'

They all turned to Zhenka. He didn't like this – I could tell that by his face – but he soon had his face under control.

'It depends on many factors,' he said in a businesslike and dignified way, 'on the print-run, for example – that is, the number of copies printed. And other factors: the paper, the binding.'

But his ruse didn't come off; Mishka broke in impatiently:

'But at the most – how much?'

An even greater silence descended around Zhenka. He raised a shoulder, tugged at his beard and finally forced himself to say:

'Well, I reckon, around six thousand . . .'

From the way Zhenka had reduced the figure I realised how touchy a subject it really was. I glanced around quickly at the company and saw that they were all in a state of mild shock, and the way the hero's wife parted her hands and then clapped them together in amazement was like a slap in the face for me.

'Six thou . . . sand!' Mishka repeated. He was no longer looking at me. Meanwhile my hero was staring down at the table, and I could not tell what he was feeling. The atmosphere at the table had changed completely, and I could see now the wariness on Zhenka's face.

'Six thousand!' Polina Mikhailovna repeated with a sigh.

'Ye . . . es,' said Mishka meaningfully. 'There you are, Andrei, you'd have been better off with the six thousand in your pocket than all this fame and fortune.'

'But how can it work out like that?' Polina Mihailovna said complainingly. 'He fought in the war and was wounded and nobody offered him that kind of money, but a little book about it's worth that much!'

'Daylight robbery!' the fisherman exclaimed, almost with a snarl. The men sitting near him nodded in agreement, not looking either at me or at Zhenka. All my hopes were on Zhenka but he was obviously at a loss; it was the first time I'd seen him like this.

'But you have to realise,' he said, trying to maintain a pleasant expression, 'writing a book isn't easy, you have to learn . . .'

'Oh, sure. And do you think it was easy dragging Jerries out of their trenches?' My hero, my modest, embarrassed hero, Andrei Semyonich, had now joined in. His face was red, his eyes angry and his fist lay clenched on the table. I could see he was drunk.

'By law the money should be split fifty:fifty!' the fisherman said, banging on the table.

'What are you talking about? What law? Papa, don't listen to them!'

'Why shouldn't I? Don't you think I've got cause for complaint?'

'Quite right – of course you have! Fifty:fifty! One man risks his life and another comes along and makes money out of it! There should be a law against it!'

'Stop it!' The nice daughter was trying to bring them all to their senses.

'My goodness, Andryukha,' the fisherman refused to let up. 'Just imagine what you could have done with that money!'

'Plenty,' muttered Andrei Semyonich, but then his wife shook her fist at him.

'What would he have done with it? For eight years he just couldn't leave the booze alone, and I was slaving away like a horse . . .'

'Mummy, please!' her daughter shouted desperately.

Zhenka nodded towards the door and we both stood up. Somebody took me hesitantly by the hand, but I freed myself and quickly covered the few feet between the table and the door. Zhenka and I grabbed the door handle at the same time, getting in each other's way, and then Andrei Semyonich's daughter came between us.

'Wait a minute! Please, don't go. It's all so stupid. But you must understand – my mother held down two jobs, and when she fell ill we didn't even have bread to eat, just potatoes . . . Please don't be offended. I just don't know what to say . . .'

I didn't know what to say either.

'We understand,' said Zhenka reassuringly, 'and that's why we are leaving. We understand. Let them all calm down, then we'll sort things out.'

Zhenka was lying: nothing could possibly get sorted out. I

tried to calculate quickly how much of the advance I had already spent; I would have to return it.

The daughter was weeping into someone's coat hanging in the hall. Zhenka took a step towards her and made a move to take her by the shoulders, but his hands stopped halfway and he had to make a hasty pretence of smoothing his hair down, because our hero's son-in-law had just appeared in the hallway.

'See what money does to people,' he said with good Communist sorrow in his voice.

'Perhaps it's not the money,' I argued glumly, 'but the lack of it?'

While the son-in-law was consoling his wife, Zhenka pushed me towards the door. For some reason I resisted. I was still very drunk and not capable of taking any decisions. Then, all of a sudden, I turned my back on the two of them, pulled a wad of money from my pocket and stuffed it into the pocket of a coat hanging by the door. Zhenka grabbed me by the arm, abruptly and angrily but without a word. I snarled at him like a dog – and my hand was empty. He pushed me out of the door, dragged me down the stairs, and only when we were outside did we come to a halt.

'You fool!' said Zhenka. 'Do you really think they'll take the money from you? Sentimental fool! All you've done is condemn them to the further humiliation of returning the money to you.'

'I won't take it.'

'Then you're an idiot twice over! They will continue to humiliate themselves until you forgive them and take the money. And you'll take it! And it's then that they'll really loathe you.'

'Zhenka, isn't life disgusting?'

'Oh sure,' Zhenka declared. 'Can you walk as far as a taxi?'

'I want to go to Uryupinsk.'

'Anywhere else? You don't want to go back to mummy and daddy?'

'I'd visit my mother, but she has no time for me. My father

I don't want to see. He's just like you. I hate both of you!'

'I see,' mumbled Zhenka, leading me off somewhere.

'One of us is a bastard. Is it you or me?'

'One of us is a fool,' Zhenka replied calmly, 'and that's you. And you'll always be one.'

'And you'll never be one, is that it?'

Zhenka left my side and rushed into the roadway so quickly a taxi nearly knocked him down. He said something to the driver, stuffed some money into his hand, opened the door for me, and I flopped into the seat. The taxi took off at top speed, and I had no time to ask Zhenka why he wasn't coming with me.

'Where are we going?' I asked the driver, and he gave me my address.

Good. I needed to go home. Life might be objectionable, but at least it was better in one's own flat.

By rights I should have relaxed in the taxi, but the closer we came to where I lived the clearer my head became, and I was overcome by such a mood of despair that I was afraid even to creep into my own empty flat. What could I do there? It was only late afternoon, and if I slept now all sorts of depressing thoughts would descend on me in the night. I peered out of the taxi at the streets, recognised that we'd reached the district where I lived and finally made up my mind.

'To the right now at the traffic lights. We're going somewhere else.'

'Fine with me,' said the driver calmly. 'Where?'

'Carry on round the ring road and I'll tell you where to turn – I don't remember the name of the street.'

I felt hastily in my pocket and was delighted to find a ten-rouble note tucked away there. If Yura the poet wasn't home, as was likely, I would still have enough to get to some other address. I ought, of course, to have phoned before dropping in on him, but I decided to take a chance.

All the windows in the taxi were open, so I stuck my head out and gulped the air rushing by. At the speed we were moving it felt cold and clean. Even when a Chaika limousine sped noiselessly by in a cloud of high-octane exhaust, I didn't wrinkle my nose or splutter; I was brought up on engine fumes. They had the same effect on me as the wind has on a son of the steppes. I was an urban child, a mushroom that pushed its way up through the asphalt, a mutant in a machine civilisation. You could spit in my face and I wouldn't take offence; I was a social mutant, too.

As my head cleared I tried to understand what had happened in my hero's home. Had they insulted me or not? Of course they had. But had I the right to be insulted? It really had been a silly business over the money. Splitting it fifty:fifty would have been fair, but that would have been just a gesture, not a moral act. I would only have done it under pressure, and I was thoroughly in agreement with the law that did not oblige me to make such a gesture – and I was grateful for that.

Frankly, I was fed up; worn out with this – or, more precisely, so primed for my new life that all the fuss and bother and unpleasantness of this business would soon be shut out of my consciousness, like a neighbour's pop-music on the other side of a wall.

A quiet woman with a stoop opened the door to me. Yura Lepchenko's mother. She didn't recognise me.

'Yura is working!' she warned, leading me to his room. It was quite clear that when her son was 'working' his mother did not dare to knock on his door – it was up to me to take that risk. I banged with my knuckles on the door and walked straight in. Our poet was lying on a couch, his legs crossed, holding a note-book and a pen. Would you believe it – he actually *was* working! The moment I appeared he jumped up from the couch as if I had caught him doing something improper.

'Creating?' I asked him and poked my nose impudently into the open note-book. A whole page covered with verse! Yura clapped the notebook shut.

'I understand – it's a trade secret.' I shook him by the hand

and apologised sincerely to him. 'I felt sort of sick, sorry for dropping in without warning.'

Yura hastily put away the paraphernalia of the creative process. He had bookshelves on all the walls, as was the fashion. They contained, naturally, Tsvetayeva, Pasternak, Blok and, would you credit it, even Gumilev! In the eastern(!) corner were the inevitable icons and on one of the shelves were candlesticks encrusted with wax. Everything just as you'd expect in fact, in the average Soviet flat.

'Do you want anything to eat? Drink?' Yura asked.

'I'm full up with food and drink. Listen, is going to church with a hangover a great sin?'

'Better not to go,' Yura replied delicately.

'It's only four o'clock . . . I'll be over it soon.'

Yura eyed me suspiciously. 'As it happens, I am going there today . . .'

'Great. Make me a cup of coffee before we go and I'll be fine. What's going on there today?'

'The usual. The service, then a sermon . . . A talk . . .'

'Just what I need. You'll take me along?'

'Well, so long as you're sure you're OK . . .'

'I'll be all right. Have you got some pickles?'

'You'd be better having a sleep – I'll open the window.'

I wasn't all that sure that this wasn't just another of my whims. Another act? I didn't know. Anyway, I decided to follow Yura's advice and lay down on the couch; he threw the window open and slipped out of the room. I slowly relaxed and sank into a dreamless sleep and remained in that state for what must have been quite a long time, because when I came round again the sun was no longer shining in through the window – it had gone down behind the parapet across the yard. That minute Yura burst into the room.

'We've overslept!'

He had been snoring away too – in the other room – and it was now six o'clock. Yura was in a state of nervous indecision for some time – was there any sense in going so late? His little

face was lined with concentration like a child's. Finally the
wrinkles in his forehead smoothed out and he said calmly:

'Let's just go along for the sermon. Want a shower?'

'There's nothing I'd like more.'

Yura took me to the bathroom which was gleaming with
foreign tiling (no doubt thanks to Zhenka Poluëktov), in-
structed me how to work the imported taps and handed me a
vast bathtowel. The ice-cold stream of water descending on
my head made me catch my breath, but once I got used to it
my breath and my *joie de vivre* soon came back. My body
rejoiced in the cold and its own self-awareness, and felt that it
was only a thing not fully mine, a thing that hadn't merged
completely with my 'I'. It was a strange sensation, as though
I was outside myself and my mind and body had not come
quite into line with each other. But now that I was alert and
full of life, the disagreeable thoughts which had also revived
and were moving around slowly in my mind had also been
more or less suppressed. My body was ready to enter into
communion with other worlds, but my mind – what kind of
spade would be needed to scrape that clean?

Yura was urging me to hurry up, but I still had time
to notice that he'd undergone a sort of transfiguration: his
movements were confident, his look assured. I was amazed,
but I still couldn't believe it: Yura just couldn't be a believer,
that was impossible! So what was going on?

'Are you wearing a cross?' he asked.

I had to smile. What intellectual could possibly be without
a cross? Mine was no ordinary cross either, it was a gold one
and on a gold chain, and had actually been blessed in Zagorsk
itself. It was a naïve question for Yura to ask, like asking if I
had read Hatha Yoga or Kafka.

But in the Metro, as we came closer to our destination, I
found myself not wanting to display my mental agility, but
instead to clear my mind of all the smart remarks that poison
one's pure perception and permit no single sacred thought to
survive. But what about my will? I was obliged, after all, to

approach the church with purity of heart. So I tried to fix my mind on something pure and simple. I told myself: you want to think of what is pure and simple! This was where I might of course have turned my thoughts to the priest's daughter, but in fact, alas, nothing in my relationship with her was either simple or pure, and remorse, rather, came into my mind with the words 'fool' and 'bastard'. Why hadn't I started my new life with a clean slate, without error? What wonderful tranquillity I'd be experiencing now! But no, we had sinned. And how must Tosya feel going to church, if I, an unbeliever, wished the earth would swallow me up?

A hundred yards away there was a crowd gathered in front of the church.

'Go on – push your way through!' muttered Yura, and his elbows became sharp and pitiless as he squeezed his way energetically through the crowd. The people made way for him, and I was sucked into the vacuum that formed in his wake; I simply floated through the crowd as if I were being towed, and in a few minutes we were inside the church. Even then Yura pressed forward, and we finished up practically at the front with the priest standing above us with a Bible in his hands. Yura crossed himself and I did the same though with less zeal.

The priest was rather short, plump and bald; he had a round face and narrowed eyes and his fingers on the binding of the Scriptures were white and stubby. He was saying something about atheists; he appeared to be condemning them, and his voice, which was as soft as a woman's, was yet bold and forceful. The metallic tone and his interjections alerted you and seized your attention, and with the first sentence that I understood completely I began to feel emotional. I had already guessed that this was no normal service I was attending, no ordinary priest I was listening to. Yura turned his head to me and winked conspiratorially, which told me my guess was right. The priest's voice grew stronger and he moved his hand vigorously above the heads of the congregation and kept it there.

He held the atheists up to shame, denounced them and called down on their heads God's judgement, God's wrath and God's forgiveness all at the same time. He spoke about those who were suffering in the Russian land, and I heard him give the names of prison camps – Solovki, Kolyma – and couldn't believe my own ears. It was like a dream. I wanted to tug at Yura's sleeve and to ask him what was going on, who this denouncing priest was, and why he could speak at such length without anyone bursting into the church, interrupting him, without the dome of the church going up in smoke! I heard a call that was practically a command: 'Let us pray for those who suffer in the Russian land, for the innocent who have been murdered . . .'

There were tears in my eyes. I made the sign of the cross, once, twice, three times, and I caught a glimpse of others doing the same, and the whole church was filled with the sound of hands moving up, down and across. It was like a whisper not so much of prayer but of something more serious, able to grow from a whisper into something bigger. It needed just one more sentence from the plump, balding priest and something quite extraordinary would happen to everybody, and to me as well. I was also ready for whatever it was, and I waited trembling for the summons. But the priest's voice was prudently restrained, his tone mobilised people to a state of readiness, warning them in a fatherly way against any hasty action. I lost my individuality; my will was a minute particle of the general mood, drawn towards some wholeness that I took to be a transformation, a discovery, and along with the general will I was straining forward with all my being, towards the white chubby hands of the priest.

'What is this? What is happening?' I asked myself, without presumably wanting a reply, because a reply would only simplify and minimise everything. I was not looking for understanding: I wanted to *feel*. More than once I dreamt of that feeling of belonging to something greater, but was convinced when I woke that such a state would be humiliating, not elevating, and I could not believe that it could give me a feeling of happiness.

'Well, what do you think of it?' I heard Yura's voice; he'd made his way across to me and was whispering in my ear.

I didn't know what to reply and I didn't want to reply. I simply wanted to preserve that unprecedented feeling of happiness within myself but Yura had already brought me back to earth and it was in vain that I tried not to return. The service was coming to an end, as was apparent from the rustling and shuffling in the crowd.

People began pushing their way to the front for the priest's blessing, while Yura and I were squeezed back against the wall. Noticing a number of elderly women who were also pressed back into the corners, I was surprised first of all by their stolid silence. But I was even more surprised to see in their faces a look of barely concealed annoyance. The church was full of young people, or rather people of my age, and all the rest were pressed back against the walls and into the corners. I recognised the faces of the young: they were Moscow intellectuals – young men with beards, auburn hair and swarthy complexions who worked in stupid, pointless institutions; nervous young women with menial office jobs; bearded Jews belonging to literary and philosophical circles; and, of course, the dissidents. The dissidents I recognised by their expression, the way they hung together in a group, the way they talked – I couldn't hear them but I could sense their conspiratorial manner; and now I could see they were passing some paper from hand to hand, probably collecting signatures for a petition against something or other. Yura had the piece of paper, but hastily handed it on to me. I was right! It was an appeal by the parishioners in defence of the priest who was threatened with some unpleasantness. I took out my pen and signed my name and, without much thought, handed the paper on to an elderly woman in a grey scarf standing behind me. Uncomprehendingly she looked first at me and then at the piece of paper. A young Jew tried to explain it to her, but I heard only

'Father . . .' before she said crossly: 'I don't know why you have to come to church on Saturday. The place is so full we can't get to the altar! Why don't you stay in your blessed theatres?'

I was beginning to feel ashamed. I tried to revive the feelings which only a few minutes previously had carried me right up to the dome of the church, but I failed.

The crowd moved back and made way for the priest, who passed through making the sign of the cross and blessing the congregation. Behind him, like bodyguards, were several young men with long hair. On the streets of Moscow I had taken them for hippies, but I saw now that their hair was cut in the same way as Christ's was in pictures. Peering into their eyes I discovered to my surprise no sign of pretence in them, only an undisguised admiration for the priest and faith too, perhaps? . . . I wanted to ask them: 'You, with the long hair – how do you come by it, this faith of yours? And where do you come from? Where is this place I haven't found in the land of victorious socialism which produces people with faith?'

I envied those young men, but just a trace of doubt broke my consciousness: 'Perhaps you are nothing more than a Russian version of the hippy? In Russia, too, from time immemorial every kind of crazy idea and eccentricity has been practised in the name of religion.'

The priest stopped in front of me, I automatically pressed the palms of my hands together, and he quickly blessed me. But he was no Father Vasili! I felt nothing! To be honest, just then I was incapable of feeling anything. A half hour earlier I would have fallen on my knees and burst into tears. But that would have been deception, for not faith but emotion would have caused my breakdown. And the priest would not have realised that I had misled him.

But how many of the others there were deceiving him, like me, and why had they come? In my case it was purely by chance. But what about the others? What did they want of the rebellious priest? Experience of the faith, or experience of revolt?

Somebody gave me a sharp jab in the side – it was the woman in the grey headscarf who was pushing her way through to the priest. She was obviously telling me something with that jab. The priest gave her his blessing in the same businesslike way as he had blessed me. Couldn't he, a shepherd of souls, sense the difference between me and that woman? Indignant on her behalf, I looked disapprovingly at the back of the departing priest. My thoughts turned to Father Vasili, the smiling priest of a little Siberian church, and I experienced a sense of pride: I knew of something greater and better, at least something that I needed more. I headed for the exit.

Outside it was already dark. Under the lights in the porch and from the door to the gate there was a crowd of people. Outside the gate as well. People were smoking out there: some respect for the church!

And what was it that had actually happened to me and all the others in the church? I was quite relaxed now, but I could remember the tensions then, the sense of shock, almost of hysteria. Supposing the priest had gone on talking and the excitement had increased, what would I and all the others have experienced, what might it all have turned into? What might I have been capable of in such a state – I, who was incapable of responding to any appeal? I was rather frightened, because I would not only have responded – I would have joined in the rush as an inseparable part of the crowd. What was the secret? Could words acquire a special power over the spirit beneath the dome of the church? You know, if it had all happened on the street or inside a theatre – where that woman had wanted us to go – I am sure I would have stood to one side, observing the situation with a mocking grin, as becomes a modern intellectual today.

What explanation could a really expert observer suggest? Maybe the shape of the church, its decoration, the phonetic peculiarities of the religious lexicon combine to create a special environment, a kind of four-dimensional space, and perhaps in those conditions the human consciousness may display an unexpected aspect of itself, unusual qualities and unsuspected potentialities. Which wouldn't be bad. It would mean that something was happening in the world, in my Moscow at least, that was new and which could not have been there before. I hadn't noticed it until now. I had been swimming in too shallow waters, too preoccupied with myself. But now I had been drawn into contact with the phenomenon. We were witnessing the beginning of what might be (and possibly was) a historical event. So perhaps we, this pitiful generation of hacks and sycophants, were capable of doing something after all?

In short, optimism. Highly unusual. Indifference and lyrical pessimism were the trademarks of our caste; we regarded our being sacrificed to the social Moloch as one of the ramifications of tragedy on a worldwide scale. But that was a lie, an attempt to justify our own internal emptiness, our insignificance. We had no self-respect.

'I've been looking everywhere for you!' said Yura, in reproach, appearing from nowhere. 'How was it?'

'Interesting,' I said in a tone of indifference.

'There are lots of politicals here.' For some reason Yura said this in a whisper. 'Former camp prisoners. Shall I point them out to you? Some have done ten years for their political views.'

'No need, I've spotted them already.'

'Oh, of course,' Yura acknowledged, remembering that I was close to the dissidents.

'What about the Jews?' I asked, 'there's a lot of them here – are they interested in Orthodox Christianity too?'

'That's the sort of people they are, my friend – they've a nose for what's going on.'

'And what *is* going on?' I asked the question out of genuine curiosity.

'If you were to have less to do with the Poluëktovs and the dissidents you'd soon find out.'

I was taken aback by the way he said this, and I replied uncertainly:

'There are no Poluëktovs here, but certainly plenty of dissidents.'

'Oh, of course!' said Yura with aggressive sarcasm in his voice. 'They'd like to stamp this whole thing out.'

'What whole thing?' I asked in some irritation.

'They need a leader, someone to worship. But it won't work. They're not going to get the priest.'

'I still don't understand what sort of affair you are talking about, but I can tell there's some kind of squabble going on. At least they've issued a letter in defence of the priest; I don't think I saw you sign it.'

Yura's little face suddenly became very sad. He mumbled, obviously rather hurt:

'That letter will only make things worse. It makes him out to be a political activist – it's an old trick of theirs. Someone gets sacked from his work, so they draw up a petition, collect some signatures and the fellow gets it in the neck again. What else can he do? He joins the dissidents . . .'

'You should have written a different letter.'

'Oh yes. Do you know how many informers there are around here?' Yura twitched and looked over his shoulder. 'The dissidents have nothing to lose.'

I placed my hand on his shoulder and tried to say something without irony or point-scoring.

'Yura, do you or I have anything to lose? Is there anything in our lives of value?'

He cast me a glance full of distrust and suspicion, and anyway I was aware how full of empty rhetoric my words were. No matter how insignificant and wretched life may be, there is always something to lose. Everybody loves life: the mind may stray, but the instinct gets things right. I could see that instinct in Yura's eyes. I had signed that piece of paper only because I *knew* that there was no danger in doing so now. Yura did not know that, he hadn't been given that information. Instinct, too, needs information.

People came streaming out of the church doors and divided

into two lines. Then the priest emerged and passed along the passage between. He was already in an ordinary suit and he looked even shorter than before, but you could see now that he was still in good health, and probably not much more than fifty. The light fell right on his face and I could see in it an expression of unconcealed joy, almost of triumph. The bearded young men surrounding him prevented the rest of the crowd from taking their leave of him. At that moment, as if by command, a little 'Moskvich' car drove up. The priest got in next to the driver. A couple of bearded lads dived into the back seat, and the car shot off.

'They've certainly got things well organised!' I thought admiringly and gave Yura's sleeve a tug.

'Tell me: why do *they* let this go on, why do *they* tolerate it?'

'Our priest is not afraid of *them*,' Yura replied loftily. 'Let *them* be afraid of him.'

I studied him attentively. Surely he didn't believe in their fear? Was it all self-deception? The excitement of the moment? How long would it last? What would it lead to?

In any case I felt the need to thank good old Yura for the experience. He was no longer the person I had known for several years; I saw him now in a different light.

I put my arm round his shoulder.

'Thank you, Yura. It's a pity I didn't know about all this sooner.'

Yura was obviously proud.

'Sometime or other I'll read you some poems that I've never read to anyone yet.'

I thanked him as best I could for that, hoping that it would never happen. I could already guess that they would be poems about FAITH, and bad poems about faith really are awful. He was right about one thing, though. I hadn't been moving in the right circles and I'd missed something important, something I had to do some thinking about.

It would have been nice to go off on my own now and reflect on what I had seen in the course of this unusual evening. But I was reluctant to part from Yura. He was seriousness itself and a look of concentrated inspiration illumined his face. Perhaps, at this very moment in that poetic mind of his, lines of real poetry were carefully adjusting themselves to each other; I could well imagine how a single word might be knocked out of a line by another, and that one by a third, how the rhymes form at the end of the lines, and how the whole structural image emerges, comes to life and becomes something quite different from the sum of the lines. I could also imagine the rapture one must feel at such moments.

Perhaps it doesn't happen like that at all. But how Yura's eyes shone in the darkness! No, he certainly had something – he was a remarkably fine chap. It was a pity I had not taken him seriously and even made frivolous jokes at his expense, quite sure that my target was unlikely to take offence. We, the ordinary Soviet people have something very good and genuine in us. Perhaps we are not rogues and scoundrels at all. Considering what we have been called upon and forced to do, we could have turned out a lot worse. If, after our childhood in the 'Pioneers'* and our youth in the Young Communist League, we are still capable of being interested in religious ideals, isn't that a miracle? And the fact that we have lived to see priests in revolt – isn't that to our credit?

In the Metro I parted with Yura most cordially. I felt like embracing him, but he wouldn't have understood, he wasn't in the right mood. He said goodbye to me rather distractedly and hastily, obviously in a hurry to be alone, and he disappeared in a flash into the crowd.

'According to the law, the money should be split fifty:fifty!' these words suddenly came to mind – the ones that had struck me like a slap in the face a few hours previously. I just could not imagine the next meeting with my hero after what had

* Communist Party's organisation for children.

happened. 'To hell with him!' I muttered all the way in the Metro. 'To hell with him!' And I heaved a deep sigh into the ear of a passenger who fell up against me as the train braked.

I opened the door of my flat and my father immediately popped his head out of the door of his room.

'You've got a room-full of guests.'

I could hear the sound of men laughing, and a woman's voice too.

Zhenka and Andrei Semyonich were sprawled on the couch with their feet up. The old soldier's daughter had drawn up an armchair. They were playing cards.

'Gena,' said Andrei Semyonich's daughter with a laugh, 'They're cheating: I've lost six times in a row. Come and join us – we'll teach them.'

As though nothing had happened, they dragged me to the couch and Zhenka dealt the cards for the four of us. The last time I'd played cards was when Stalin was still alive.

Andrei Semyonich patted me on the back, Zhenka shouted in triumph, my lady partner cursed, and in a matter of minutes I had lost the game.

Andrei Semyonich put his arm round me and whispered in my ear: 'Forget what happened. It was a lot of nonsense.'

'You know . . .' I tried to say something, but he cut me off.

'We understand. Your book will be read by my grandson and maybe by my great-grandson. You will extend my life. Can that be measured in monetary terms?'

I guessed this was Zhenka's doing, but I was touched all the same. Embracing Andrei Semyonich I said quietly: 'I'll write a really good book. I promise it won't be a sloppy job!'

His daughter drew me closer to her. 'We didn't offend you, did we? Don't be offended, there's no need.'

'Please . . .'

'My father is a good man and I've always felt sorry for him. He deserves more, don't you think?'

'Of course! Everything I write will reflect the kind of man he was and still is. It's only the way he's been living . . .'

'That's right,' she nodded happily. 'Then you're not offended?'

'That's enough whispering!' Zhenka called out. He was no longer playing the well-turned-out intellectual-cum-businessman that he'd been in Andrei Semyonich's flat. He was almost being himself. And he had done it all for my sake, so as not to upset my affairs.

'That's it, friends!' he exclaimed. 'I've overstayed my welcome.' He tapped on his watch. 'I must leave you.'

'It's time we went too,' my hero hastened to say, and his daughter hurriedly agreed. As they said goodbye to me and wished me well, Zhenka gave me a meaningful look and whispered, practically without moving his lips:

'There you are, old boy. Get down to work and keep your emotions under control. The money's in your desk. You owe me a dinner at the Prague.'

The three of them dawdled noisily in the entrance hall and I kept glancing anxiously in the direction of my father's room.

At last they left, though I could still hear them talking and shuffling outside the front door. I felt I ought to apologise to my father, and I was just approaching his door when it opened suddenly and I almost collided with him.

'Gena,' my father asked me, 'what are your plans for tomorrow?'

I didn't quite understand – usually we didn't ask each other questions like that.

'Valentina, you see, is coming here around five o'clock. Will you be in?'

Poor Father! I sensed how difficult it was for him to talk like this, to put himself in the position of a suppliant, and I was only too glad to help him out of an awkward situation.

'Of course. It so happens I have nothing much to do tomorrow. In any case,' I hastened to correct myself, because actually I wasn't sure what was happening tomorrow, 'I will certainly be home by five.'

My father nodded, nervously doing up the top button of his shirt. Poor man! He was facing a most difficult undertaking. But I would make it easy for him; I would be the good little boy; I would be just what he wanted me to be. Moreover, I was far from uninterested in the woman he called Valentina: in fact, I was extremely curious about my father's choice of woman; I was even afraid of appearing nervous, because, after all, I was very fond of my father.

'I'm afraid we made rather a lot of noise – sorry.'

My father threw up his hands as if to say he had not even noticed, and in fact I think he was anxious about the next day – for my sake. I was glad that I would be the object of his anxiety for the whole of the next day – perhaps for the first time in our life together.

Having nothing more to say to each other, we parted, somewhat awkwardly. I went into my room and stood at my desk. The money was stacked neatly in a drawer. I took the notes out, threw them on to the desktop and wondered what attitude I ought to have to the money now. What I had been through today – from the quarrel in the flat to the extraordinary church service – must have left its mark. After all, I was a thin-skinned creature, and moreover I was on the threshold of a new life. I attempted to get some sense of my state of transition, and for that purpose I made myself sketch out an idea of the new life I was so eagerly yearning for. What would it be like, this new life of mine? A devout family with firm moral foundations? One. Steeping oneself in religious truths? Two. Renunciation of the empty bustle of life in Moscow? Three. What else? Surely that wasn't everything?

Of course, without the mention of a certain name there was no point going on. But once the 'Tosya' was pronounced the cup of my new life was filled to the brim. There were no longer any doubts, and I knew precisely what I wanted!

All the same, my mind was not at peace: an unaccustomed dynamism had invaded my life and I just couldn't cope with the speed at which things were happening. The very next day I would have to settle down to my hack work again. I knew how much I could do: I could work fifteen hours a day, but earning the money was only half the battle. I would have to find someone with enough influence to get me a flat which meant that I would have to approach my mother.

I hadn't been to see her since that crazy day when we'd all quarrelled with each other – I hadn't even phoned her since then. I was ashamed of myself. In the rush I had forgotten about them all. I had forgotten about Lyuska and about Irina, and I'd just let things slide. I would, of course, go and see Irina again, but not now – a little later, when my own situation was a little clearer.

I had to admit that Irina's name caused an agitation in me, which so far I had been able to suppress – or, at least, ignore. But I needed to have solid ground beneath my feet – I needed certainty.

*

Dear Gennochka!

Two letters from you the same day – what a treat! I held the envelopes in my hand and danced round the room. I was lucky – I read the second letter first, and the first one afterwards. The letter still distressed me. I didn't understand all of it and gave it to my father to look at. You don't mind, do you? He is such a good father – he understands everything. He says your mind is in a state of confusion, and that that is very hard to bear. If only I could help you even in some little way! But you are so far away that it sometimes seems to me that you're not in this world at all.

We've had so much rain here for the last three days that all the streams have turned into rivers. I sat at the window and there was water all around, and I imagined I was sailing in a boat to you and had lost my way on the ocean.

Sailing on the ocean is like standing in one place, because whether you travel for an hour or a day you still see nothing but water.

I am not going to rewrite this letter, though for some reason it's not turning out as it should. I want to cry all the time, but don't get the wrong idea – I don't actually cry at all and it's only in the evenings that this mood comes over me. I'm now spending the days haymaking. Papa has cut the meadow beyond the bridge – do you remember it? I'm drying the hay now but it's rained three times, so the hay has to be spread and turned all the time. Volodya helps me sometimes – the deacon – but I don't want him helping – he keeps looking at me as though there was something wrong with me.

This year the wild strawberries are so big and juicy – I keep gathering jarfuls and not being able to eat them, because I imagine I'm really picking them for you . . . So I give them all away.

I've read the book you left behind. Maybe I haven't understood it all, but anyway I don't like books like that – somebody somewhere always has to be attacking religion and the clergy – I had more than enough of that in school and I could never understand why everybody got so angry. After all, we don't interfere with anybody, Papa doesn't order people about or drag them into the church – it's they who are always forcing people to go somewhere – to meetings, to do voluntary work on Sundays – yet they attack us. And then there are all the jokes, like the ones the engineer in that book of yours tells – he knows nothing about us and yet he makes fun of us.

You want us to live in Moscow, but I'm afraid, from what I see on television, that Moscow is too crowded and that the life there makes it impossible to believe in anything. People's faces are all so ugly, as though they've got no souls – all they do is to fulfil various plans and pass resolutions. They scare me.

You're used to it, I suppose. But shall I get used to it? The buildings in Moscow are so big and you can't see anything beyond them. But down here, wherever you go you can see our church, or at least the bell-tower, and so you needn't ever get lost.

Up to the ninth class in school I also used to dream of being someone important and living in a different place where there were a lot of different and interesting things going on – I even dreamt of being an astronaut – but later, when we bought a television set and I saw the faces of those heroes when they were talking about their own lives as if they thought they had a thousand lives or life that never ended, I always wanted to cry out to them that there was only one life, and that the most important thing was what came after it, and if you didn't believe in that then what was the point of living at all, what was it all for? I know you told me that the most important thing is to have an interesting job, interesting work, but I don't understand why that should be the most important. What is important for me is that I love you, that comes second to what is most important of all. But you couldn't be like that, could you? And it makes me sad ... just a little.

What about your father and mother? They won't like me, will they? And there's no remedy for that, although I already love them all, and your sister too. But I'll tell you something else that frightens me. It sometimes seems to me that the Lord brought us two together not for this life but for another life, because everything that has happened between us is somehow contrary to all the laws. You ought not to have fallen in love with me, and as for what has happened to me, how could anybody have foreseen it – you descended on me like a bolt from the blue!

No! No! No! – I am not going to write any more today. In fact I ought not to have written anything today. I am terribly tired, from all the haymaking. Three times we had rain, and the clouds kept sweeping over. I'm simply very tired. But you will keep on writing often, won't you?

It's a pity that it'll soon be autumn, not spring. It would be easier for me to wait for you if spring were just ahead.

I kiss you. I've even forgotten what it was like to kiss you, but I know it was very good!

Your Tosya.

IV

Andrei Semyonich rang me at ten o'clock the next morning. He seemed to want to confirm the restoration of our relations. He told me he had recalled a very interesting episode that had taken place in the Königsberg operation, which had slipped his mind for some reason but now he even remembered the name of the army newspaper in which it had been reported. I spent twenty minutes on the phone recording his voice on a tape-recorder, holding the receiver close to the microphone. When Andrei Semyonich tapped on his phone to indicate he had finished I thanked him and fixed our next meeting. I suggested it should be in my flat, and that prompted Andrei Semyonich to enquire hesitantly whether that was because I didn't wish to go to his home. I reassured him, pointing out that I had all the materials to hand in my flat and that it was much more convenient. The fact was, though, that I didn't really want to go to visit him; I knew that his wife would start apologising to me too, though she had nothing to apologise for. He went on talking for some time and just couldn't bring himself to stop, as though he was afraid to be the first to put down the receiver. I made it easy for him by saying that I had to start my work.

I really did have to get busy with my work. Easy to say that, though, but when I played the tape back and listened to it I realised that it was now going to be much more difficult to complete, especially since I'd promised on the previous day not to turn out another hack job but to produce a really good book. Now I would have to go through everything I had written again and probably rewrite it too!

I tried to put myself in the mood for work – I made my bed, took a shower, drank some coffee and said aloud: To work! To work! But when I was face to face with my papers I knew that I could not work that day. I checked once again the money I had received as an advance, put aside what was already committed, and then worked out whether, if I wished, I could return the money to the publisher. I very much wanted to do just that. Do that and then depart for Uryupinsk, to the wonderful little world of Father Vasili! That would be the sure way to cut the Gordian knot of all my problems.

Only the previous day I could have done it. The joke was that I was tied now to Moscow by a hasty promise to turn my first rough draft into a conscientious memorial for the benefit of Andrei Semyonich's descendants.

I had intended to spend the day writing the chapter covering the final victory: lying in hospital, my hero learns that the war is over. This sort of thing had been written about and filmed a thousand times before, and I had to hit on some new angle, some new element, something not invented but genuine. I wanted to experience it myself! But first of all I had to define my own attitude to the war – what it would have meant to me if I had been there. But if I had lived then, I couldn't have known about everything that had gone before – the prison camps, the torturing, the peasantry reduced to starvation and the uneducated power-crazed thugs, could I? No – in order to be a hero like my Andrei Semyonich I would have had to know nothing, to understand nothing, about all that. Of course, there was another possibility – I might have known a little and even had my own opinion about it, but the war might have allowed me to hope that after it was over we would sort everything out and see that justice was done. That would have been a funny sort of idiocy. Or another, singular possibility – that the war had been the very factor making me aware of my own personality. What would have been my attitude then to the victory and the return to the job of building that very same socialism?

But this had nothing to do with the real Andrei Semyonich and with this book of mine, commissioned by an official publisher? None of these possibilities was open to me. So what was I left with? The hero's joy on hearing of the great victory and his grief for those who had perished. Somehow, though all this had taken place, and on a massive scale, it didn't even help when I made some really strong coffee. I was not a copying machine or a monotonous echo of Party directives but an individual with my own needs. They'd paid me a fee, and my conscience was not supposed to matter: but I did have a conscience after all, even if it was rather pock-marked, like a face recovering from smallpox.

I dialled Zhenka Poluëktov's number, heard his confident voice in the receiver, and, envying him his assurance, I mumbled: 'Listen, Zhenka, what if I were to drop this whole idea and return the advance – would that be very improper?'

Zhenka spent some time clearing his throat. 'Genya, man,' he said in the tone of an infuriated diplomat, 'if anybody knew what I put up with from you they would think I was some kind of homosexual. What's the matter – going through a psychological change of life are you?'

'It's just the opposite – it's a psychological rebirth.'

'Wonderful!' Zhenka growled. 'What's it got to do with me?'

I gave a deep sigh – loud enough for Zhenka to hear and realise how difficult things were for me.

'Come to think of it, why do you bother with me anyway?'

'Why?' He seemed to be grinding his teeth, or chewing gum. 'I want your plans to be carried out in every detail.'

He stressed the words *in every detail*, and I giggled stupidly.

'So that you can marry Irina?'

'Yes,' he replied laconically.

'Is it really only a question of what I think? Have you consulted her about it?'

'Listen, man – we've said a lot too much already . . .'

But there was no stopping me now, and I broke in: 'I think you ought to know: Irina's pregnant. And get this: it's not mine, and it's not yours either.'

I was blushing; I knew I was behaving very badly.

'What the hell are you talking about?' Zhenka's voice went hoarse.

'Forget it. I blurted it out. Be a friend and forget it. That's what she told me. Maybe she made it up. We had a fight . . .'

'Shut up, Gena, will you!' For a time Zhenka was silent. Then he hung up.

I hated myself for it, I wanted to smash the telephone. What is it in us intellectuals that makes us do such mean things? God, it's so revolting! I ought to call Irina and warn her: who knows what Zhenka, such a practical man, would do. He'd set his sights on Irina as a partner in life, and now I'd really upset his timetable – how would he react? I didn't like Zhenka setting his sights on Irina. Of course he was a big operator, but he was congenitally lacking the mechanism of human feelings. He could receive stimuli, nothing more, and life for him was only the composing and solving of an amusing crossword puzzle, Irina was only a handy word in the puzzle, down or across.

I silently abused Zhenka and came to some pretty caustic conclusions about him. That was quite natural, after all, because there's nothing more boring and unrewarding than cursing oneself . . . and I couldn't make up my mind to ring Irina.

Then the phone rang. I started back from the instrument. It would be Zhenka, of course. He must have finally understood, and be wanting to clear up the situation . . . I took the receiver and breathed a sigh of relief. It was Lenochka Khudova – I could tell by the sound of sobbing, and for a

whole minute there was nothing but more sobs, so I waited
patiently.

'Gennochka,' she mumbled at last, but quite distinctly,
'marry me, will you? I'll make you a good wife.'

'Fine! Right now? But I've no time. What on earth has
happened? No more tears though, they only rust the phone.'

In a way I was glad she had phoned. Lenochka went on
sobbing and snivelling.

'Come on now, tell me all about it.'

'Can I come and see you? I can't talk over the phone.'

Why not? Let her come. I needed to kill time till evening,
when this Valentina was due to appear, and maybe even . . .
What a wonderful idea! I would make Lenochka stay until
then and include her in the company. It would make everything
easier, she had a way of putting people at their ease, and she
was such a friendly, easy-going person. We could sing old
Russian love songs together.

I explained to her how to get to my flat, and she promised
to take a taxi.

I didn't want to think about anything in particular now, so
I thought about Lenochka. She was one of those people whom
you couldn't take seriously. Compared with Irina she was an
amoeba – very sweet and good, but an amoeba nonetheless. I
conjured up her little snub-nosed face with its button eyes and
compared her with Irina, whose every smallest feature, the
least movement of the eyes, the slightest gesture, betrayed a
confused world of feelings hidden from outsiders. Irina could
be charmingly feminine, but only when there was someone she
wanted to be feminine for. I had often been surprised by her
ability deliberately to fade and then in a flash to blossom,
transforming herself before your very eyes. She could rivet the
attention of one person while remaining invisible to everybody
else. However much her businesslike manner used to annoy
me, she as always had the wit to detach herself from everything
extraneous – in other words, she knew how to 'belong'.

There I was, thinking about Irina again, and again I felt

agitated. There was Tosya who was more than all of them put together: her you couldn't analyse; you could only dream about her, you had to see and feel and sense her – she was life itself.

I decided that all this uncertainty was confusing me, getting on my nerves. And *I* was getting on my nerves. For example, I started to hate my habit of tapping my watch with my fingers, and there were certain expressions I saw on my own face that disgusted me. Even my handwriting now seemed vulgar and affected. There was something new in my awareness of myself, and it worried me.

There was a ring at the door. I opened it, and Lenochka Kudova fell into my arms. It was amazing how she was able to turn on the tears – presumably she hadn't been weeping in the taxi.

'Help me, Gennochka!' she whined into my ear, watering it with her tears.

'Let's go into my room.'

I sat her down in an armchair, took a paper napkin and dabbed at her cheeks. She pulled herself together, drew a handkerchief out of her trouser pocket and filled the room with the fragrance of expensive perfume. A minute later she was all smiles and watched as I, looking very serious, squeezed out the napkin into an ash-tray.

'Really, Genka!' she said, pouting. 'My life is hanging by a thread and you're just laughing at me.'

I sat back on the couch and said in a businesslike way: 'What's the story?'

'Oh, what can I say? Zhukov has gone completely mad. Papa is threatening to find out where I am at night.'

'And where are we at night?' I asked out of curiosity.

'Stop it!' I'm sure Zhukov is going to give me the push. Gennochka, how can I make him marry me? You're going to get married – how did Irka do it? Tell me.'

'It's very simple,' I said with a yawn. 'You need a third person.'

She fluttered her long eyelashes, then said, disappointed:

'No, I tried that. I told him that a producer at Mosfilm had made advances to me, and all he said was: "Fine, go ahead."'

I got up from the couch, went up to her and bent over her.

'You little fool. A third person, but not like that. You need a very, very small third person, not much bigger than my hand and not much smaller than your face.'

Again she fluttered her eyelashes. Something resembling a thought process took place inside her little head; her eyes opened wide and her lips spread into a broad smile.

'Irka's pregnant!' she exclaimed with joy, for some reason best known to herself.

Now it was I who blinked. Yes, true, if the child was mine, then . . .

'Irina's nothing to do with it,' I replied, quickly. 'But for you it's the most reliable way of getting Zhukov's name on your passport.'

Lenochka sank deep into thought.

'And if that doesn't work, what then?' she said, now thinking quite calmly, though there were still tears in her eyes, and I went again to the table for napkins. She appeared to be reaching some conclusion or else had cried herself out.

'Your room looks like a professor's,' she said, nodding in the direction of my typewriter and the piles of paper scattered around. She stood up and went across to the shelves and ran her fingers along the backs of the books as if they were a keyboard.

'Who's that?' she pointed at the portrait of Solzhenitsyn.

I told her.

'So that's what he looks like!' Lenochka said, surprised, screwing up her eyes at the picture. 'I didn't imagine him like that. Very ugly, isn't he? Looks bad-tempered, too.'

I had no intention of discussing the subject with Lenochka and tried to steer the conversation elsewhere, but she just stood there screwing up her eyes at Solzhenitsyn.

'My father says some awful things about him.'

'Does your father know him personally?' I enquired sarcastically.

Lenochka nodded affirmatively.

'What is your father, then?' I asked, my curiosity aroused.

Lenochka hesitated, cast a final, rather angry glance at the picture and turned away from it.

'My daddy is a lieutenant-colonel,' she said with unexpected pride and even defiance. 'He works in the Lubyanka. You're not one for gossiping, are you?'

I now saw Lenochka Khudova in a new light. So this very inoffensive girl was cast on our shore from a world we considered to be inhabited not by real people but by functions instead. For example, since childhood I had always thought of the well-known 'Iron Felix'*, the first head of the secret police, as some kind of functional apparatus made of iron and not as a person at all. So Lenochka was a black sheep that had somehow turned up in our circle. I looked at her in silence. She misinterpreted my silence and said in a rather hurt tone:

'*That* man,' with a nod at the picture, 'and a lot of others like him have said such a lot of awful things, but my daddy is so honest and just, and I won't read that man,' she said with a further nod at the picture.

It was time for me to say something, but I sat there like an idiot, unable to take my eyes off her face. She started to blush and seemed offended.

'My daddy says that if we let them have their way everything would collapse and that's what they want to happen. Then the Chinese would gobble us up bit by bit. What do you think?'

I just couldn't discuss topics like that with Lenochka Khudova, whose main purpose in life was to get a mediocre television producer to marry her. Fortunately, Lenochka herself was tired of the subject by now.

'I'm sick of all that! I just want to get on with my life. I – hate – politics!'

* Felix Dzerzhinsky.

I was ready to believe her – I believed she hated even the political line that her 'daddy' stood for.

An interesting question came into my mind.

'What is it that attracts you to Zhukov?' She looked at me in surprise. 'Is he so talented?'

Her glance wandered in embarrassment.

'Apparently not very . . .'

'Then what is it? Are you just imagining you're in love?'

'Perhaps,' she agreed quite calmly. 'But I want to marry him, and only him. Do you think there haven't been others?'

Poor daddy, poor lieutenant-colonel! Imagine what he thinks of his daughter becoming the wife of a second-rate producer, especially one with rather dubious acquaintances, like me, or Yura the poet, or Zhenka!

'Does Zhukov know who your father is?'

She shook her head.

'Fine! Then you're as good as married.' It was not only that I wanted to make Lenochka happy: I also secretly relished the idea of playing a dirty trick on this lieutenant-colonel whom I had never met.

Lenochka was trembling all over. She believed me. She had placed her hope in me.

'You scratch my back, I'll scratch yours,' I said. 'I've got a tough meeting today. I'd like you to be there.'

She threw her arms round my neck, presumably with the idea of kissing me – her main, indeed her only, occupation.

'We've got four hours with nothing to do. Shall we go to a cinema? Or go and sit in a restaurant?'

Lenochka was beaming, but she had a different idea.

'Let's go to the Manezh.'

I grimaced. The Manezh picture gallery was at the time exhibiting the works of a very fashionable and socially-minded artist, and I had no desire to hang about in a mile-long queue or to look at manifestoes of canvases.

'Without waiting in the queue,' Lenochka promised, and I could sense the powerful influence of her father behind her.

Then I recalled that on more than one occasion Lenochka had arranged similar queue-jumping and no one had suspected the source of her influence. Oh well, even a mangy sheep yields a handful of wool – a remark directed not at Lenochka of course, but at the source itself.

And Zhukov, if he weren't too much of a fool, would, in a year or two, become head of the television studio, wait and see! That self-satisfied blockhead had no idea of the trump card that was being thrust into his hand! We had to help him to understand!

*

There was an enormous queue of people going right around the Manezh. But Lenochka led me confidently to a side entrance where a queue of people trying to avoid the long wait had already formed. My friend pushed her way to the front without difficulty, showed something to the policeman on duty, snapped her handbag shut and shoved me through the door.

I knew this artist. He offended me. I'm no great judge of painting but I resent being told how to respond. This is understandable: I'm an intellectual and like to assemble my own system of values, including aesthetic values. And now this artist grabs me by the scruff of the neck and shoves my face up against his canvases, leaving me with no possibility of doubt about his work. He thought of me as a simpleton who, having once grasped his original discoveries, ought immediately to spring to his defence. But I don't need that sort of thing. I need the sort of art that leaves me free of obligations and opens up new horizons to my own view. For example, I can look at what some avant-garde painter has smeared over a canvas and I can make it out to be whatever I please – and that suits me and it suits the painter too. There has to be mutual respect.

Lenochka elbowed me. She was standing there lost in admiration before a vast canvas on which strangulated feeling was screaming away in vivid colours. I suppose I would have been more in sympathy with the painter had he painted so as to suggest I was telling him shocking truths. But no – he thrust his fist in my face and told me what to think – anyone who didn't agree with him was scum.

I ·looked around and could see the same resentment at being bullied reflected in every intellectual face. The outraged visitors to the gallery were attacking the artist's work and destroying him with their professional commentaries, and I was sure they would leave the gallery firmly set in their contempt for the painter. And he deserved it too, since he hadn't respected the intellectual's self-esteem and had been so stupid as to make his appeal to the masses. That was equivalent to spitting in our faces. The unfortunate artist would learn how the intellectuals could take their revenge, grind him into dust and reduce him to zero.

Lenochka nudged me again. 'Just look at that – how marvellous!'

'What about your daddy – would he agree with you?' I asked her, not without malice. Lenochka frowned.

'No matter what you say, as far as I'm concerned Daddy's the very best,' she said defiantly. 'Not once in his life has he raised his voice to me or to my mummy.'

'Comrade Lieutenant-Colonel Khudov is a good family man' I imagined his superiors saying, 'and as morally sound as a mausoleum!' But I didn't want to needle Lenochka. I was sick and tired of jostling through the labyrinth of stands in the gallery and my eyes hurt from looking at the paintings and the faces, but Lenochka was dragging me off into the thick of the crowd in the centre of the hall where, it was clear, the artist himself, half-suffocated and half-crushed, was dispensing autographs. The shy smile on his face struck me as false when his paintings screamed arrogantly at you from the walls and seemed to hurt your eyes. I looked at his smoothly shaven face and came to the certain firm conclusion that, if he had his way, he would grab all those people by the scruff of the neck, because he knew just what they were worth – the ones who were singing his praises and those who were inveighing against him – they were all no more than slaves of the moment, and when did that moment end? When you get outside those walls! What would my companion, a KGB lieutenant-colonel's daughter take away from here? And the others? I'd have loved to look inside their heads. I'm sure I'd have got inside info on the future. Though I hoped that no one there, including the artist himself, had any chance of building the future. If I'd been allowed to know, for example, that the perfectly respectable, fashionable young man opposite me had definite plans for our *common* future in his mind, I would certainly have tried to interfere with it! Because how was this crowd, or anyone in it, better than I? Down with people who claim to know the answers. They shouldn't be believed at any rate. After all you may not believe them, but somebody else may. And that was the most important truth that our minds had produced in the course of fifteen years of dissidence. Whether it was good or bad, the fact remains that we're happy or unhappy, alive, and have the chance of beginning a new life on Monday – but the sociopolitical enthusiasts would deprive us of even that last remaining possibility. Take this artist, for example . . . Oh, to hell with him!

Oh yes! There you are – the gallery was full of people who thought the same as I did. Lenochka was reading the book in which people had written their comments. She was obviously upset, nearly in tears.

'Really – the thugs! 'Look at the awful things some people have put!' I could see, written in large letters: 'Hack painting! A disgrace to the Manezh! Mediocre!'

Lenochka snatched up a pen and wrote nervously: 'A great artist! Really great!' She wasn't alone – the book was filled with comments by equally naïve and enthusiastic folk, and I felt sorry for them.

I caught sight of the artist's face again and it prompted me to think that both those who praised him and those who blamed him were hitting the same nail on the head and that the whole show was being produced and directed by the artist himself. Oh well, it was none of my business – I was not going to do anything about it – long live the non-doers!

Lenochka looked at me in disappointment. I made it abundantly clear by the expression on my face how bored I was with art and how I longed for some fresh air.

'We can go if you want to,' she said, hoping that I would show some consideration for her feelings. But I didn't.

'Yes, let's go.'

On the way out we ran into the Skurikhins. Instead of saying hello, Maria gave me a meaningful glance, as if to say: where else would intelligent people meet if not at a picture exhibition.

'Leaving already?' Oleg asked, as though we had parted an hour before.

'Yes,' I said, trying to sound noncommittal. But the question came at once:

'What do you think of it?'

I pushed Lenochka forward. The pupils of her eyes were still large.

'Gennochka,' she whined, 'we still have time. I'll go back in with them for half an hour, and you can wait for me, OK?'

'No more than half an hour,' I agreed. 'We mustn't be late.'

She looked like a ruffled sparrow.

'Come on,' she said to the Skurikhins, 'I'll show you where to begin.'

I made my way out through the row of policemen and took deep breaths of the stuffy, malodorous air of the city.

I was unsettled and very tense. I loathed that artist whose daubings I had spent an hour staring at. I loathed his face, too, and I wanted to go back in and say something really nasty to him. Alas, I couldn't now, without the help of the daughter of the lieutenant-colonel in the Lubyanka. I weighed up in my mind what I might have said to that house-painter. I would have told him that he was just a noisy hooligan in terms of painting and that the idea about which he made so much noise with his uncontrolled use of colour amounted to nothing at all, and finally that I'd known everything about his subjects long ago – the murder of the *tsarevich* and the destruction of the churches. But the question was: did he, the scoundrel, believe in the mystique of the church? And if he didn't believe, then what right did he have to upset me? Did this dandy in his foreign clothes know that I had long since been ashamed of my passion for Russian songs and the typically Russian faces of people from Ryazan, that I had already become a *homo esperantus*. And wouldn't he start shouting in Esperanto himself when his admirers ripped his French-made suit off his back and decked him out in red shirt and dragged him from his comfortable flat and into the church he'd painted and make him perform a thousand genuflections? No, damn it, he hoped that nothing like that would happen, that all this was nothing but words . . .

People were already staring at me: I was waving my arms about, making faces and moving my lips. Stuff the bloody artist! The question was: what did I want most of all here and now, standing on the Manezh square? I felt happy, because I knew what I wanted: to find myself in Father Vasili's house, or by the overturned boat at the edge of the lake and for it to be night with only a sickle moon. And I would take Tosya by the hand, and be a little tipsy and close to tears!

I looked around me, saw the Kremlin and screwed up my eyes so as to blot out everything that didn't fit in with those walls and towers. The result was an idyllic picture almost like those hanging in the Manezh, and Father Vasili and his daughter would have been at home in this scene produced by my squinting view of the Kremlin. Moreover, it was only they, so out of place elsewhere, so funny and so dear, who could complete the picture, because they were made of the same stuff. And I – would I fit in there? My God, I would, so long as I was hand in hand with Tosya.

I opened my eyes wide and looked around me at all the rushing, rumbling, stinking traffic and said 'Begone! Begone!

Oh Lord, if You exist, send me a miracle – this minute! In thirty seconds! I know I don't deserve one, but I beg You to send me one anyway, because I am on the brink of an abyss, cars to the left and cars to the right and the Kremlin stars above me, and I can't take a step without it being fatal. Help me to make a step! One step!'

'Are you feeling ill?'

Very ill, my dear officer!

'In there' – I waved my hand in the direction of the Manezh – 'it's very stuffy.'

The policeman – about my age or a little younger – sized me up with an experienced glance and his manner became less official.

'A lot of people in there? This is the second week they've been crowding in. Must be a very good artist, eh?'

'Go on in,' I said, 'and have a look.'

'I will. There'll be a whole unit here tomorrow. We'll get in somehow. Feeling better?'

He was asking about my state of health, and I was grateful to him. He was a human being, and so was I.

Lenochka came running up and under the benevolent eye of the constabulary we made our way from the Manezh to the Metro. We were already late and when I burst into the flat my father immediately stepped out of his room. He had his best clothes on, but his calm manner seemed to have deserted him, and when he caught sight of Lenochka he frowned anxiously. I left my companion at the door, took my father by the arm and led him into the kitchen.

'Is that your new girlfriend?'

'She's not new and she's not mine, but I thought she would make things easier. If you don't approve . . .'

'Well, why should I . . .?'

'Don't worry,' I tried to calm him down. 'I can send her packing any time if need be. That is our style.'

'Oh, well, if that's it,' said my father, smiling. 'Perhaps it will be better having her.'

'And, er . . .' how could I put the this? 'Valentina . . . is she here already? What is her patronymic?'

'Nikolayevna,' my father muttered.

Poor man! It was the first time I had ever seen him so unsure of himself – his nervousness was quite contrary to his nature.

'And please,' he entreated, 'try to be understanding and tolerant – I know you can.'

For goodness sake! – my father entreating! There was nothing I wouldn't do for him now. I had long dreamt of hearing a request like this from his lips.

The three of us went into my father's room, and I had a pleasant surprise: my father's lady friend was young and very charming, and when we all shook hands and introduced ourselves she behaved very simply and naturally. Not the grim academic lady I'd feared. It was only when we were seated at the table all laid in readiness and I found myself facing Valentina that I noticed that she resembled my mother a little – she was the same type, although it was difficult to say exactly where the resemblance lay. I looked at Valentina with a friendly smile, and thought to myself that it was possible my father still loved my mother and that that might explain his present choice of companion. Lenochka was wonderful, already chatting away easily with both my father and Valentina – about the art show and the artist, of course. Valentina was rather cautious about expressing her opinions, but Lenochka was, on the contrary, very sweeping in her judgements, and I watched with pleasure the way she took to my father's friend. Some women have the happy gift of being able to talk about everything with anybody as equals and without appearing to be stupid, that is to say, overstepping the bounds of femininity. Strangely, the conversation had become serious, almost professional.

My father, although reserved as usual, was already at ease because everything was going off well. So I decided to rock the boat a little: it seemed to be sailing a bit too smoothly.

'Don't you think,' I said as I sipped my wine, 'that we are

quite unnecessarily overburdened with information? Take me, for example – I have a mass of things stored in my head: I can give you the names of all the members of the Convention at the time of Robespierre, of all the singers who have sung the part of Boris Godunov, all the paintings of the early Van Gogh and late Cézanne – I have thousands of names and numbers in my head – would you like to know how many light years it is to the sixty-sixth star in the Swan constellation? Or in which year the battle of Crécy was fought?'

'Which year was it then?' asked Lenochka, trying to catch me out.

I spread out my hands as if to say: do you think you can trip me up with such little things?

'In fact, I don't remember even myself how much I can remember about everything. And why should I? It's quite senseless to remember so much history. Knowledge is self-deception.'

'How can you say that?' It was Valentina now who intervened, and I was glad that she'd taken the bait. 'You are quite wrong!'

Valentina clearly had Ukrainian blood in her veins – she had the arched eyebrows and the oval face of a Ukrainian, but she had light blue eyes such as one finds in Cossack women of the Don or the Kuban. If she was older than I, I thought, it was only by very little. But then I had more than once made a fool of myself over a woman's age. I knew exactly how she would reply to my arguments: the whole discussion was as old as the hills.

'Cultural phenomena are just as real as you or I. They have an independent and lasting value, and a person has the right to inhabit the world of these phenomena and be considered not only a useful member of society, but even . . .'

'Even more useful than others?' I interjected.

Valentina became confused and blushed like a young girl, and Lenochka came rushing to her aid:

'So what? If cultural values are the highest of all, then a

cultured person is no ordinary person. I can't stand hypocrisy. Ordinary Soviet people! Just let somebody try to call me that.'

'Relax, Lenochka, you're no ordinary Soviet person.'

She paid me no attention.

'Everybody is taken up with politics – one thing today, something else tomorrow. But Bach and Raphael are for all time, and I would even say more . . .' Lenochka was quite radiant – I had never seen her like that before. 'The whole human race exists for Raphael, and for those who understand him, because all the rest is nonsense.'

'It's rather a radical view to take,' Valentina commented quietly.

My father gave me a gentle nudge and we went out into the kitchen to make the coffee.

'What does Valentina do?' I asked my father.

'She's a doctor of philosophy.'

'If it's not a rude question, what was her thesis on?'

'I think the subject concerned the main link in the chain of historical events – there is such a subject in Marxism.'

The irony in his voice was so finely pitched that it was impossible to identify it precisely but also impossible to overlook it.

'And what was the most important link?'

'In those days it was known as "plus chemisation".'

'Of course,' I said with a grin. 'To pursue that subject at the level of a doctorate must have been difficult, with all the dialectical wavering of the Party line.'

My father shrugged in a way into which you could read anything you liked.

'Well, do you want my opinion?' I asked rather cheekily – of course he did!

He gave another shrug of the shoulders, but this time I could tell he was nervous.

'I think she's wonderful. And amazingly pretty.'

My father shot a glance at me. It lasted no more than a hundredth of a second, but in that hundredth he managed to thank me and did it in such a way that I would never be able to take advantage of his gratitude even if I'd wished to.

We carried the cups and the cake into the room which was now filled with laughter. The women had changed the subject; to judge by the sly looks they gave us it had been very much a women's conversation. I was enormously pleased with Lenochka and more determined than ever to land Zhukov for her.

The box with the cake was opened and the women's delight was gratifying to my stern father, because it was quite clear that this cake came from no ordinary bakery. It was an aristocrat among cakes, obtained through string-pulling from one of those special shops that served the powers that be. We sliced the cake with a brightly polished knife and distributed it on the monogrammed plates; even in its dismembered state it was magnificent, and the women – both the professional Marxoid and the professional wife – eagerly extended their elegant fingers, all displaying identical pale rose-pink nail varnish.

Everything was going wonderfully, but I still had no idea at all what my father's relationship with Valentina was. There was in their behaviour no evidence of intimacy, though they used the familiar and affectionate form of address to each other. Knowing my father, it was clear this meant they had known each other for a long time, had come to an understanding and there was no need now to emphasise how close they were to each other. But just occasionally my severe and composed father would give a tiny glance in my direction.

For some time the women were completely absorbed by the cake like a couple of sweet little kittens at a saucer of cream. It was such a happy sight – their eyes bright, their fingers twinkling, but not a single movement diminished their charm, in any way. A total perfection of movement and gesture. My father and I were so much cruder and more primitive!

The conversation soon became more animated: there was a rather emotional exchange on the subject of the preparation of some recherché dish or other, and my father became uneasy –

I think he may have been afraid Valentina was lowering herself in my estimation by getting so carried away by a mere matter of cuisine. Meanwhile I had a nagging urge to complicate the situation, so I asked Valentina in a casual way:

'So you and Father work together?'

My glance addressed the question to my father as well. I could sense how in an instant everything changed and an atmosphere of tense alertness descended.

'In the same department, even,' Valentina replied. 'Though it's not work so much as a service, wouldn't you say?'

It was her way of turning for help to my father.

'In a sense,' my father said. 'As people employed on the ideological front we are, I suppose, really civil servants.'

He wanted to avoid the subject, but I wasn't playing.

'So you've known each other for a long time?'

'Five or six years.'

'Seven,' my father corrected her, and no longer looked in my direction.

I had no desire at all to spoil their mood, but I was looking for some indication of what they felt for one another. Would it be unpleasant for me to see what my father felt for another woman? Would it reawaken in me some family feeling? But out family had fallen apart so long ago and so completely that all the protective family instincts had perished. I sincerely wished my father happiness and was convinced that he and my mother would never come together again, and, finally, I knew that it was impossible either to spoil or to improve my relations with my father. In the end, what was there in my power to do? All I could do was smooth my father's path to possible happiness. I got up from my chair and patted my father's shoulder, respectfully, then looked into Valentina's cool eyes and said in a sufficiently natural voice:

'I'm glad. Honestly. It's great.

Filled with a sense of the 'greatness' of it all, I slipped out and went into my own room. There I looked up Zhukov's telephone number, dialled it and a severe female voice informed me that Anatoli Dmitrevich was in his studio, so I phoned there.

'Hello,' I said, 'how's life and all that?'

Zhukov was surprised at my call and put on his guard.

'Listen,' I said in a friendly but conspiratorial tone, 'I'm ringing about your Lenochka. Do you know who her father is?'

'Is that of any importance?' Zhukov asked cautiously.

'For me, no. For you, I'm not so sure. Her father is a colonel in one of the departments in the Lubyanka. And informed sources say that his beloved daughter has been spending nights away from home. The Colonel, deeply concerned, what is more, intends to use his intelligence network to get to the bottom of the case.'

'You're not serious?'

Wonderful! I had floored Zhukov with one blow! Now I could help him up.

'You don't joke about the Lubyanka. So there you are – please appreciate my service, that is to say, my information, for what it's worth, and just remember, when you are joined in wedlock to our mutual friend and begin moving in higher spheres, don't forget who tipped you off about the approach of your good fortune.'

'Bloody hell!' Zhukov spluttered. 'If you're not lying, this is more serious than you think.'

'I'm not lying; I am simply, for purely selfish reasons, providing an old friend with some information.'

Zhukov was breathing heavily. I could picture that smug face bewildered and dismayed as plainly as though I was watching him in a mirror. But I knew that he had understood my allusion to higher spheres.

'Goodbye for now!' I said. 'I've got a whole load of problems myself, brother, so let's meet in happier times.'

Who would have the face to condemn me? Lenochka

Khudova wanted desperately to get married. Was it wrong for me to wish the best for her? Zhukov, the producer, was carving out a career in television, and that was by no means the most contemptible of ambitions. We all want a good life; we all have the right to have it. Somewhere there were other worlds where people lived according to other rules and laws, but they were probably not perfect either. 'All honour to the madman who inspires mankind with a golden dream.'

I could hear laughter coming from my father's room. Those were happy people sitting in there. And I also wanted things to go right for me. My desires did not interfere with anyone; I didn't stand in anyone's way. My twisted trail avoided other trails, and the world wasn't packed so full of people that you had to elbow one another.

Standing at the door to my father's room, listening to Lenochka's animated chatter, to Valentina's soft twittering and to the relaxed drone of my father's pleasant speaking voice, I thought to myself how nice it would be to put a chair right there at the door, sit down in it and doze off to the murmur of the happy voices of those nice, agreeable people. I like Cerberus, I'd bite anyone who came near that threshold with something nasty. Wasn't there a noble rage within me that sometimes wanted to bare its fangs?

Dostoyevsky's St Petersburg dreamer was the greatest of human beings. He found within himself the strength to turn his dream into a source of life and in that way freed himself entirely from the demands of the real world. In his new state it was man himself who became the central figure, the cause and the consequence: man was a god without a capital letter, and that was better than being Man even with a capital M; the glorification of man always turns into another example of his enslavement and humiliation.

But I, but we – we don't need glorification: we just need peace and quiet. And as for those three on the other side of the door – what did they want out of life?

When I entered the room, there was nothing left of the cake

but crumbs, but there was still some wine. Lenochka – sensitive as a cat – looked questioningly at me. But I ignored her; let her worry and be anxious for a while, it suited her.

'We're discussing philosophy,' she announced. 'Your father claims it's a closed book for me.'

'And what do you say, my lovely one?'

'What do I say? I say it's all nonsense – any kind of philosophy. A person makes up his own terminology and then goes rattling on about things everyone knows. But since each philosopher uses his own terminology they appear to be arguing about very profound subjects, whereas the truth is they just can't understand one another.'

I looked across at Valentina. She might be a philosopher by profession, but she was a woman first. She wasn't going to take offence on account of philosophy; I even suspected that she didn't really give a damn about it; in any case both her face and my father's were now glowing with remarkably similar smiles.

'I have read Schopenhauer,' Lenochka went on. 'Lord, what a fool! You just can't imagine the sort of things he says!'

'And what does the foolish Schopenhauer say?' I laughed.

Lenochka glared at me. 'That no woman – this is what he says – no woman would ever offer herself to a man because, no matter how beautiful she might be, she would run the risk of being rejected. Men, you see, are often not interested in love. But when the man makes the first move, then she should comply. Doesn't that make Schopenhauer a fool?'

'Yes, I suppose it does. It's hardly his greatest thought,' Valentina agreed with a smile.

Lenochka shook her curls vigorously. 'A man who doesn't understand anything about women is incapable of saying *anything* intelligent. He is just a male. Also, according to this "philosopher", the cleverest person shows no compassion, knowing he will not meet with any himself. Still, I'm sorry for him, and that means all his philosophy is nonsense.'

Lenochka pursed her lips and then said in a half-whisper: 'And your Marx was also a fool.'

Now they were all laughing, Lenochka along with the rest of them.

Valentina and my father exchanged glances. Apparently it was time for her to leave. But something in my father's look held resentment or disappointment, leaving me unsure again of their relationship.

The women took the dishes out into the kitchen, glancing in turn at their reflections in the hall mirror, while my father and I stood admiring their fuss. But something still bothered me, and I could only hope that my father would find nothing to complain about in my behaviour.

At that moment, as I left the room last, the telephone rang behind me like a stab in the back. I hesitated, and then dismissed the phone with a wave – let it ring. But my father was, as always, quick to act.

'We'll wait for you downstairs.'

I went back into the room. I recognised my mother's voice at once.

'Gena,' she said in an unnaturally calm voice, 'could you come round to see me at once?'

To be honest, I had no wish to see my mother at the moment: I wasn't in the right mood at all.

'Right now?' I asked. 'Won't tomorrow do? I've things to do . . .'

My mother was silent.

'Is it something serious?'

Again she was silent. It was as if the phone had been cut off.

'Hello!' I shouted. 'Mother – what's the matter?'

'Lyuska's been arrested,' she said in a hollow voice. I didn't grasp the meaning of her words at once.

'Why?' I asked stupidly and then shouted: 'When?'

'Today. Please come.'

I choked on my words: 'Of course, of course, I'm on my way.'

I was confused; I felt dizzy, even shaky on my feet, as if I was on a swing or looking down from a height. Lyuska arrested!

What an absurd statement. It had to be a practical joke, because the word 'Lyuska' and the word 'arrested' were incompatible. Whether it was good or bad didn't concern me – all I knew was that she was my sister, no matter how wild and eccentric she might be; I didn't take her seriously, and so was unable to imagine that anybody else could. Lyuska under arrest – it was simply ridiculous!

It was only as I walked out of the building and gulped down the cool evening air that I suddenly realised quite clearly that my crazy Lyuska had gone too far and that this would be on my record, too.

My father and the two women were waiting for me. I went slowly towards them and they could see something was wrong. I took my father to one side and said without looking him in the eyes:

'Lyuska's been arrested.'

As I said it I could see only my father's hands, delving rather nervously into the pockets of his jacket. It was not a typical gesture of his: it was either fright or something else. I raised my eyes and saw his stony expression and heard him say in a half-whisper:

'So she went too far.'

The very same words as I myself had on the tip of my tongue.

'Are you off to your mother?'

'Yes.'

'I'll be at home. Give me a call. All the details, please.'

He stood there, so stiff and pale. I was amazed: I had never seen him in such a state before. The women, now very concerned, came up to us. I took Lenochka by the arm, nodded goodbye to Valentina, steered my friend across the road and told her that I had to attend to something very urgent. I jumped into a passing bus, leaving Lenochka standing on the pavement.

*

The door was opened by a woman I didn't know who eyed me in a hostile but inquisitive manner, and behind her I could see my mother's face, tear-stained and covered in red blotches. She stood there with her fists clenched beneath her chin, just shaking her head. Then she led me without speaking into the room. It was full of dissidents, sitting, moving, standing and practically all smoking. Although the windows had been thrown wide open there was a dense curtain of smoke hanging in the air. Some of them I knew – had seen them here or elsewhere – others I was meeting for the first time. They all looked grim and paid no attention to me. Judging by the mess I guessed that the room had been searched.

'Did they find anything?' This was the first thing I asked my mother.

She made a feeble gesture. There had been nothing of importance in the flat. My mother sat down by the window. Someone gave her a cigarette: there was the click of a lighter, followed by complete silence, as though someone had died.

A big crowd, but no Lyuska – she alone was missing from the room, but it felt as though she had disappeared completely. I couldn't imagine Lyuska in a cell. I had heard and read so much about those cells and about the prison procedures that to me it all seemed to belong to another planet whose civilisation I'd read about but couldn't really grasp. And now little Lyuska, fragile, highly-strung Lyuska was there, too.

'What did they say?'

My mother looked at me, tensely raising her eyebrows. I repeated the question.

'A warrant . . . under article seventy* . . . a preventive measure . . . taken into custody.'

She had difficulty speaking. I put my hand on her shoulder

* Article 70 of the Russian Criminal Code refers to the crime of 'Anti-Soviet agitation and propaganda'.

and I would have put my arm around her, but there were too many people in the room. Then the doorbell rang, and my mother jerked so convulsively that I felt a sympathetic stab of pain; she was still hoping for something, not rationally but instinctively. I couldn't help but hope, rather stupidly that, well, they'd only meant to frighten Lyuska and intimidate her. She was just a hysterical young girl, nothing more, nothing at all – I knew that for certain. It was just her romantic attachment to the renegade and dissident. They weren't fools, those fellows down there, they could surely understand something so elementary!

It was the foreign correspondents who had turned up. How keenly and professionally they looked around, taking in the disorder in the flat, and I could already imagine their dispatches: 'According to reliable dissident sources . . .'

The woman who had opened the door to me was dictating a prepared statement to the correspondents. I was surprised to hear that my hysterical little sister had been practically the founder of the Movement. She was credited with having done all sorts of things, and her arrest was declared to be a violation of international conventions. Thus anathema, again, upon the state which, ever since time immemorial, had been famous for cruelty to its people. Now to the long list of its victims, from Radishchev, the Decembrists and the followers of Petrashevsky onwards was added the name of my Lyuska.

If the forces of law and order saw things as I did, then it was certainly necessary to remove such a dangerous person as my sister as far away and for as long as possible. But I was even more surprised to learn that according to her friends, none of the things that Lyuska was supposed to have done was in any sense a violation of the existing laws. On the contrary, it was her arrest that violated the law, and consequently they ought to release Lyuska at once, unless the powers that be wanted world public opinion to get a wrong idea of the Soviet legal system.

In times gone by I had signed dozens of such documents without reading them carefully: it was sufficient to be moved by emotion and pity, but the strange thing was that whilst in the past I had regularly signed in defence of people I did not know, now I would not for anything have agreed to sign on behalf of my own sister.

I looked at my mother. There was pride written on her face and even her eyes seemed different: the despair had gone from them. One correspondent, full of sympathy, darted eagerly up to her and kissed her hand. Whatever he was saying to her he apparently let his curiosity go too far, for she suddenly shuddered, put her hands to her face and ran out of the room. Everybody made a dash to follow her, but I pushed ahead of them, shouldered back the confused reporter and slammed the door in his face. My mother had taken refuge in the kitchen. She was not crying, she was just standing there with her eyes closed, rocking gently to and fro. Suddenly I felt no sympathy for her. I closed the kitchen door and said in a tone of calculated harshness:

'And you never expected this kind of thing to happen?'

My mother stared at me and bit her lips. 'Why are you saying this to me?'

A note of annoyance was creeping into her voice. So what? Let her lose her temper. She was better off angry now than miserable.

'I can't believe it!' She said, turning away towards the window. 'I just can't believe that you're not sorry for Lyuska.'

'Father asked us to phone him.' I said, for some reason.

'I suppose he's worried about his official position?'

'Maybe, maybe not.'

'I'm not calling him!'

'Then I will!'

She shrugged her shoulders almost in my father's way, and I could hardly refrain from smiling.

'What can I do to help?'

She wouldn't look at me. 'Stay with me today . . . for a little while.'

'What about all those . . .' I nodded in the direction of the other room. 'Do they have to be here?'

'They are friends of Lyuska's. They're genuinely concerned . . .'

'And the foreigners? Do you actually believe they can help? If they can't, then all their noise only makes things worse.'

'I don't think so. Nothing has any influence on those boys in the Lubyanka – either way.'

'Tell me – did Lyuska's little boy-friend grass on her?'

'Please, I can't talk about it any more. You go in. I'll sit here for a while . . .'

When I returned to the room they all rushed towards me asking questions. I told them that my mother needed to be alone. Then I asked the foreigners, who were waiting about with note-books in their hands:

'Tell me – who in the West is likely to be interested in the arrest of a silly girl in Moscow?'

One of them, sporting a camera and a Nordic look, replied calmly, choosing his words carefully:

'People in the West sympathise with your movement. Everybody understands what human rights are.'

'And how long has the West understood that?'

'Understood what?' the question came back.

'That we have no rights here.'

'People in the West have never liked total-it-ar-ian-ism. Did I say the word correctly?'

The woman who had obviously taken charge here drew me aside. 'Gennadi, you will agree that this is no time for debating?'

'And who are you?' I asked brusquely.

She gave me her name. I had, of course, heard of her. Had read the stuff she wrote and read about her; I even knew her whole life-story and some interesting gossip as well. It's a small world!

'I wasn't debating,' I said, moving away from the correspondents with her. 'Only isn't it obvious that my sister is none of their business?'

'You're wrong!' she snapped. 'They sympathise with us, and their help is not ineffective. You know very well that a court's verdict has been influenced by public opinion in the West. We have to make use of every means.'

I fell silent and retreated into a corner. This dissident poet, that dissident 'refusenik', this wife of a dissident now in prison, that editor of a dissident periodical, and two or three other protesters from the same 'circles' – I knew them all, though not by their surnames. Here they were all just Mishas, Sashas, Laras, Leras, and there was even one Stepanida, the wife of a dissident scholar. Some of them already had invitations in their pockets to emigrate to Israel. Others were being kept under surveillance by the secret police.

It would seem that these people had a cause, courage, and camaraderie. All that, somehow, was alien to me. I had no need of the rights they were making such a fuss about. I had nothing to say, nowhere to emigrate to, and as for the right to shout my head off – would that help me to start a new life? And what had these intellectuals, with their invitations to Israel or summonses to the Lubyanka, to do with all the millions of people living in our vast country? They had nothing to do with me, anyway. I wasn't a politician, I wasn't a hero. Without great ambitions I could make myself a place in this society within the existing legal framework or at least hide in it. I had no need either of foreign correspondents or of human rights. What I needed was another life, a completely different life.

It's odd, but the only thing that my sister lacked in this life was personal happiness. She fell in love with her Shurik first and only became a dissident later. Now she had become an 'initiator', a selfless activist and so forth. Only I knew that she was none of that, she was just Lyuska. If I had succeeded in packing her off to the distant land of Father Vasili, if only that had come off, she would have calmed down, would have taken some long walks and had some good sleep, and perhaps she might even have fallen in love with Volodya the deacon, because my little sister responded readily to kindness – she might even have become a believer.

Too late, now. I wanted to go to wherever people's fates were decided and explain everything, tell the judges that my sister was not a threat to this age of 'advanced socialism'! But perhaps she *was* a threat? What if her arrest was intended as a lesson for the others? How could you possibly penetrate the logic of their penal system?

The telephone on the window-sill suddenly burst into life. I wasn't quick enough to reach it first: somebody else had already grabbed the receiver, and my mother, standing in the doorway, was listening to what was being said. Someone wanted to offer their condolences. She refused to take the phone so the expressions of concern and hope were passed on to her, and she smiled wanly.

Two years ago, at the height of the dissidents' success, she hadn't been like this. But after all, what had these people been hoping for? Or counting on? The ones who had more sense had cleared off to other countries whilst there was still time. Their friends had given them an enthusiastic send-off but secretly held them in contempt. The emigrés were well aware that they were making the path to the police cell a little shorter for those who stayed behind; they tried to keep people's spirits up or they became even more active, but they got out just the same, instinctively grasping the essence of the game being played by the mighty, indestructible government of workers and peasants, the most stable government in the world. Those who were left behind had not understood that – at any rate, my mother and Lyuska hadn't. The whole of freedom-loving humanity was on their side – such illustrious names! such distinguished people! such strength! But now that the people who had started and inspired the movement had been granted the privilege of emigrating, the freedom-loving West had rather cooled off. Yes, the correspondents still rushed to the flats of people who had been arrested at the ring of a telephone and the radio stations in the West continued reporting the persecutions and the prosecutions at regular intervals, but the idea itself had gone back to where it had come from – to the West. And my mother and Lyuska were still here.

Mother came up to me. 'What do you think – should we send a letter to the person at the *top*?'

She really had no faith in any such letters. But she could not accept the fact that Lyuska would be shut away for a long time and that there was nothing she could do about it.

'You do realise,' I said, 'that if you write a letter like that you have to beg. What would Lyuska think of that?'

There were tears in my mother's eyes.

'And the correspondents won't be any use for that . . . it has to be done alone . . .'

My mother rocked her head from side to side. My throat tightened as I watched.

'Lyuska's done for,' she said in a whisper. 'Done for . . .'

'Stop whining. She's not buried yet,' I cut in brusquely.

I was sorry for my mother, but at the same time I felt a certain malicious satisfaction; hadn't she played a part in Lyuska's activities and didn't she realise the extent of her own complicity? If she did realise then I didn't envy her. The fact that there was already talk of addressing an appeal to the authorities meant that the thirst for battle was on the wane. In whom could she now place her hopes? She had only me, who was no use, and my father who, if she was to be believed, trembled at the thought of losing his job.

Again the tinkle of the telephone and, strangely enough, this time it was for me.

I shuddered at the sound of Irina's voice. I'd literally forgotten her existence. Why did I seem so moved, hearing her voice? It could only mean I was not totally indifferent to the woman with whom, as they say, I had broken off.

'What have you heard?'

This must have been the end of a sentence. I'd missed the rest. There was a sort of gurgling in my throat as I replied:

'Article seventy. That's really all . . .'

'Can I do anything?'

She meant that she was ready to sign anything that would help my sister, despite the fact that, with the intolerance typical of dissidents, Lyuska had always despised Irina for her 'too official grovelling' – that is, in Lyuska's language, the fact that Irina worked for television.

'We're all right, thank you. How are you?'

It seemed to me strange that such unexpected warmth should creep into that short, uncomplicated question.

'I'm all right.'

I was disgusted with myself for wanting to see Irina that very minute, to run to her or ask her to come to me. But it would have been wrong to do either. I was not such a bastard that I could love two women at the same time; at least I ought not to be – after all, it was unnatural and insulting to both of them!

'Listen, Ira,' I said anxiously, 'listen . . .' But I didn't know what I wanted to say.

'Go on, I'm listening,' she said in a studiedly businesslike tone.

'Ira, there's some sort of misunderstanding between us . . .' I could hardly have said anything stupider.

Her reply was cold: 'There are more important problems than that now. I am asking you' – and she laid stress on the word 'asking' – 'if there is anything I can do . . . Well, you understand . . . You *will* give me the opportunity?'

I knew she was about to put the phone down, but I was struck dumb – I could think of nothing to say.

'Of course,' I muttered. 'Naturally.'

'I'll be at home all day. Today and tomorrow.'

She hung up. I could, of course, have called her back and carried on with the conversation, but I didn't like the way everybody in the room had ostentatiously turned their backs on the telephone. And what did I have to say to Irina anyway?

I dialled the number of my own flat instead. Straightaway my father answered.

'No details, Dad. It's the usual thing: they came, did a search, and took her off.'

'They gave no reasons?' He knew the question was pointless. 'Why should they?'

'Ask your mother to come to the phone.'

He was wasting his time, I knew. But I went to the kitchen and found my mother sitting at the kitchen table, her chin resting on her hands. In that position at that moment she looked amazingly like Lyuska, really it was the other way round, of course, but at that moment she really did look like her daughter.

'What does he want?' she asked almost inaudibly as she stood up.

Following her, I could sense something sharp and angry in the way she walked and in all her movements, and I was quite sure, from the way she took up the phone, uttered the word 'Yes' with pursed lips, that there would be no conversation between her and my father.,

'I don't need any help from you,' she hissed through her teeth, and I could only wonder at how much people could hate each other who had once been close. 'And she doesn't either.'

This was patently untrue. If my father had been in a position to offer Lyuska any help, my mother wouldn't have spoken to him like that. But she knew that my father was powerless, so she twisted the knife. I could just imagine my father's face turning rigid, like an eyeless mask; after all, he did love Lyuska, too, in his own way. How could a father not love his daughter? How could he suppress that love so completely that it could not surface at a time of misfortune?

My mother was still holding the receiver, which meant that my father was still saying something. But unfortunately her back was to me so that I couldn't see her face.

'It's not for you to be the judge of that!' she said suddenly, in a harsh voice. Everybody turned round to look when they heard her speak. If only they would leave the room, leave us alone. But it was hopeless. And now, in the bathroom, with the water running in case of microphones, a memorandum of protest was being drawn up which was going to make the whole of progressive humanity tremble. The room was so crowded there was almost nowhere for me to go, so I went back to my mother. She cast a look of alarm in my direction, as though she was afraid I would hear what my father was saying.

'All right, that's enough!' She was in a hurry to end the conversation. 'This is a pointless conversation. Goodbye.' With that she put the phone down.

'Will you allow me to give you my opinion?' I asked her quietly.

'What?'

'Your high principles are out of place just now.'

She eyed me from beneath lowering eyebrows and I knew she was about to lash out.

'You don't love him either,' she said. Her arrogant assumption that she could see through people infuriated me. It had since childhood.

'It's not a question of my loving or not loving. Is it really so difficult for you to grasp that I don't have any other father, that he has never done me any harm, and that my relations with you and with him . . .'

But my mother was no longer listening to me. Her attention was on a group noisily drafting an appeal in defence of Lyuska. Then the phone rang again and for the umpteenth time: somebody else offering condolences. I was not wanted. Not wanted at all!

I listened carefully to the wording of the document. My ambivalence towards my mother's and my sister's way of life was so clearly defined in my mind that I was almost reduced to despair. Everything in the text seemed true enough, but as a whole the document aroused in me not only irritation but a desire to ridicule it, to demolish its arguments, and to translate it into another language that would make its cunningly constructed imbalance between words and deeds overwhelmingly manifest. This appeal to the emotions rung hollow for me, as had so much of the behaviour and so many of the events of the last few years: all the accusations and tribulations, granting of permission to emigrate followed speeches on arrival in the free world, allegedly because of pressure by the authorities; on the other hand the courageous and stubborn behaviour of the ones left behind, which I could understand but never achieve, and the brave conduct in court and the ruthless sentences . . . And now Lyuska. I gave myself a test: if they were to offer to let me go to prison in Lyuska's place what would I do?

I knew a man had to have something in life for which he was ready to sacrifice himself. If it were not politics then it could be something very personal, but there had to be something, otherwise a man was an animal, not a man. So would I be capable of enduring the cell, the court and the prison camp in Lyuska's place? I tried to imagine how Lyuska would look as she came out of the gates (why must there always be gates?) of the prison, squinting into the sun with a confused but happy expression on her face – now at this moment, could I go there, into the hole, myself? I imagined how I would feel to be without freedom, to be without it for many years, and enduring all the other aspects of camp life that I had heard about – no, I just couldn't do it! It was easier for me to imagine death – one moment everything would be there then suddenly it would all be over – that wasn't difficult to imagine. But life in prison!

Did that make me a coward? I remembered Lyuska the last time we met, how her eyes blazed in anger – you could see in them that she was ready for anything and without fear: for her, prison was as nothing compared with the treachery of the man she loved.

But for me there could have been nothing worse than losing my freedom.

It came to my turn to sign the 'document' and they all watched me, but I signed it without demur, although an hour previously I'd been sure I wouldn't. I was a coward. I confessed this to my mother with a sad smile, which she interpreted in her own way, looking at me with gratitude. Had I not signed it they would have regarded me as a coward, and I was too much of a coward to be recognised as one. I put my signature to something that was utterly alien to me – all the clever terminology, the blatantly political rhetoric disguised as humanity, and the humanity compromised by politics.

Still holding the piece of paper, I said – I hadn't given up the idea of defending myself – as seriously as I could:

'This is fine, but I think we should just say at the end: "Down with the Communist dictatorship and its bodyguard the KGB!"'

They stared at me as if I was a complete idiot. I tried to explain:

'We want democracy, don't we? And what stands in our way? You should call a spade a spade. What's the point of beating about the bush? Here, I'll write it in here at the bottom . . .'

The sheet of paper flew out of my hand. It was the poet-dissident who'd grabbed it. All the luxuriant growth on his head and his face seemed to have stood up on end. Nobody even tried to argue with me. Only my mother, who had guessed that I was just fooling, shook her head and gave me a reproachful look.

'Oh, I'm sorry,' I said calmly, 'I forgot. We don't dirty our hands with politics: we're only concerned with the human rights granted us under the constitution. So let's say: "Long live the constitution of the USSR – the most democratic constitution in the world!" After all, even Berdyaev believed that.'

'Stop it, Gennadi,' my mother cried.

The poet-dissident said with a grin: 'Why don't you write your own personal appeal and expound your views there?'

'Thanks,' I said, 'I hadn't thought of that. Maybe that's what I'll do.'

My mother, now alarmed, beckoned me to follow her out.

'What's the matter with you, Gena?' she asked after I closed the door.

'It's disgusting, Mother, really disgusting! It's all a game. You and I know perfectly well that Lyuska wasn't a fighter: she simply fell in love. Besides, if you're going to fight, you ought to fight properly. We're demanding that the political system should be changed but that's not a political demand. Oh dear no! We're only humanists. What a farce! But listen, maybe they're right. Why *don't* we go down to the blasted KGB headquarters? It's ridiculous for a powerful organisation like that to be fighting a woman. I'll just take Lyuska away from them and that'll be that.'

My mother said nothing, and neither did I. I knew there wasn't a chance we would really go anywhere.

'I thought it might be easier for both of us to get through today if we were together,' she said hardly audibly. 'Go away, Gena. I don't know what I was expecting when I rang you.'

'Mother!'

'Go to your father. He probably needs you more. He's at last realised, apparently, that he has a daughter.'

'I'm sorry, Mother.'

'I'll ring you if there's any news.'

I went off without saying goodbye to anybody.

*

My life hasn't worked out too well. I have no family. The two people whom I love hate each other. But I was made for a life of comfort. The very word 'comfort' has such a pleasant, warm sound, like a favourite fair of slippers. Say it ten times over and you can doze off. In the last century I would have been an ordinary conscientious not very high-ranking civil servant, my favourite writers could have been Walter Scott and Zagoskin; I would have had a quiet, sweet wife and a houseful of much-loved children, whom I would have brought up to appreciate the virtues of simplicity and comfort. I would have been a pillar of the state, a state where everything was in its place.

And yet in Russian literature there is no type more despised than this. Everyone scoffs him, Chekhov especially. He must have been a sour man, Chekhov: he hated life and the people who lived it. His characters are bilious caricatures, and after reading his stories you have the feeling that he was that kind of a doctor too: treating people like corpses and interested only in the most loathsome diseases. At all events, it was the Chekhovs who destroyed Russia; the revolutionaries did no more than make an airborne landing on the ruins.

In my mother's flat they were yapping away about human rights, but all I wanted was to live in peace. Hadn't I a right to that? Or was my desire not human? To which international organisations ought I to send a complaint about my parents for hating each other so much? Who knows which rights mankind most needs, in Russia at least? If they were to hold a referendum, to buttonhole every passer-by and ask him or her what they needed most in life, I am sure the majority would ask for peace and comfort.

The most important thing for Lyuska's friends was free speech, but I needed a different kind of life. Other people could get up on their hind legs, but I wanted to be able to mind my own business without anyone calling me an egotist. I'm no more an egotist than Lyuska. At least I'm more honest about my interests and about frittering my life away on them.

I was terribly sorry for my sister, but, when all was said and done, she has, as a sister, left me nothing but the right to be sorry for her.

*

I didn't want to go home. I eyed the telephone kiosk nostalgically, felt in my pocket for some change, stepped inside and dialled Irina's number. On the last digit I halted – I had no idea why I was calling her, and when I let the last number go and heard the familiar voice in the receiver I coughed and said in a strange voice:

'Actually there's nothing new . . . I'm on my way over.'

'No,' she said firmly.

'Why not?'

'You can't come here.'

'Ira, I need to talk to you.'

'I said you can't come here. Isn't that clear enough?'

'Sod you, then!'

I had no more two-kopek pieces, so I put in ten kopeks and heard the voice of good old Yura Lepchenko inform me that he was alive and kicking and would be glad to see me. Thank goodness there was somewhere where I could still drop in.

*

'I know everything,' said Yura in a whisper as soon as I walked in.

'Where from?'

'Oleg Skurikhin phoned.'

'Where did he get it from?'

'Irina phoned him.'

'And who phoned Irina, I wonder?'

There was no gainsaying it, times had really changed! Would anybody have admitted the brother of a girl who'd been arrested into his home? Twenty years ago would they have fussed over him with such eager concern as Yura's mother was fussing around me now offering food and drink and somewhere to sleep? Yura was a lucky man – he had just the kind of mother that a poet needed; he had a nice, comfortable mother who breathed tranquillity and a quiet warmth, and was herself small, slim and noiseless; she had very beautiful hands, a pleasant voice, and she said only what was absolutely essential, not one word more.

Once everything was ready she left Yura and me in the

kitchen alone. I ate everything on the table, while Yura drank tea and delighted in my vast appetite.

'How many years will she get?'

'Article seventy. Six months to seven years. How can you tell what they'll make of her case?'

'Look, Genya – have *they* gone right off their heads? Sending little girls to prison!'

I agreed with him. No doubt *they* had an answer to his indignant question but I could only guess what it might be.

'Listen, Yura, who is running everything among the dissidents these days? Women. The authorities have been reading their history books, and *they* know how many men tried to kill the Tsar and failed; it was a woman who took the job on and managed it.'

'Your sister is no Perovskaya.'

'How do you know? At any rate, she's capable of doing things that you and I aren't capable of. You and I were in that church yesterday. Suppose tomorrow they grab me by the scruff of the neck, haul me off to a cell and ask me about you. Are you sure I wouldn't inform on you? Be honest, now.'

'Why should you do that?' Yura mumbled.

'Don't dodge the question. I wouldn't be that sure about you either. But I would certainly vouch for Lyuska. Tell me why that should be, why women are stronger than men?'

Yura hesitated before answering. 'Dissidents are like revolutionaries: their cause is built on hatred.'

'Maybe; I'm not so sure. So what?'

'Hatred is a powerful emotion that suppresses the instinct for self-defence. I haven't given this subject much thought, but, in my view, a normal person cannot kill another human being – it would go against a law of nature. But he can do it out of hatred.'

'Then what about the idea of elementary decency – how does that fit into your argument? Is it a strong emotion or a weak one?'

Yura sighed. 'You know,' he said, 'a man once – it was a

long time ago – offered me a drug to try. He told me what an interesting experience it would be what wonderful visions you had. I was so scared that I broke out in a sweat. It was because I knew for certain that taking drugs is a terrible thing. Although there would probably have been no harm in trying it. Out of curiosity.' Yura broke off, and I still hadn't got the point of his story. 'Or take another case. It was when I was a child. Someone dared me to jump into a hole in the ice. So finally I jumped. And now I know I'll never do it again. I know for sure that it's not for me.' He broke off again. I drank my tea and looked at him. 'It had nothing to do with decency. When I jumped into the ice-hole, I shouted so loud that they all laughed at me. I didn't know what it was like in the hole, so I jumped. And I suppose it was, well, not proper, not the right thing to do, to shout out. Not everybody knows his limits. The person who does know is a smart guy and he can make good use of his knowledge.'

'I'm having trouble following you today.'

'I don't think,' said Yura, changing the subject, 'they'll give your sister a long sentence.'

I hoped the same, but preferred not to talk about it.

'Why don't you recite some poems,' I suggested. I hoped he would refuse, but, alas, he stood up, went across to the window and stared fixedly at the flowers on the painted shutters. He recited his poems in a confident and even rather pleasant way. Some of the lines were technically quite accomplished about the meaning of life, its disillusionments and doubts, and I really took them seriously, even though in the course of the whole history of mankind miles and miles of such verse had been written. Another yard wouldn't hurt. Anyway, human wisdom isn't a quantitative concept, it isn't even a qualitative one – it is a constant, proportional to a unit of time. Every moment of history has its own ration of wisdom, but from the perspective of any other moment it is merely another monument of the past, an object for aesthetic contemplation. Had not Shakespeare said long ago that life was 'but a walking shadow . . . a tale told by an idiot', and had that ever convinced anybody sufficiently for them to give up life?

> My unbelief grows stronger
> Than love. I choke on it!

These were the last lines of one of Yura's poems. He turned to me, his eyes ablaze.

'They're good!' I said and almost meant what I said. 'But have you written any about how you would like to live? Poems about a different kind of life?'

I was sure Yura had poems for all occasions. But I was wrong.

'No. There's one by Ibsen.'

'Well?'

He was immediately transformed – he even seemed to grow taller and, there was a childlike mischief in his eyes as he recited:

> My sail is spread out like a wing in the wind,
> Above the live world like an eagle I soar,
> The seagulls are screeching in panic behind,
> My ballast of reason has gone overboard.
> Maybe my craft is already aground,
> Still, I managed to fly as long as I could.

'Yura, my friend, you're a real romantic!' I said, genuinely surprised. 'But what prevents you from "soaring like an eagle"? Oh, I suppose the "ballast of reason" is not so easily tossed overboard by a person today. But listen to this: I'm going to marry a priest's daughter and will soon bid a fond farewell to all of this. How about that?'

I made no attempt to conceal the boastful note in my voice and I could see the envy showing clearly in Yura's face.

'Well, get yourself married, and then we'll see,' he said.

'My future father-in-law may be a priest, but he's not in the same class as your rebellious clergyman.'

'Why?' Yura asked, rather offended.

'Why?' And, to tell the truth, I wasn't sure why I'd wanted to compare Father Vasili with the priest in Yura's church who'd made such an impression on me. I tried to explain it to myself and to Yura at the same time.

'It's something like this . . . There's a banner waving above your priest. I don't know what it stands for, but it's a banner. Over mine, you see, there's just a halo, if you know what I mean. Your priest makes one feel ready to die, mine makes you want to live, and live well. Am I making myself clear?'

Yura did not understand, but he was offended. He put on his offended face, sticking out his lip and flaring his nostrils.

'Come on, don't be cross,' I told him in the voice I'd have used to Lyuska or Irina. 'Your priest is an event, a phenomenon, whereas mine is just an individual and probably not unique. What's more, I don't think I fully understood what was happening. When are you going to see him next?'

'The day after tomorrow.'

'Let's go together. I mean it!'

We went on talking for a long time about all sorts of things, drinking tea, and listening to radio stations broadcasting from the wicked West, hoping we might hear something about Lyuska. At last we did. Those foreign correspondents certainly worked fast. I found it strange to hear our surname on the radio; it seemed as though they couldn't really mean *our* Lyuska, but they did, and although it didn't make things any better it was reassuring to know that my little sister was not rotting away in obscurity all the same. Perhaps it would make things easier for her if she knew that her name was already being mentioned in broadcasts from Europe and America and that someone would hear it and all her friends in Russia would listen to every bit of information about her.

It was going on for three o'clock when we went to bed, but for a long time I was unable to sleep: I had a feeling that I had something on my conscience. I wore out my weary brain even more by digging about in my conscience, and at last I fell asleep from exhaustion.

Sometime after mid-day Yura and I got up and drank some coffee, and I phoned my mother. We agreed to go the next day to the Lefortovo prison with a parcel for Lyuska.

It was Wednesday. Yura was apparently in no hurry to go anywhere, so it was after three when I left his flat and made my way slowly home. The sky was overcast and it was cold for a summer's day. As I came out of the Metro it began to drizzle and I ran for shelter to a row of poplars at the entrance to my building. I snatched the newspapers out of the post-box, opened the door, dropped the newspapers, swore, picked them up, threw them down on the table and went into my room. Then I froze stock still in amazement.

There, sitting in my chair, was a stranger reading . . . my Bible! I was literally struck dumb in the doorway, but the man calmly put the book aside, stood up, gave me an odd little bow, and said:

'Hello. Don't you recognise me?'

When he spoke, I did recognise him. It was none other than Volodya the deacon from the distant land where Father Vasili lived. He was wearing modern city clothes, though the suit and the tie and the neatly pressed trousers were clearly giving him some trouble. But for me he was like a visitor from another world, and for some time I did not reply but simply stared at him.

'Why are you here? Has something happened?'

He smiled serenely. 'Your father allowed me to wait for you here, and gave me permission to look at the book. Nothing has happened to us, everything is just as it was . . .'

'Can I offer you something to eat, a drink, a bath?'

'No thank you, I had something to eat with your father and I'm not at all hungry. Don't worry about me.'

At last I brought myself to go up to him and shake him by the hand, but I still couldn't get over his being in my flat.

'Did Father Vasili send you? Be honest.'

'No,' he said, smiling, 'He was against it at first, but later agreed.'

'What are you here for then? Do you have a letter for me or what? Maybe you'd like a cup of tea or coffee all the same?'

He refused. 'It was my own idea to come here, so to speak . . .' At that he lowered his eyes.

'Listen, Volodya, if you've got something to say to me, say it. You can't have come here just to have a look at me. How did you travel, by the way?'

'By air,' he sighed. 'The first time in my life. One's closer to heaven, you know, but it's a bit frightening.' He laughed and I began to get rather annoyed. 'In fact, I have come precisely to have a look at you. Tosya asked me to.'

'And you have nothing to say to me yourself?'

'All I want to ask is . . .' he said, with the same smile as before, 'why are you tormenting her like this?'

Well, that certainly went to the heart of the matter. I considered. Was it worth replying? Worth continuing the conversation with this lovelorn deacon?

'Can it wait, what you're busy with at the moment?' said Volodya. 'Or maybe there's something I don't understand? Surely you realise how hard it is for her?'

Perhaps I really didn't realise. 'You are right by and large, of course. Everything could be left for later. But I wanted everything to be on a sound and solid basis from the very beginning.'

I was putting it badly.

'But you did begin, didn't you?' he asked, casting his eyes downward again.

He was right. We had already begun, of course, and far from brilliantly. I turned my eyes away too. But my intentions had been perfectly honest; I had wanted to atone for the dishonest beginning, to put things right, to prepare for our life in the future. But she was suffering, so the deacon was right, and I was wrong. I would have set off that very day with Volodya, if it hadn't been for Lyuska.

'There have been some rather unpleasant developments for us here . . .'

'I know,' he said, 'your father told me. We shall all pray for your sister.'

It was only with difficulty that I suppressed a bitter smile. Of course I couldn't deny that praying was essentially a release of spiritual energy and, who could tell, perhaps that energy does have the power to influence things.

'We shall pray,' I repeated the deacon's words. 'Other people say: we shall fight; others still: let us hope. I belong to the third lot. I haven't lost hope, you know. You can pray and hope down there in your backwoods but you can only fight here. So, Volodya, tomorrow I'll go with my mother to the prison to leave a parcel for my sister, and the next day you and I will set off together. We'll see the job through properly, I'll bring Tosya here and we'll do battle together for our new life.'

Volodya frowned. Didn't he believe me? Or perhaps he still had hopes?

'Now then – before God: what would you like to happen to yourself?'

The deacon blushed. 'I cannot speak to you as I can to God.'

'All right, then – a direct question. You don't want me to marry Tosya – do you?'

'It's not that.'

'Then what the hell is it?'

At the mention of hell he started and cast a quick glance at the icon.

'I don't trust you!' he said it with a sigh, then took fright at his own words and looked guiltily at me, as if asking for forgiveness.

'What is it you don't trust? My love for her?'

'I don't know. Don't torment me.' He rose and went across to the icon. 'The Lord knows I want her to be happy!' He crossed himself slowly and then turned to me. 'So we'll return to our village the day after tomorrow?'

'The day after tomorrow. But now, you'd better tell me how she is. And how everyone's doing.'

'What's the point, if we're going there tomorrow?' He sat down in the armchair, his hands on his knees. 'Tosya is working. We're all working. We're doing up the church now and we're doing it all ourselves. Father Vasili, Tosya and I and a couple of men from the village to help us. It's hard. We can't get paint anywhere, or linseed oil . . . but bit by bit it's getting done. Then there's the vegetable garden and the hay and, um, all the other things we do, so many worries and problems.'

'You think *you've* got problems!' I thought but I said nothing, because actually I wasn't sure that other people's problems were any easier than my own.

'See there,' I pointed to the desk with the tape recorder and all the paper, 'I've got a pretty difficult job to do, but it pays well. We'll buy a flat, or maybe a house in the suburbs.'

I was making it up as I went along. It was the first time I'd ever thought of getting a house in the suburbs.

'Houses are cheap down our way. And there are plenty of empty ones, you can even get one for nothing.'

He said this very matter-of-factly, but I was stung by his implication.

'It's not out of the question, Volodya. I'll have to think about it. But it's not easy, all this.' There was a ring at the door.

'It's probably my father.'

'He said he would be back late. He also asked for you to wait for him. Forgive me, I should have told you sooner.'

I went to the door and opened it. Zhenka Poluëktov burst in.

'You're home? Good! Which direction do your windows face?'

He pushed me aside and dashed into the kitchen. I followed him: Zhenka opened the window, stuck his head out, whistled and waved his hand.

'I had to get rid of the taxi. I came over on the off-chance. We must have a talk.'

I led him into my own room. Seeing the deacon, Zhenka frowned and spent a moment weighing up my guest.

'I see. A messenger from the other world.'

I introduced them. The deacon looked embarrassed, hesitated and then shook hands shyly. Zhenka slapped me on the shoulder.

'Well, you and I, Genya, man, will have to leave your other world for a moment. We've some private talking to do.'

He was about to walk out, but I stopped him. I had a premonition that something had gone wrong; there was a strange restless look in Zhenka's eyes.

'Sit down and speak out. What secrets can I have from him?'

Zhenka looked at me, then at the deacon, and coughed as if to say it was none of his business and he washed his hands of the matter. He sat back on to the couch and gestured for me to sit down too. I remained standing.

'Right, Genya, this is where you get what's coming to you. So pay attention.' I looked at Zhenka as I might have looked at the wheel of a truck about to run me down.

'As I understand it, you do not intend to marry Irina?'

I replied slowly, feeling like an actor in the wrong play: 'That's right. I intend to marry a priest's daughter, the fiancée of this person here. His name is Volodya . . .'

Had I really guessed already what Zhenka's next pronouncement would be? Probably, otherwise why should I have talked like that.

'In other words, Genya, you don't want to marry the woman who is expecting your child?'

Of course, it was not a complete surprise. Perhaps I had guessed it long ago, but had not admitted it, had pretended ignorance. I couldn't see my ears but I could feel how red they were. I think Zhenka was surprised at my reaction.

'You must realise, Genya, I gave her my word of honour that I wouldn't tell you. And I wouldn't have said anything about it if she'd agreed to marry me, but, there it is, she sent me packing. So what does that mean? She loves *you*, you bastard. What the hell for, I wonder?'

My neck creaked as I turned to the deacon Volodya, who was staring into the corner, blinking.

'You see what's happened – it's like a complicated geometric figure: two adjacent triangles with a common side. How can we separate them from each other?'

And then, in desperation to Zhenka: 'A bastard, am I? You're the rationalist, define the situation. You came here to give the bastard what's coming to him. Fire away! I'm knee-deep in it already.'

'One could say,' Zhenka replied coldly, 'that you're a dog in the manger. And a very lazy dog at that.'

'And I'm not even house-trained. Well, deacon, what will you say to this shocking sinner?'

He was afraid to look me in the eye, but I burrowed into him with my eyes like a tick – there was no way he could avoid me.

'With the woman who, well . . . that was all some time ago, wasn't it? And you don't love her any more?'

'Look, my dear deacon, you're talking like a wretched humanist. And a dishonest one too, so far as I can see.'

'I know nothing!' The deacon cried out, almost in a howl. 'Don't ask me questions. I don't know anything!'

The telephone rang so suddenly that it seemed almost to jump up and down on the spot. I signalled to Zhenka to answer it.

'No, I am not Gennochka. Gennochka? In theory I suppose he's here.'

The deacon looked at the telephone in horror. Zhenka put his hand over the mouthpiece.

'Lenochka Khudova in person, and in a state of great excitement.'

I hadn't time for her now, but Zhenka handed me the phone.

'Gennochka, you're a magician!' the daughter of the

lieutenant-colonel from the Lubyanka was beside herself with joy. 'Gennochka, if you ever need to cross a puddle without getting your feet wet, just let me know; I'll lie down and let you walk on me.'

'It worked?'

'Zhukov made me a formal proposal. Just when I had decided to try the third-person idea! Billions of kisses!' Lennochka made kissing noises into the phone and said goodbye.

'What did she want?' Zhenka asked.

'I've arranged her happiness. I'm not a completely lazy dog after all.'

Zhenka rose from the couch, went across to the deacon, sat down on the arm of his chair and put his arm round him in a friendly way.

'So what have we decided?' Zhenka asked. 'Who are we marrying?'

The deacon clutched his head in horror.

'Lord, the way you live! The lives you all lead! Why do you live like this?'

'Let's not panic, Comrade Religious Worker. We do our best.'

Really, Zhenka's sometimes so crude. But the deacon calmed down immediately. He tugged a few times at his tie, which was obviously annoying him, made some strange noises in his throat, detached himself from Zhenka's embrace, and got up.

'I'll sit in there, in the kitchen. You don't need me.'

But I couldn't do without him! I didn't know why, but Volodya's presence had become essential. I took him by the hand and sat him down again in the armchair.

'Volodya, please.'

The three of us sat there, each unable to look at the other. It was an unspeakable situation. I had to decide whom to marry. The banality had vanished: the situation was straight out of hell. Zhenka wanted to marry Irina, the sacristan wanted to marry Tosya; I had to marry one or other of them.

Best to start with what was absolutely clear to me. And what was clear to me was that I could not bear to lose Tosya. To lose Tosya meant to lose everything, both myself and the life to which I had become attuned with all my consciousness. I loved Tosya: I had loved her before and I loved her after all this had happened in my life There could be no other choice for me.

After this first thing had become clear to me a second thing followed: I had to see Irina. Thank God. That was already something like a decision. I must go immediately, this very minute.

I pulled the phone across to myself, dialled the number and put the receiver straight down when I heard her voice. She was home.

'I'm going to see Irina now.' The two heads opposite me swivelled round and two pairs of eyes seized on me like pincers. 'And the day after tomorrow Volodya and I fly off to Uryupinsk.'

'Where?' said the deacon in surprise.

I looked at Zhenka, who kept his silence, biting his lips. The deacon blinked. My decision had satisfied neither of them. There was no tidy solution to this dilemma that life had thrown in my way. At least; it was not in my power to solve all the unknowns in the equation. And at this point, with an egotist's unerring instinct, I was pinning my hopes on Irina. I was going to see her. Irina would be able to bring things to a full-stop. It was mean, I realised, but I was determined to do it.

'You,' I said to the deacon, 'wait for me here. Tell my father I'll be late.'

Then I called out to Zhenka: 'Come on, let's go!' and walked straight out of the room. After feeling my pockets I went back to grab some money off the desk and caught up with Zhenka on the stairs.

'Count me out,' said Zhenka. 'I'm not going with you to Irina's. I gave her my word of honour!'

'Relax, there's no need for you to come along.'

*

Of late I'd mostly been seeing Moscow in the half-light. Or to be more exact, I had the impression of that I was moving in a limbo, from problem to problem. I tried to tie them together, but there weren't enough fingers on my hands for me to hold all the threads. I felt like the nutcase who let himself down from the skies on a short rope and who cut a piece off the top when the rope ran out and tied it on to the bottom.

'All right, then,' Zhenka said in the taxi, 'so you're going away, but what'll happen about the book?'

'When I've got married I'll return with my wife. It may not take more than a week. It's not all that urgent, is it?'

'There is time,' Zhenka replied rather uncertainly. 'If you change your mind you can sell the job to me and I'll finish it. We can agree a price.'

What a sharp fellow! I really liked him.

'Just look what a mess I've got myself into,' I said. 'I'm not such a bastard really, but this whole situation is quite shameful.'

'If I told you what I think,' Zhenka muttered, 'you'd be furious.'

'Go ahead. I'd rather hear it from you than from Volodya.'

'The most harmful people in the world are those who don't know what they want,' said Zhenka. 'They stick their noses into everything: they meddle in other people's affairs, screw up other people's games, ruin things for everyone and get themselves into a mess at the same time.'

'I get you. Thanks.'

'There you go – you say thank you. You're so damn smooth I can't stand it. Give me your little sister the dissident any time. At least they stuck her in prison. But the law doesn't provide for you.'

I bridled at that. Zhenka *was* a sod, after all.

'I suppose in her place, you'd have wriggled away like an eel.'

'In her place?' said Zhenka, surprised. 'How could I be in

her place? But I wouldn't half mind being one of the people who shove such people into the camps.'

'You talk too much, Zhenka!'

'No, I don't. I'm sorry for you, but I'm not a bit sorry for your sister. Naughty children get rapped on the knuckles. And your dissidents are very naughty. As for those know-it-all Jew leaders, they're asking for a pogrom!'

'Don't tell me you're an anti-Semite,' I said, laughing.

'I am a Semite who has to live in this country, and who likes living in it. The ones who fuss about this state and this government are my enemies, whether they are Jews or Armenians or mad Russians. I'd like to see the lot of them put away in the camps!'

'You don't really mean it . . .'

But who could tell – maybe Zhenka was a genuine child of the existing order.

'OK, this is where I want to go,' said Zhenka, 'I'm getting off here. Will you pay?' He was already out of the taxi but he peered in at the door again. 'I hope Irina slaps you in the face.'

And he slammed the door – just like a slap in the face.

*

Irina opened the door a few inches only.

'What do you want?'

'Would you mind letting me in first?'

'What do you want, I asked you.'

I pushed the door, brushed her aside and went in.

She was in her dressing gown, and the first thing I noticed was her stomach: She was four or five months pregnant for sure. When she caught my glance, she gave a peculiar little wriggle and the stomach disappeared. But meanwhile angry red blotches had appeared on her face. I knew she was furious, but I didn't care. She stood there in the entrance hall clearly without any intention of moving from the spot. I went into the sitting room and sat down.

'You're a pig,' I heard her say.

There was a jar of pickled cucumbers on the table; so far as I knew, Irina didn't much like spicy things so I decided it must be a peculiarity of her condition. At last she came into the room, holding her hands so as to disguise her altered figure. I stared at her. She was like herself and yet altered. There was something different about her, something that I hadn't seen before. There was a look of softness, vulnerability or something else indefinable in her face, though there was anger at the moment too. It was as though an unknown Irina was facing me, and I felt intimidated. It wasn't her gaze, it was my own, fixed now on those familiar but transformed features.

'Well?' she said.

'Sit down . . . please, and be quiet.'

I needed her to sit down facing me without speaking, and I also needed to be silent and listen to my inner self. I felt something very important was about to happen, perhaps the most important thing that had ever happened to me; I was full of alarming premonitions, one of which was that this was the end of my freedom. I felt as though I'd been swimming free and was now caught up in a current of circumstances which were too strong for me. More than that, they were the only reality, and in them I would have henceforth to continue my existence.

I made myself remember why I had come. It was in order to clear up an ambiguous and dishonourable situation for which I myself was responsible, though I hadn't intended to hurt any one. Why else had I come? Did I want Irina to help me get out of the mess? That would be too naïve and too unkind of me. So what had I reckoned on? I wanted Irina, the future mother of my child, to say to me: 'You are free to go and I do not need you.' I'd believe what she said, or at least pretend that I did.

Irina eased herself down into the chair. She seemed to shrink and lose all her anger and all her hostility towards me. Opposite me was nothing more than a little pregnant woman, a woman whom I knew through and through, so thoroughly in fact that this knowledge became the decisive factor. I could feel my long-cherished idea of a new life slipping away from me. I was making no more judgements, nor offering any opinions or verdicts: everything was working itself out on its own, with my participation but without my prompting.

All the same, I had to find the right word for it: the woman sitting facing me was my wife. How simple, how obvious! My wife! It wasn't just the word, it was the feeling too that was born in those few minutes. I could hear the rhythm of my life changing, I could feel my own pulse beating evenly and clearly, my steady, quiet, regular breathing. I was filled with regret for something lost for ever: I was taking leave of something, but at the same time I rose and went across to Irina. I touched her cheek with the palm of my hand and I felt something warm on my fingers. It was her tears. With unaccustomed gentleness I lifted her by the shoulders and brought her face close to mine. She covered her eyes, and I silently wiped away the tears from her cheeks – there weren't many after all, only two little ones. Holding her by the shoulders, I felt her trembling body ready to yield to me, and I knew that this was the final point in our confused relationship. For another minute or so I kept fate at arm's length, but then my hands made a tiny movement and Irina pressed herself close to me. I stroked her hair as my mother had once, a hundred years ago, stroked mine, and we stood there silently because too much already had been said. I only asked:

'How long?' She understood at once.

'Four months.'

'Everything normal? Have you seen the doctor?' She nodded.

Where on earth had she, this proud, arrogant woman, acquired this bashfulness and this submissive manner that I had never seen before? In the end I lifted her face and looked into her eyes. There was no joy yet, it's true, but there was readiness to respond to affection and I kissed her on the eye-lids and said with a firmness unlike me:

'So, that's that.' I found it strange and surprising that there

was such firmness in my voice, so I repeated it for my own
benefit:

'That's that.'

I said it as if I were the master, like a man. Hearing it was
unsettling, but not unpleasant.

'I could eat a horse!'

In no time we were busy in the kitchen, just as if nothing
had ever come between us, except that I wasn't sprawling in a
chair as I'd always done before, I was bustling about more
than she was. It was hard to say who was trying to feed whom
in that happy confusion.

*

I feel such pity for this life of mine – the only one I shall ever
know! It oozes away through open fingers and I cannot make
a fist. Why was life given to me, then, if pity is my only
achievement? What's the use of pity? You can't express it or
share it; it's just an empty, fruitless thing. What must I say to
myself to stop being scared as I see the milestones flashing by
on my pointless journeyings from night to day, from week to
week and from year to year? My great mistake was probably
to invest other people's epochs and other people's lives with
meaning and to try to measure my own life by theirs, suffering
from the comparison between real and imaginary. Foolish,
because there was no more meaning in other times and lives
than there was in my own epoch. I had to remind myself that
a man can acquire freedom only when he realises that lives and
epochs cannot be compared and that it is meaningless to impose
such meaning on his own life. And I have to acknowledge to
myself that the search for a meaning in life is a form of torture
invented by people who, by virtue of their birth or upbringing,
are prisoners of ambition or pride; that such people remain
forever slaves of their complexes.

I could tell myself a lot more to justify and console myself,
but all the same I regret my one and only life. If only I could
at least envy someone to the point of desperation, perhaps I

might work myself up to do something decisive but, unfortunately, I don't envy anyone, no-one on earth. When one looks closely at a man's apparently enviable success, one sees the costs and losses, which no success is worth. Comparing the course of your life with others' lives is pointless; now that conclusion gives one something to live by, and one needn't regret one's own one and only life!

This morning, on such and such a day, month and year, a woman was sleeping at my side, a woman who was already my wife, but the choice which had come about in apparently such an ordinary way involves bigger things. The crossroads had been reduced to one narrow path, the variants had fallen away until just one was left, the mist of uncertainty had been dispersed, two necessary points have been made, and a straight line drawn between them; and the future stands revealed in a sober morning light. Here is the peace of mind I have been longing for.

I quietly passed my hand over Irina's face and she pressed her hot cheek against it.

'Is it time already?' she asked.

I wasn't sure she hadn't said it in her sleep. Her expression was quite peaceful, and that meant she was happy. There was no other face I wanted to think of now. I had the right to tell myself that it was in my power to make at least one human being happy. That right could give me the will to live.

'Do we really have to go there?' Irina asked, and then I realised that she was not only not asleep: she was preparing herself for the ordeal of our visit to my home would cause her.

Irina asked me to look away – she was embarrassed by her changed shape. She rushed off into the bathroom in her dressing gown, but for some time I went on lying there, just staring at the ceiling. A sentimental tune of Vivaldi's which I didn't like but Irina did was going round in my head.

I got up when the smell of coffee drifted in from the kitchen. Irina had already washed and put on clothes which cleverly concealed her condition. I looked at her and said to myself, by way of information only: 'I like her, I will always be able to love her, and as the future mother of my child she evokes in me a feeling of tenderness.' But one can't utter the word 'tenderness' with impunity, so I embraced Irina with this new tenderness, as the mother of my child, and I kissed her in a new way, and she responded shyly and chastely.

In fact Irina was unrecognisable. She was altogether so domesticated now, so relaxed and unhurried that you could hardly believe that a month ago she had been rushing through the stairways and corridors of the television studios full of shocking ideas, rowing with her bosses, twisting arms, unmasking and damning corruption. Only women have this ability to transform themselves so quickly and so completely, without plans for a 'new life', without introspection or hesitation. Now there was something to be envied! But tell her that the fuss of her former professional life was just that – empty fuss and no more – and she would be offended. One state did not reject the other after her transformation.

We drank our coffee quickly – we were late. Outside the house Irina protested violently against taking a taxi, not yet knowing that I had some money. Of course, she was only four months gone, we could still use the Metro, but why should we when I had money in my pocket? I made a show of firmness, and she gave in, looking surprised and even pleased.

I stayed silent in the taxi. I was preparing myself for an extremely difficult meeting and I wasn't entirely sure that I would be able to keep the situation under control and not lose my head completely. In my head were the first, most difficult and unavoidable sentences.

Irina didn't know exactly what I had to face but had obviously sensed that it would not be easy, and so she said nothing, but I could see the anxious look on her face when I glanced sideways. Of course, I could have done this on my own and perhaps should have, but with her at my side it would be easier for me and, to be honest, I was now afraid to make a move without her. So long as she was at my side I was capable of asserting myself.

We let ourselves into the flat and I knocked on the door of

my own room. The room was neat, and Volodya was sitting in the armchair in his smart suit, with a book in his hands. When he saw that I was not alone he quickly stood up and put the book down on the side table. I let Irina enter before me, took a deep breath and said in a hoarse voice:

'This, Volodya, is Ira, the future mother of my child and consequently my wife.'

The deacon's eyes were out on stalks. He moved his lips without saying anything. From behind Irina I threw him a pleading look that he should be magnanimous and wise. Only his pure and undefiled soul was capable of understanding me and of condemning me with half the severity I deserved at any rate; condemned more stringently than this, I might lose the will to live. Irina sat down on the couch leaving Volodya and me to stand facing each other, or rather leaving me to stand before him as if I were before the Lord God, ready for judgement but hoping for wisdom and magnanimity.

'So there it is, Volodya. This is how we live. And you, whether you like it or not, will have to put everything else to rights. I believe in your special strength and I believe that you will be able to put things right and save us all, myself included. You see, I'm trying to unravel the knots, but not everything is in my power; you, though, will find the necessary words and . . . prayers.'

I dared say no more of this kind. It could be dangerous.

'The day after tomorrow we'll have a kind of wedding and I hope you'll stay, and give us your blessing.'

The deacon shook his head.

'I can't do that . . . I have no right. I'm not a priest.'

'But couldn't you give me your blessing simply as a person – I need your blessing. I need it, you understand.'

He looked down. He didn't dare to look in Irina's direction.

Good, kind, unhappy deacon! What a burden I've unloaded onto your sensitive soul! But I know it's your profession and you will be able to bear it.

I cast a glance at Irina – she understood everything. The old Irina might well have exploded at this point. The new Irina said nothing.

'So you'll stay on for our wedding?'

'I don't know,' the deacon said, almost in a whisper.

Then Irina took matters into her own hands. She stood up, went up to him, took his hand and kissed it. The deacon, frightened, snatched it away.

'Please, please!' he said plaintively with a self-deprecating gesture. 'I am nobody. I am a greater sinner than any of you.'

'I beg you,' Irina said quietly but urgently, 'please stay. If you go away things won't be right here. I ask you, I who have wronged no-one.'

Beads of sweat were on my forehead. Irina had understood everything; probably even more than she was letting on. Perhaps Zhenka had had time to spread the word. In any case she knew where the deacon came from.

'All right, all right,' he agreed hastily. 'If you wish it, I can, of course.'

'So that's that!' I announced, for the first time in a normal voice. 'Now let's call on my father and get his blessing. Is he up and about?'

'He . . .' the deacon hesitated strangely. 'The fact is, he waited for you all night and, well, he went away.'

'Went away? Where?'

Volodya picked up an envelope from the table and gave it to me. It wasn't sealed and I took out a folded sheet of paper.

Gena! I have been obliged to leave town. As soon as I get things settled where I'm going I will drop you a line. If you get married, why not have this flat? I don't need it any more. Please take the money as my wedding gift to you and your wife. It's in your desk.

Papa.

What on earth was this? Where had he gone to? And why? I read the note again and could make no sense of it. If I hadn't known my father as well as I did I would have thought it was some kind of a joke. I pulled out the drawer of the desk. Beside my money from the publishers there were two neat bundles of money from my father and on each one was written 'I thou.'.

I dashed into my father's room. Everything was tidy and apparently in place. Even the typewriter. But no, not every-thing. A few books were missing and there was nothing on his desk. I could have looked in the wardrobe, but why bother when it was clear the owner had vanished?

'But why?' I shouted to Volodya from the corridor. 'Did he tell you anything?'

'He told me nothing. He was waiting for you. I only know that he is a kind and unhappy man.'

'What?' I said in amazement. 'My father kind and unhappy? My dear deacon, you're fantasising, my father doesn't know the meaning of the word. He's the calmest, the happiest man in the world.'

But Volodya did not agree and shook his head.

'Irka, can you figure it out? He didn't take his typewriter! And you know he was planning to get married too? He had only just introduced me to his . . .' I clapped my hand to my forehead and dashed to the telephone. I dialled my father's number at work. 'Excuse me, I think you have a Valentina Nikolayevna working there? Unfortunately I don't know her surname . . .'

'You mean Korotkova?' a man's voice enquired, not too politely.

'It could be.'

'She's teaching a class. Ring back in ten minutes.'

So Valentina was still in town! What on earth was going on? You patch up life in one place and it comes unstuck without warning in another.

'So what made you think my father was unhappy? How did you make that out?'

The deacon looked at me guiltily. 'I don't know . . . It's obvious . . . You can see it in his face . . .'

'Rubbish!' I threw the envelope down. 'My father is happiness itself.'

'Perhaps you don't love him?' Volodya asked.

'My dear deacon! How on earth could I not love my own father?'

'I'm sorry – it seemed to me . . .'

The deacon's eyes were meekly apologetic. I went right up to him. 'Try to recall what he said! After all, you had a long talk. Why is he unhappy? Ira! You knew him – did my father ever strike you as an unhappy man?'

'He is a very reserved man.'

I was in complete confusion. All my life my father had been the same for me – calm, self-confident and well adjusted. I couldn't imagine his being anything different.

Only that morning I had enjoyed a brief taste of peace, and now look! How, I wondered, had our lives managed to get into such a mess? We'd lived such quiet lives, I thought, without taking many risks or having fancy ideas, then suddenly bang! – the most idiotic complications.

I dialled the number again. They summoned Valentina at once.

'This is Gennadi,' I said, rather aggressively for some reason. 'What has happened to my father? Do you know?'

'Put down the phone,' Valentina replied, in a muffled voice, 'I'll call you on another line.'

I waited, strumming on the desk with my fingers. As soon as the phone rang I seized the receiver.

'He's given up his job and gone up north somewhere. He didn't tell anyone where he was going. There's been the most massive row here.'

'But what was the matter?' I cried out impatiently.

'It's all very complicated . . .' Valentina seemed about to burst into tears. 'You understand, Gena, you're old enough, you ought to understand . . .' I could tell she was in tears. 'He wanted us to live together. He said he couldn't go on like this any longer.'

'And you turned him down?'

I could not conceal my amazement. I had been sure that Valentina was out to net my father.

'I couldn't make up my mind. You see . . . well, I already have a family – a husband, a son.' So that was it!

'Believe me, Gena, it's not that easy . . . breaking up every-thing and starting again from the beginning. I'm not a young woman, after all.'

'What about your husband . . . did he know?'

'Good heavens – no!'

What a woman! Living with two men for years? 'The lives you lead!' – I recalled what Volodya had said the previous day.

'In short, you gave my father the push and he's gone off to the north.'

I thought my tone of voice would rile her, but if it did, it wasn't apparent in her voice.

'That's not it at all!' she objected, snivelling like a little girl. 'I didn't make any decisions. I simply couldn't break up my family.'

I was beginning to understand her now. She wouldn't have minded going on living with two men, but my father had rebelled. My God, how utterly unlike him it was! It was as though we were talking about an entirely different person.

'I'm so afraid for him,' Valentina was now weeping openly into the phone. 'He said no-one needed him.'

'That's not true!' I cried angrily. 'I need him!'

'But he thinks no one wants him. You should have heard the way he said it!'

I couldn't imagine my father saying such a thing – not the father I knew.

'What's he going to do up there?'

'He said he'd been invited to take up some job as an econom-ist, not a very important job as far as I could tell. Gena . . .

please forgive me – I know that I . . . but there was nothing else I could do . . .'

'Didn't you love him?'

'Goodness, you really are still . . . ' – she probably was going to say 'a baby' – 'very young, aren't you? Haven't you learnt that there are more things to life than love? For example, my son has a father and he needs precisely *that* father, no other will do. Don't you understand?'

I could understand that all right. But what I couldn't understand was how a woman could live with two men for several years and not choke on her own lies. That was something only an extreme rationalist could do.

'If he writes to you, please let me know. Because he won't write to me.'

'I'll let you know,' I promised, knowing I wouldn't.

'Only don't be angry with me, please, promise me that.'

'What is there to be angry about?'

'You all – I mean your family . . .' Valentina paused for some time, perhaps was simply wiping the tears away, 'none of you knew him at all.' Another pause. 'You didn't know him, and you didn't understand.'

What was the point of arguing? I had no further need of her, and I waited patiently for her to finish.

'Please don't think badly of me.'

'I won't.'

'And you'll phone me if there is any news?'

'I'll phone you.'

With that, I hung up. I looked at Irina and the deacon. She was lost in thought: the deacon appeared embarrassed.

'Fine goings-on,' I muttered. 'Soviet reality is coming unstuck. Instead of me going to Uryupinsk, my learned Marxist papa has dashed off there.'

'*Where?*' they asked in unison.

I went to my father's room and settled into his chair. So what was it I had overlooked in him, my father? I hadn't overlooked anything. Perhaps something just snapped, like an overloaded spring. In any case, I now was without a father, and Lyuska was in prison. My mother was alone. There was no family left. There hadn't really been one before, what with one thing and another, but now the collapse was complete. But – my father! Had he really not understood my feelings for him? I hadn't created the coldness there was between us – he had. Then suddenly I realized what had happened. He had said nobody needed him. But whom did he need, apart from his twin-bedded doctor of philosophy? One kind word and Lyuska would have stayed with us. Perhaps even my mother wouldn't have left him. Actually, no, she would have left him in any case. I was sure of that. I knew everything, but what an emptiness I felt inside me!

The phone rang, but I didn't want to touch my father's phone so I went to take the call in my room.

'Well, Gena, man, any good news?'

Poor Poluëktov! Good news indeed! 'There certainly is! You are invited to come here the day after tomorrow to attend a modest gathering of friends on the occasion of my marriage to a person with whom you are not unacquainted.'

I handed the phone to Irina.

'Zhenochka, you must come. You're my very best friend.'

That's a woman's way of giving one a slap in the face. I could imagine Zhenka's expression just then and I felt genuinely sorry for him. After all, he had been a damned good friend. Most important – you could rely on him.

'It'll only be our friends – eight or ten people at the most.' Irina passed the phone back to me.

'Tell me, Gena,' Zhenka asked in a very subdued voice, 'Is this your final incredible trick or the last but one?'

'The last, Zhenka. It's all over. I'm home and dry.'

'And so what is this, a Pyrrhic victory?'

'No, Zhenka,' I replied in a serious tone. 'It's no victory. I've arrived, that's all, and I've nothing more to say. So you'll come?'

'I'll wash my hands and come,' he snapped, and hung up.

'Is he coming?' Irina asked anxiously.

'How could he not?'

*

Nobody knows how to have such a good time as we ordinary Soviets. How could they? What has a wealthy American, for example, got to celebrate? He's quite content with life as it is!

We honest Soviets, on the other hand, dive into a good time as if it were alcohol or drugs: half-hearted rejoicing doesn't suit us and doesn't satisfy us – it makes us either moody or violent. We know something that non-Soviet people do not – the degree of celebration needed to produce enough happiness to tide us over to the next celebration. It's not a question of alcoholism. God forbid! I'm talking about people who aren't drunkards, ordinary Soviet people. My love for us is sincere, whole-hearted. It's adoration! So we're not pure, but we *are* harmless. We live this strange life of ours, that's not of our making; but have we any choice? Do we need to have a choice? Is a choice really possible?

Every one of us goes about his everyday affairs, and if anybody says that it's not up to much, then we'll go for him: we have the right to live in just that way and in no other. Who presumes to make us live otherwise than the way we live now? If anyone claims to have a moral right like that, then we demand equality of rights – let him live as we do. They swear at us, curse us, ridicule us and expose us – but what right have they got? Just let us know what that right is, and we'll make sure we have it too, and then look out for yourselves!

I love us simple ordinary Soviet labourers, able to live in two dimensions: we render unto Caesar what is Caesar's, but we keep what is ours to ourselves, and no totalitarianism will stop us switching off now and then to have a good time.

And the faces! You just look at our faces when we are having fun! Could anyone else have such open, such happy or such kind faces as ours when we're having fun – when we're dancing. It doesn't matter what we dance to – the Beatles, the *kalinka*, the *lezginka* or the seven-forty – we stopped worrying long ago about the form or the means of our rejoicing – the rejoicing itself is the thing, and we don't care how we get there.

In what words can I describe to the uninitiated the state of gaiety and happiness, of genuine happiness, that we experience when we are in our own circle, among our own people, surrendering to the raptures of the moment or of the hour! What goodwill and love we have for each other then, and how trusting and sincere we are in our feelings.

At those moments we are more than beautiful. Our faults, the filth of our everyday lives do not intrude on our enjoyment. Yes, I really believe that only Soviets know how to enjoy themselves properly!

And here they are, my friends – and here I am, looking at their happy faces and happy as can be myself.

Zhenka Poluëktov, the new Soviet man, with the future at his feet; dear Yura Lepchenko, the conspirator-neophyte-poet, to whom the past undoubtedly belongs, and that's already something; Lenochka Khudova, radiant as an icicle in March, and Zhukov, the rising star of television – they belong to each other, and that's something too. The dependable married couple, the Skurikhins, the owners of the flat where we're celebrating, because we're used to it and continuity of surroundings is an important condition for unrestrained rejoicing; the swarthy Felix with bald patches in his curly locks, to whom belong the unique ancestral rights of the Chosen People, and whom I love like a brother, no anti-Semite could diminish that love in this atmosphere of universal philanthropy; and our guest, the marvellous deacon Volodya: I'll ask him, as the plenipotentiary representative of heaven, whether he condemns us from the height of his purity, and what will he say? He'll say: 'I do not judge you!' and that must be regarded as forgiveness. Then, at my side is the hero of my prospective book, which I will definitely write now, Andrei Semyonich, who shed his blood and risked his life so that we should have the right to live as we are living. Suppose I asked him if he fought the war so that this party and tomorrow's hangover could happen, he'd say, yes he did, and that it would have been right and proper even if millions laid down their lives fighting for our way of life and for our complex and difficult existence. Let nobody criticise it. He'll get his head smashed in!

My dear, kind friends! Wonderful Soviet people! How much I love you, how grateful I am that you are so undemanding!

From the first moment when we sat down to table and throughout the whole evening every toast, every word and every look – everything did so much to simplify my far from simple situation. Irina and I kissed each other as though we'd just met, and there was nothing affected or unnatural about it on our part; it was because my good friends had recreated a sense of youth and renewal for us.

God knows what a foul mood I had been in when I arrived at the party. The three of us – my mother, Irina and I – had just delivered a parcel to Lyuska. I had only come briefly into contact with Lyuska's present world of thick walls, wire netting and warders, and it had upset me so much that Irina had noticed it and told me how pale I looked, but she didn't see the almost uncontrollable trembling that had seized my whole body. As an ordinary Soviet citizen I may not know what real freedom is, but I wouldn't part with my unreal freedom for any cause under the sun. As far as I am concerned, no cause is worth exchanging for my right not to hear the clang of the prison gates. I suspected that Lyuska felt the same way, and I was horrified at the thought of what she was going through behind those brick and concrete walls.

They agreed to accept some of what we brought, but some they refused, and my mother had hysterics. She called them fascists, Stalinists and *oprichniki*, and we had trouble dragging her away, even when we'd been forced to put our signatures on the muddled statement she handed in.

On the way back I whispered to Irina: 'Shall we join the dissidents, then, when we've had the baby?'

'Yes, let's,' she agreed, and I eyed her in some alarm.

I did not invite my mother to my wedding, or rather my party. She wouldn't have come. But now, at the height of the fun, I was sorry I hadn't persuaded her or tricked her into joining us. She wouldn't have been able to hold out against the general mood and might even have stopped weeping and scolding for a while.

Maria Skurikhina turns on the tape-recorder and everybody starts to dance. Actually it's neither a recognisable folk-dance nor a waltz or whatever, it's simply the last stage of liberation. We've learnt it from the cursed West, where they do regard it as a dance, but for us ordinary Soviet people it's more like a prayer, a pagan hymn of the body to our transient spiritual freedom, our aimless evening's happiness. Everybody is moving round the room to the din of foreign rhythms passing each other and following each other, and the shadows on the walls make it seem as though there are more people present than there are, there's a whole world of happy people in the room, I can't restrain myself from joining in the dancing, I start to twitch my shoulders and to tap my feet and to shake my head, I can feel my eyes light up and shine and I know that very shortly I will be completely carried away by the rhythm and will drown in it.

But there among the drowning and the dancers, gliding around the room, past the dancers and through them, is the figure of a woman who has the palms of her hands raised to her face – I can make out her face with its half-sleepy, half-smiling expression, her restrained, and graceful movements. She floats around unaided, from another world, belonging to no one.

I stand stock still in horror and then look at the deacon Volodya, to check whether he's seeing what I am, but in his eyes I see only fright, and I understand – it's only shock at seeing our musical-choreographical ritual, and he hasn't seen what I have – Father Vasili's daughter weaving sleepily through the crowd of people to her own elusive rhythm. And, so as not to see her, I close my eyes and say very quietly: 'Tosya'.

Somebody grabs me by the hand and drags me off my chair.

'Let's go!' I exclaim as I push my way into the crowd, forcing myself into it like a corkscrew, and then I begin to perform impossible steps, and there are no more mirages, only enjoyment, and now my 'other life' begins – not an invented or imagined life, but the life I was given at birth by fate, only I didn't recognise it earlier in the confusion of my empty pointless thoughts . . .

Moscow, 1981–82.